Presented By

Mrs. Jane Olsen

Bruce Alexander was a prolific author of both fiction and non-fiction. When he died in 2003, he had completed most of *Rules of Engagement*, leaving behind notes on the remainder of the story. This novel has been completed by Bruce's widow, Judith, with the author John Shannon.

RULES OF ENGAGEMENT

Sir John and Jeremy are confronted with a series of bizarre deaths on the streets of London, and when Lord Lammermoor plunges to his death from Westminster Bridge, suicide is deemed to be the cause of death. But Lammermoor's fatal leap coincides with the arrival of Dr. Goldsworthy, a student of Dr. Anton Mesmer and his research in animal magnetism. Sir John discovers that Goldsworthy's patron in London is Lady Lammermoor. Meanwhile, Jeremy's sleuthing uncovers a web of intrigue within the Lammermoor family and reveals more suspects who stand to gain from Lammermoor's death.

Books by Bruce Alexander
Published by The House of Ulverscroft:

BLIND JUSTICE
MURDER IN GRUB STREET
WATERY GRAVE

BRUCE ALEXANDER

RULES OF ENGAGEMENT

Complete and Unabridged

ULVERSCROFT
Leicester

First published in the United States of America
in 2005

First Large Print Edition
published 2006

The moral right of the author has been asserted

British Library CIP Data

Alexander, Bruce, *1932 –*
  Rules of engagement.—Large print ed.—
  Ulverscroft large print series: mystery
  1. Fielding, John, Sir, *1721 – 1780*—Fiction
  2. Police magistrates—England—London—Fiction
  3. Blind—Fiction 4. London (England)—History—
  18th century—Fiction 5. Detective and mystery stories
  6. Large type books
  I. Title
  813.5'4 [F]

  ISBN 1–84617–247–0

Published by
F. A. Thorpe (Publishing)
Anstey, Leicestershire
Set by Words & Graphics Ltd.
Anstey, Leicestershire
Printed and bound in Great Britain by
T. J. International Ltd., Padstow, Cornwall

This book is printed on acid-free paper

FOR
SONJA AND RICHARD
and in memory of
SHELBY PECK

1

In which Lord Lammermoor leaps off Westminster Bridge

The Lord Chief Justice, William Murray, Earl of Mansfield, did occasionally visit Sir John Fielding, magistrate of Bow Street Court, yet it seldom boded well when he did. Far more often than not, 'twas he, the Lord Chief Justice, who summoned Sir John that he might impose some new task upon the Blind Beak of Bow Street (as he was popularly known), or had some favor to ask, anything indeed that might put a demand upon the magistrate's time and attention.

There seemed to be a sort of routine followed by the Lord Chief Justice on those rare occasions when he did visit at Number 4 Bow Street — or so it seemed to me. First we would hear his coach-and-four pull up at our entrance. Then, only seconds later, the door would slam open, then come the rapid click-click-click of his heels upon the pinewood floor all the way down the long hall to Sir John's chambers. His quick step announced him; it proclaimed him as the Lord Chief Justice, a man with no time to waste; it asked — nay, demanded — our notice more effectively than the loudest shout would have done.

That was the usual overture to his appearance. Upon this day in the year 1775, however, he made no such bid for our attention. A coach-and-four pulled up — yet we are visited from time to time by others in such grand conveyances. The door to Bow Street opened quietly and closed just so. We heard the footsteps in the hall, which were nothing at all like the footsteps of the Lord Chief Justice. They plodded along weakly and at one point even shuffled hesitantly, as if unsure of the way. We noted Mr. Fuller's greeting to our visitor, restrained and respectful. That made us wonder. Our jailer showed such deference to very few.

'Who could that be?' I asked in a whisper.

'Just what I was asking myself,' said Sir John in the same quiet voice. 'Why don't you take a look, Jeremy?'

At that I rose, tiptoed to the door, and peered down the hall and spied, to my great surprise, none other than the Lord Chief

Justice. His head was low, and as I bellowed forth his name in greeting, he barely raised his head to acknowledge it. This was so unlike him that I was inclined to ask myself if he might be ill (I soon saw that he was not). Entering, he dispensed with all formality and sank down into the chair nearest the door. Then, and only then, did he look up at Sir John, who had risen behind the desk to welcome our distinguished guest.

'Oh, sit down, Sir John,' said the Lord Chief Justice in his usual testy manner. 'This is no time to stand upon ceremony.'

'What sort of time is it, then?' asked the magistrate as he eased down into his desk chair.

'In truth, I can only speak for myself, but I confess that I am quite overcome with grief for a friend.'

'Well, tell me just who it is you grieve for, and allow me to share your sorrow.' Sir John, who did sometimes tease and bedevil his chief, allowed no hint of that in what he spoke: Indeed, he meant what he said. 'You may thus make it lighter for yourself,' he added.

'Yes, well, it was partly for that which I came.' He cleared his throat as his voice grew hoarse, but then he pressed on: 'Lord Lammermoor was a political ally, but far more than that to me. We were friends in the truest, deepest sense of the word. We were at Oxford together, both of us Brasenose lads. We came down the same year, as a matter of fact, and remained close all these years in London. Why, I even visited him one summer ten or twelve years ago at his home in Scotland. What a great palace of a place it was! Indeed, I remember — '

At that Sir John cleared *his* throat, signaling his wish that the Lord Chief Justice ought not allow himself to stray into anecdote and personal memories. Yet it was taken in good stead.

'Quite right, Sir John,' said he. 'This is no time for reminiscence. I shall stick to the facts, I promise.'

'And what are the facts?'

'Strange enough in themselves. But judge for yourself.' And having said thus much, he told the rest of his tale only a bit better than he had begun it.

Francis Talley, Lord Lammermoor, had worked late the night before upon the drafting of a bill which was to be put soon before both houses of Parliament. It was an emergency measure intended to take the initiative from those 'vexatious colonials' (the Lord Chief Justice's phrase and not my own). Calling for the blockading of the four busiest

4

American ports, it would effectively end all commercial activity between the British colonies and the whole of Europe.

'It should only be a matter of a short time,' said he, 'until every man of affairs from Boston to Virginia is agitating for an end to the blockage and the arrest of the Adams brothers. If we but attack their purses then — '

Again Sir John gave a polite cough, and again the Lord Chief Justice took the hint: 'Forgive me. I'm to make a speech in support of the bill and I fear I was extemporizing a bit there, warming to the subject, as it were.'

'Of course.'

'In any case, leaving late from his office, he walked alone to the Westminster Bridge and started across it.'

'The Westminster Bridge?' queried Sir John. 'What business had he across the river?'

'At this point one can only guess. My supposition is that after a long day of work, he simply took a walk to clear his head.'

'Took it alone, did he?'

'Quite alone, Sir John.'

'There were witnesses?'

'Practically every step of the way, in spite of the late hour.'

'Just how late was it?'

'Only a bit after one o'clock.'

'What happened then and there upon the Westminster Bridge astonished all who viewed it, for about halfway cross the Thames, Lord Lammermoor clambered over the rail and leaped into the cold waters below. Never having mastered the art of swimming, he drowned in short order. A waterman, who had just delivered a passenger in Southwark, was not near enough to save him, nevertheless saw him drown. 'Twas he brought in the body.'

Sir John listened attentively to the report. Then, when he was quite sure that the Lord Chief Justice had finished, he ventured the word that his chief wanted least to hear.

'Suicide, then?'

'No,' said the Lord Chief Justice. 'No, I cannot believe that of him. He was energetic, young in spirit, too much alive to allow any sort of trouble to overwhelm him.'

'Are you sure of that? I mean to say, how well did you know him . . . *really?*'

'As well, I think, as two men could possibly know each other. But then . . . ' He stopped then and, of a sudden, grew most thoughtful. 'Yet it is true that I had not seen him often in the past year. He was deeply involved in this awful contention with the colonies.'

'Some call it war.'

'It had best not come to that, for if the full

might of the British Empire is brought to bear upon those hapless colonials, they will be crushed utterly.'

'That's as may be,' said Sir John. 'However, what is it you wish me to do with regard to Lord Lammermoor?'

'What indeed?' said the Lord Chief Justice with a sigh. 'I can only tell you that I am certain in my heart that he did *not* commit suicide, no matter how the facts of the matter may indicate otherwise. Look into it, Sir John — as a favor to me — and I promise to leave the conclusion in your hands.'

'Meaning . . . what?'

'Meaning that in spite of whatever decision may be reached by tomorrow's coroner's inquest, you will not be deterred from looking further.'

'Hmmm, I see.'

'But do give significance to the fact that Lord Lammermoor has led opposition to the colonials from the time the Adams brothers first raised their heads.'

'Do you blame his death on them?' I could tell, reader, from the sound of Sir John's voice that he was quite astonished at such a suggestion.

'No, no, not another word. I leave it in your hands. I'll not urge you toward any conclusion in this. That would be unfair to you and demeaning both to me and to my office.' Then did he rise from his chair and bow to Sir John. 'That said, I'll be on my way. Thank you, Sir John.'

Thus did he take his leave. We stood staring after him as he went back the way he had come. I noted that he moved with a quicker step than before and seemed somehow invigorated by his visit to the magistrate. Perhaps he felt that now, having put the matter in the most capable hands, he had done all that could be done.

'What did you make of that, Sir John?'

'I know not quite what to say,' said he. 'I sympathized greatly with him when first he entered, for I believe he did truly love that fellow, Talley. Yet when he chose to blame the colonists for his friend's death . . . '

'It seemed quite daft, did it not? I should say that indeed his death seemed quite like suicide to me — even as the Lord Chief Justice tells it.'

'For what it's worth, I agree, but I must caution you, Jeremy, *daft* is a word you dare not use in reference to the thoughts and intentions of the Lord Chief Justice.'

'Yes, sir,' said I. 'You may be sure that I'll remember that, sir.'

★ ★ ★

In my defense, I could only say that I had come comparatively recently to my position as Sir John Fielding's clerk there at the Bow Street Court. Mr. Marsden, who had served long and faithfully, had died the year before. He had, in fact, left a modest legacy of a few pounds. Far more important, he had left me his job. Though I should gladly have performed Mr. Marsden's duties without compensation under ordinary circumstances, Sir John would not hear of it. And so I, who had then not yet reached my majority, was now earning near as much as Mr. Marsden had when he died the year before at age forty-seven. At first I felt unworthy, but soon I convinced myself that Sir John could not have found another so young in London who knew as much of the law as I (much less one who knew more). And so I was content that what I was given I deserved.

There was, I confess, another reason why I so eagerly accepted Sir John's largesse, and that had to do with Clarissa Roundtree. She and I were orphans and had been taken in by Sir John and Lady Fielding to help out in our different ways — she as Lady Fielding's general factotum, and I as Sir John's dogsbody. To put it briefly, we two were betrothed. We had courted in our own clumsy fashion; extorted the blessings of Sir John and his Lady from them by devious means; and posted the banns of wedlock. The date was set for a month in the future. I looked upon the prospect of my coming marriage to Clarissa Roundtree with all the terror which young men of my age (eighteen at the time) are expected to feel. Would we get along? Could I make money enough to keep her? What about children? When would they come? How many would there be? I was as fearful and frustrated as ever I could be.

And so, reader, you see that I had much at stake. Above all, I wished to please Sir John as his clerk — which, by and large, I had thus far done. Yet in addition, I would keep hard at my legal education so that I might be welcomed into the profession as soon as it were permitted.

I well recall that at that time I went about my business as one quite single-minded in demeanor but secretly scattered in his intentions.

That, I take it, is how I may have seemed to those unfortunates who, having spent the better part of the night in the strong room, would appear before Sir John that morning. It was my duty to interview each of them and get the particulars of the misadventures which had put them behind bars, how they would plead, et cetera. Sir John and I would then go over the notes that I had taken before he began his court session so that he might know better how to deal with the reprobates and sinners who came forth in our section of London (which included Westminster and the City) in never-ending supply. As magistrate, he had a reputation among the criminal population for his fair treatment of them. They knew he would not be taken for a fool, which is to say, he would not tolerate being lied to in such a manner as would not have tricked a ten-year-old. As a result, he usually got the truth from them. It was given to him to award sentences of up to ninety days for misdemeanors. More serious crimes are passed on for trial to the Felony Court at what will ever be known as the Old Bailey. Following the trial, it then fell to me to write a brief report on each of those who had appeared before Sir John during that session — and the disposition of each; these, of course, were kept for the files.

There was, of course, an additional sort of legal proceeding in which Sir John, as magistrate, was obliged to take part. In these he sometimes seemed to take honest pleasure. These were the disagreements — and there were many — between men of business which had to do with matters of business. Or do I speak too quickly? More often than not, they were quite simple and unimportant and had little to do with commercial matters. Still more often than not, they were simple disagreements. At first I thought that the one brought before Sir John on that day of the visit to us by the Lord Chief Justice was just such a one. Yet the importance of it, not immediately evident, seemed to grow.

Though there was no necessity to question them as I had those arrested on matters to do with misdemeanors and felonies, still, I had a few words with them before the session began simply to make sure they would be present when their case was called out from the docket.

'Oh, I'll be here,' promised one of the disputants. 'You can be sure of it.'

'Your name, sir?'

'Deekin's the name, Joseph Deekin.' I noted that he had an uncommonly deep voice.

'And you're the complainant?'

'The complainant?' He looked uneasily about him. Though at something of a disadvantage at that moment, he had strong eyes and a manner that bespoke a certain intelligence and wit. 'I fear,' said he, 'that I've no clear understanding of that word, *complainant*.'

Just as I opened my mouth to explain, an older man, well dressed and somewhat arrogant in attitude, stepped forward and with an all-knowing nod, declared, 'I am he. I am the complainant.'

'And your name, sir?'

'Doctor Hippocrates Grenfell, and I am come here to present my case against this . . . this bumpkin of a fellow. And what choice was I given but to complain? To take my plaint to court? My surgery is located in the north corner of Covent Garden, you see, next to the Theatre — '

'Please, please, Dr. Grenfell,' said I, interrupting, 'don't tell me your complaint. Save it for Sir John. I am here simply to make sure that you and Mr. Deekin are also here. I must also warn you that your dispute is last on his docket, so you must wait your turn.'

'How long must we wait, young fellow?'

'Oh, not long. No more than an hour.'

'An *hour!* Have you no idea of who — '

Again I interrupted. 'That will be fine. May I advise you to sit in the front row? And do, please, remember to keep your comments brief and succinct.'

By this time Dr. Grenfell had turned away in annoyance. Joseph Deekin, however, who had kept his silence throughout and had listened carefully to every word I had to say, gave a nod to me and muttered a proper thanks.

Later, though not much later, as I hurried through the docket with Sir John in his chambers, I took the opportunity to comment upon complainant and defendant.

'What did you say that fellow's name was?'

'Joseph Deekin?'

'No, no, the other one.'

'*Doctor* Hippocrates Grenfell. That's as he put it.'

'Hmmm.'

'Not that it matters,' said I, 'but I liked Deekin and thought Grenfell a conceited ass.'

'Well, indeed, you're right about that,' said Sir John.

What? Had I missed something? 'Sir?' said I in puzzlement.

'You're right when you say it doesn't matter.'

★   ★   ★

As for the session that followed, there could be little doubt that it went well. There were but five cases preceding the complaint lodged by Dr. Grenfell against Mr. Deekin. Sir John had heard four misdemeanor cases which he had settled with fines of no great consequence. 'Twas only the felony matter that gave him pause, for the accused felon, a Mr. Richard Nash, a great hulking fellow, had by his own admission beaten a man to death.

Sir John lingered over this matter, questioning him at great length, for he did not really believe that the fellow was guilty of the crime to which he had confessed — for that crime was murder. I myself had been shocked when, in making my survey of the prisoners, he had insisted that I put him down for 'murder.' And how did he plead? 'Guilty,' said Nash. 'The man's dead, and it was my blow killed him.'

After hearing Nash's own detailed account of the affray, Sir John set to work interrogating the man.

'Mr. Nash,' said he, 'now, you stated that the disagreement which led to your altercation took place in a dram shop. Is that correct?'

'Yes sir, at the King's Favorite in Bedford Street. I always gets in trouble when I drinks.'

'But never like this?'

'Oh no, sir.'

'Tell me, were you intoxicated . . . drunk?'

'Yes sir, wobbly legged, or so I was told.'

'Then you must answer this in all truth. Was it your intention when you left the dram shop to kill the man you left with?'

Nash hesitated. Then, having thought the

matter through, he said: 'No, sir, I can't say it was ever my intention to kill any man — or woman. But those who'd gone out there, they was eager for it, all excited for the fight, y'see. And he was followin' me real close, so close that just as I turned round I got his fist right in my face. Now, that made me angry because, y'see, I wasn't ready for it, not at all, and everybody who came to watch started laughin' at me. And so I just came at him. It didn't take more than two or three blows, and the fellow fell down. But even then I never wished him dead. I wouldn't want to murder anybody — but I did.'

'The constable who arrested you — who was it, Jeremy?'

'Mr. Bailey, sir.'

'Ah yes, our chief constable, he said that he found you sitting alone by the body. And what was your victim's name?'

'The truth is, sir, I never found out.'

'Well, Mr. Bailey himself said that the victim's body was in remarkably good condition. There was a bloody spot at the back of his head and a possible skull fracture. He certainly wasn't beaten to death. In other words, Mr. Nash, you didn't kill him — 'twas the fall to the cobblestones did him in. I would like you to revise your plea. Let me make it that you plead guilty of manslaughter,

16

which is to say that you are guilty of unintentionally causing the death of another.' Sir John withheld the final comment until Mr. Fuller came forward to claim the prisoner. Only then did he say, 'You see, Mr. Nash, the law does recognize that intentions matter.'

Then to me in a whisper: 'Jeremy, we must get off a recommendation for leniency to the Lord Chief Justice on Mr. Nash's behalf — transportation, et cetera. You know the sort of thing. Perhaps you could write it and read it to me.'

'Yes, sir. I'll put it together this afternoon.'

'What have we next? Call it out.'

That I did in loud and distinct tones. 'Grenfell versus Deekin,' I cried. The two men rose, and I gestured them forward till they stood just opposite us with naught but a table between.

'Mr. Grenfell,' said Sir John. 'Since you are the complainant — '

'That's Doctor Grenfell, if you please,' said he, interrupting.

'What will you?' asked Sir John, as if in disbelief. 'In my court, all are equal.' Not waiting for a response, he began again. 'Mr. Grenfell, since you are the complainant in this affair, will you move things along by stating your complaint against Mr. Deekin?'

For just a moment a frown moved fleetingly across the medico's face, a frown which I took to mean that he was considering trying once more to browbeat Sir John into addressing him by his honorific. It was fortunate for him that he dismissed the notion.

'Yes, yes, of course,' said he instead. 'I come before you, sir, as a last resort. I have tried to reason with this . . . with this *quack*, yet — '

With that did Sir John interrupt. 'Sir, I have always considered that word, *quack*, a term of opprobrium, as most do. Since nothing has been proved against Mr. Deekin as yet, please refrain from characterizing him so. Is that understood?'

'Quite understood, yes.'

'Proceed.'

'Ah . . . well, where was I? Now I recall. I have tried to reason with this *person*, yet he will do naught that I have pleaded with him to do.'

'And what is that? What is it you wish him to do? Or, conversely, what is it you wish him not to do?'

'I'm getting to that, sir!'

'Well, get to it more quickly, man!'

'All right! I am a doctor of medicine, fully empowered by the Crown to advise, treat,

18

prescribe, and otherwise do all that needs to be done to bring the sick body back to a state of good health. My surgery lies just above Covent Garden and right below it, there at the north corner of the Garden, Mr. Deekin has pitched his . . . his tent. And there, too, the noise that issues from that tent is sufficient to drive away my patients.'

'That is what you object to? That Mr. Deekin makes too much noise?'

'Well, no, it is the sort of noise that is made — and who makes it — that disturbs me.'

'You must be more clear.'

'I'm trying to be, sir.'

'Well,' said Sir John, 'what, for instance, is said by those inside the tent that disturbs you so? Is it some manner of religious ecstasy, a tumult of shouting, et cetera, in strange tongues?'

'No, not that exactly, though there is a bit of oohing and ahing done by the audience within. It's the cries of 'I'm cured! Praise God, I am cured!' That disturbs me and disturbs my patients, as well. And then when he comes out into the daylight to gather a crowd and sell his nostrums, he himself has a voice like unto a foghorn, or a growling bear, yet it seems to attract many. He has so far disrupted my practice that I scarce seem to have one — and I a true doctor.'

19

'All right, I have one last question for you before I allow Mr. Deekin to speak in his own defense. The question then is this . . . What result do you seek against him? What will satisfy you?'

Dr. Grenfell bowed his head slightly and put a hand to his brow as if thinking upon the question put to him by Sir John for the first time. I hoped this were not the case.

'To my mind,' said he, 'this man should be cast out of the Garden, together with his tent, his nostrums, and all his accessories, not least the slut he travels with.'

Quite of a sudden Mr. Joseph Deekin turned upon the good doctor and raised a fist, which he shook at him most threateningly. With that, there was an outcry from the courtroom crowd, which covered up most of what was said between them. And Sir John leaned to me and demanded to know just what it was had caused such a stir. I explained as best I could. 'Deekin said something about his wife and shook his fist at Grenfell. It looked for a moment as if he might indeed do more than shake it.'

The magistrate nodded. He beat hard upon the table with his gavel, though things had by then quieted down. He was agitated and angry.

'There'll be no more of that,' he shouted.

'You, Mr. Grenfell, sought to provoke Mr. Deekin with your language. You knew better than to insult him in the way you did. And you, Mr. Deekin, if you dare to raise your hand in my courtroom again, you will regret it most bitterly. You have my promise on that. If any such incident happens again, you will both be sent to Newgate for a month on a contempt-of-court charge — and I swear to you it will be thirty days you will never forget.'

The crowd was stilled, and the two who had caused the commotion were properly intimidated.

'Let us continue now,' said he. 'Mr. Deekin, how do you answer Mr. Grenfell's complaint?'

'There is much truth in it,' said Deekin in that low, growling voice of his. 'I do allow it, sir. When he says that people, a few of them, come out of the tent singing God's praises for having been cured of their pain he tells it a-right. And when he says that he scarce has a practice because of me, he also says it true. But the reason for that is because all, or nearly all, who was his patients are now my patients.'

'And what has brought them over to you?' asked Sir John. 'Is it the medicine you sell — what he calls your nostrums?'

'No sir, it ain't. Truth to tell, that's another one of those times when he got close to telling it real. You might say my medicine is just another one of those quack remedies.'

'You admit that?'

'Oh, I do right enough. It won't hurt anybody, but on the other hand, it won't do them much good, either. But that's not what I offer people. What I offer is treatment. It doesn't work on everybody, and I don't say that it does. But I let them all in to watch the treatment, and maybe take the treatment, too. And whilst they're on the way out, that's when they buy the medicine. People like to carry something away with them.'

I could tell at this point, Sir John had become interested. He leaned forward in his chair and said, 'Tell me about this treatment of yours. Of what does it consist?'

'Well, it's like this, sir. First, I put them to sleep.'

'But how do you do that? You have no pallet there in the tent, do you? No bed, certainly?'

'No, just chairs is all we got, and chairs is all we need — if it's going to work.'

'How do you mean that?' asked Sir John. 'You've said that your treatment, so-called, doesn't work on just everyone. Why is that?'

'Well, getting people to go to sleep is the

hardest part. Or maybe I shouldn't call it sleep. Maybe I should just call it a trance — that's what somebody said it was once. People in that sort of shape, it's like they could only hear my voice and were just waiting for me to tell them what to do.'

'But what about those who *don't* respond to your treatment? How many are there? *Why* don't they respond?'

'Well, what about them?' Mr. Deekin asked. 'How many? I'd put it about half, maybe less. I can't say exactly because I really don't know. Why don't they respond? Again, I don't know. Maybe they would if I worked on them a little longer, a little harder, but I can't say. There's an awful lot about this business I don't understand myself.'

'So it would seem,' said Sir John in a voice dry as dust. Then did he continue: 'All right, I accept what you say, but you must tell me now how it is that being put to sleep, as you put it, benefits them medically. You called it a treatment, after all, and it's that aspect to which Mr. Grenfell objected so fiercely. What good do you do those you manage to put into a trance?'

'Yes sir, I think I can answer that. It's like this, y'see. You may or may not have made note, sir, that a good many of the illnesses and pains people have come from inside them

— from their minds.'

'You mean headaches?'

'Not specially headaches, though that's one kind cert'ny, but I mean back pains, pains of the stomach, all kinds of pains. Now, I don't mean that the mind is the only cause — could be something that's a sign of something I couldn't fix, or even help with.'

'You mean that these pains — those that you say are from the mind — are no, not real pains at all, but rather creations of the imagination?'

'Oh no,' said Mr. Deekin, 'they're real enough, all right, to him who gets them. It's just . . . it's just that my treatment seems to give those who get it power over their bodies. When I tell them they'll be free of that pain from this day forth, they believe me, and they stop it from happening. And if it does happen, well, that's what that bottle of medicine is there for. I tell them to rub a little where it hurts, or if it hurts inside, just take a spoonful or two and you'll feel right as rain — no more pain!'

'And this medicine is what you yourself term a 'quack remedy.' Is that correct?'

'Yes, sir. But it won't hurt nobody.'

Sir John sighed and pulled a long face. 'Mr. Deekin,' said he, 'I mean naught but what I say when I tell you that your presentation,

24

though somewhat confusing, is one of the most fascinating that I have heard since I became magistrate of the Bow Street Court. You have been far more open in response to my questions than any of your sort has ever been. But I still have many questions — questions that I know not how to frame, simply because I have never before heard that kind of treatment such as you describe. It makes a decision in this matter very difficult.'

'Well, maybe it does, sir, but right here in this very place I could give you a demonstration. My assistant — who's the easiest I ever knew to put asleep, or maybe put into a trance, if that's the way you want it — she's right here just waiting for you to say the word.'

With that, a girl no older than I jumped up and out of the second or third row. She proceeded to the front of the room as Mr. Deekin beckoned her forward.

'Now this little girl, sir, she had the godawfulest stutter you ever heard till she took the treatment. Ain't that so, Hannah?'

'That's her,' shouted Dr. Grenfell. 'That's the one I was talking about.'

The court audience, caught up in the excitement of the moment, was now upon its feet, cheering Hannah on, applauding Mr. Deekin. Sir John was greatly annoyed at the noise and sudden unruly behavior. He began beating upon the desk with his gavel a dozen times harder than before. He shouted for silence, directed Hannah back to her seat, and threatened to clear the courtroom.

'And as for you, Mr. Deekin, there is nothing I dislike more than to have my courtroom turned into a wild carnival. My threat of Newgate was not an idle one, I can assure you.'

Deekin hung his head but managed, in any case, to nod, and thus signaled his compliance.

'And finally, you, Mr. Grenfell, should know that I brook no such behavior in my courtroom. I do not care if this Hannah person is the one you referred to earlier. I do not care if she has been cured of her stuttering. I care for nothing, in fact, but bringing this to a fair and equitable decision, and it now seems that such is quite impossible as matters are today. Mr. Deekin, someone from the Bow Street Court will be calling you, sir, in the next few days to observe your 'treatment' — if that is what we shall call it, and no doubt to ask a few more questions as well. For matters of our convenience, Mr. Grenfell, that same representative will call upon you, sir, for by that time I'm sure I will have some questions for you, too. I believe that all this may be handled with dispatch. So let us say that both of you return in five days. Make it Friday next.'

'Must we wait so long?' moaned Mr. Grenfell.

'No, I could decide today, if you prefer, but I assure you that if I did on the basis of what I have so far heard, your complaint would be denied.'

Grenfell offered a rather sick smile. 'Take as long as you like,' said he.

★   ★   ★

Once the court session was done, the papers filed, and Sir John satisfied that nothing more need be attended to, it was the usual thing for me to repair to the kitchen above to discuss the doings of the day with Clarissa. On this day in particular I had something a little out of the ordinary to talk to her about. But as I approached the door at the top of the stairs, it became evident that I should have to postpone my discussion with Clarissa. We had a guest. Who it was I had no idea. I quite refused to knock upon any door that I considered my own, but on the other hand I wished to surprise no one, and so I stamped loudly upon the steps as I climbed them. In response, the door came open, and Clarissa stood in the open space, squinting down at me.

'Oh,' said she, 'it's Jeremy.'

'Well, you needn't sound so disappointed,' said I. 'Who is here?'

'You'd never guess.'

'Then tell me.'

Rather than that, she stepped aside to reveal our former cook, Annie Oakum. (But to say that does her no justice at all. She, having a great love of Shakespeare, had taught herself to speak proper English properly and joined David Garrick's troupe at the Drury Lane Theatre. She advanced rapidly and soon became a leading player in the company.) No older than I, she was but a year or two Clarissa's senior. Nevertheless, she was in some ways older than either of us — and in some ways much, much younger.

In surprise, I shouted her name.

'Shh! Please, Jeremy, don't announce me quite so loudly,' said she.

'Why? Is this a surprise visit? Or, well, what is it brings you here?'

In truth, she had not visited often. I had not seen her away from the theater in over a year.

'Oh, I know,' said she, 'there is little I can say in my own defense. It's just that my life has changed so I myself can scarce believe it.

But you asked what brings me here, and I'll tell you.'

There she paused, evidently knowing not where to begin. At last she found a place.

'Now, Jeremy,' said she, 'I am not sure that you know this — indeed, I think you do not — but Lord Lammermoor and I were great friends. You . . . you have heard that he is dead, have you not?'

'I have. The Lord Chief Justice came by to tell us just this morning. He was quite upset. They were very old friends. They went all the way back to Oxford together, as I understand it.'

'Yes, that's as I heard it from him.'

'Very well,' said I, 'what then have you to add to what is known already?'

'A good deal, it would seem,' said Annie. 'There is to be a coroner's inquest tomorrow afternoon. There are things that I know which would indeed surprise the coroner's jury and the coroner himself.'

'What kind of things, Annie? What do you know? How do you know them?'

'I know them because I was there.'

'You were there with him?'

'Every step of the way.'

'But Annie, you must tell them this — everything you know.'

'I can't, Jeremy. Don't you understand? If it

were known that I was with him at such an hour, it would besmirch his name and humiliate his wife during her last days.'

'She's ill?'

'Oh, very. What can I do, Jeremy?' she asked. 'I have information for Sir John, yet I cannot divulge it to him direct. Could . . . could you pass it to him without giving the source?'

'Well,' said I, '*perhaps* I could . . . ' Though how that might be done, I could not for the life of me suppose.

'Oh, for God's sake, Annie,' said Clarissa, 'tell him.'

Then did she look at our expectant faces, heaved a sigh, and nodded. Only then did she begin.

'Lord Lammermoor visited me after last night's performance, as he usually does. We went first to the House of Lords, where he keeps his office. There was some bill or other he had to check over before it went before Parliament, then were we off to my new rooms just across the bridge from the Houses of Parliament.' She turned of a sudden to Clarissa and said, 'Oh, Clare, it's such a beautiful place — and I've got it near furnished. You *must* come and see it.'

'In Southwark, is it?' I put in.

'Why, yes.'

'A bit fraught with risk that side of the river, wouldn't you say so?'

'Oh, but it's so near the Houses of Parliament. There are guards round it, day or night.'

I was becoming a bit annoyed with her. 'Well, I'll not argue that with you now. Get on with your story, Annie.'

So it was that she began again. 'Well, we were just crossing the bridge, as I said. Lord Lammermoor had little to say. He seemed to be taken up completely by that silly bill he'd left, still trying sentences one way and then another, talking to himself in just such a way. There were ever so many people on the bridge, even at that time of night, yet I recognized none of them. He, however, looked up of a sudden and spied one coming toward us he seemed to know. How could he tell? The light there was none too good — it never is. And what's more, the man approaching was so thickly wrapped in cape and coat, with hat pulled down and scarf pulled up, that I scarce recognized him as a man at all.

'Lord Lammermoor signaled me to move ahead of him,' she continued, 'that we might appear separate. I was used to such maneuvers, for he was constantly running into those who knew us not together, and so I drifted away from him, thus making it hard for me to get clear what it was happened next.'

'Annie, you must tell me, what *did* happen next.' She was telling her tale well enough — none of the previous digressions — but how I wished that she would hurry along with it.

'I'm coming to that!' (She fair shouted it out to me.) 'There was some sign of recognition that passed between them and one or two words spoken. The stranger hurried on, and Lord Lammermoor then scrambled up onto the railing of the bridge and threw himself off and into the Thames. I grasped at him, but I was in no wise able to save him. All ran to the spot from which he had jumped — all but me. For having lost him, I knew that it was most important that I not be recognized by anyone, and therefore, by some quirk, responsible for my lover's death.'

'Ah, your lover?' Clarissa crowed.

'Of course he was my lover, Clarey. We were to be married soon as ever his wife died.'

'But . . . but . . . '

'Never mind that now,' said I, interrupting. 'There are a few questions I must ask now, and you must think hard upon them. First of all — and most important — what was it this mysterious stranger said to Lord Lammermoor?'

Annie faced me square-on and fixed me with her brown eyes. 'Jeremy,' said she, 'I have no idea what was said. I heard it as little more than a couple of grunts.'

'And there was no reply from Lord Lammermoor?'

'None that I heard. He simply jumped up to the railing and off the bridge.'

'A man his age jumped to the railing?'

'Yes, he surprised me in that.'

'And what about the man who spoke to him? Did you come any closer to recognizing him? Could you describe him?'

'Not very well, beyond saying that he was of medium height, had on a proper suit of clothes, and wore cologne water.'

'A gentleman, then,' said Clarissa.

'Or one pretending to such,' said I.

Then did Annie linger only long enough to caution me to withhold her name from Sir John, no matter what. I made no such promise, but Annie left before a word more could be said, calling out her assurances that she need not be accompanied to the street, for she knew the way well.

We watched her go and heard her close the door behind her.

'Well, what did you think of that?' said I to Clarissa.

'I know not what to make of what she told you about that most peculiar matter of the dive from the bridge, but as for her conduct with that Lord whatever-his-name, I confess I am quite shocked.'

'You? Shocked?'

'Indeed I am. He sounds positively ancient.'

'No doubt he is. He is a contemporary of the Lord Chief Justice.'

'That settles it then. She's turning out as every other actress. They all want a title and a fortune to go with it, or so I have heard.' A sudden shudder took her. 'Oh, and I'd thought so much better of her.'

2

*In which I find a
surprise at my first
coroner's inquest*

Somehow — and I'm sure that the fault was mine — I did not manage to communicate Annie's strange news to Sir John until much later that day. It was indeed late in the evening, and I on my way to bed, when I heard him stirring in his closet-sized study, perhaps also intending to retire. But remembering what I had left unsaid, I stopped at his open door and tapped upon it.

'Is that you, Jeremy? Come in, lad.'

I accepted his invitation with quiet thanks and slipped into the chair just opposite his own.

'You may light the lamp, if you like,' said he — no more than a formality of welcome, for he knew quite well that I liked sitting with him in the darkened room. 'What occasions your visit? Something special?'

'Yes sir, there was something I should have

told you earlier. Clarissa and I received a visit from Annie in the afternoon, and she told us something she should have told you herself.'

'Oh? And what was that?'

Without further ado I presented Annie's story to him as she had told it to us, giving particular attention to the mysterious stranger she and Lord Lammermoor met upon the bridge, his dress, and his nearly inaudible message to the nobleman.

'And it was following this that he leaped past the guardrail and into the river?' asked Sir John.

'Yes, sir. It was.'

'Well,' said he, 'it seems that we two must now change our opinions on the matter of Lord Lammermoor's death. Yes, it would seem that the Lord Chief Justice was not nearly so daft when he insisted that his old friend would never have committed suicide.'

'Apparently so. I must tell you, however, Sir John, that Annie prevailed upon me not to tell you that she was with Lord Lammermoor on Westminster Bridge. She ran away soon as he jumped.'

'Oh? Well, I can understand that — the gossip, et cetera.'

'Yes, but it also seems that there is a Lady Lammermoor who, according to Annie, is at death's door, leaving Lord L. an eligible widower. Annie wishes to cause the poor woman no added grief.'

'And he made promises to Annie, did he?' asked Sir John. Then did he fall silent for a period of time. But rousing himself, he said quietly, as if only musing aloud: 'Perhaps it might be best if we granted Annie her wish for anonymity. Jeremy, I want you to go tomorrow to Coroner Trezavant's inquest into the death of Lord Lammermoor. Gather names, make contacts, as we should have to do, in any case, for we shall start our own investigation. Doubtless the jury will find in favor of death by suicide. Do nothing to upset the verdict. Say nothing of what you heard from Annie to them. If we do it so, we shall be able to investigate in secret and have a much freer hand.'

⋆ ⋆ ⋆

And so it was that I set out for the Crown and Anchor in the Strand a bit earlier than was my wont. It may seem odd to you, reader, that the coroner's inquests were then held in such a place, but after all, they were not convened every day of the week, and the tavern and its ballroom, which seated a great many, were unused till noon. Thus did it work well for all concerned, though it required an eight o'clock commencement when the ballroom was to be used for official purposes.

Ordinarily, at such an hour I would be interviewing those who would be facing Sir John at noon. I had glimpsed this day's assemblage in the strong room and thought them a rather hard-looking lot. So was I made somewhat uneasy at the thought of my intended exposed to the worst that Covent Garden had to offer. Strange, thought I, how I had grown more protective toward Clarissa as our wedding date grew near.

I had been to the Crown and Anchor's ballroom a number of times for various purposes. Yet (oddly, to my way of thinking) I had never attended a coroner's inquest there. In fact, except for those few occasions when Sir John took over the duties of the late Sir Thomas Cox, prior to the appointment of Mr. Trezavant as the new coroner of the City of Westminster, I had never attended a coroner's inquest. I was curious, though not specially optimistic, as to how he might acquit himself in this role. I confess that even then I had not great respect for the man. And how, if one cannot command respect as a man, can he be expected to work satisfactorily as a judge? Fundamentally, you see, this is what the coroner is. He functions with a jury and has the right to engage in colloquy with witnesses. He may also direct verdicts. Nevertheless, he is severely limited as to what sort of verdict he may render: death by misadventure (i.e., accidental); death by his own hand (suicide); or death at the hands of person or persons unknown (murder or manslaughter).

Though the Crown and Anchor ballroom was much larger than Sir John's small courtroom, the resemblance between the two was quite remarkable. In truth, 'twas the ballroom which seemed quite like a proper auditorium of the sort provided at Old Bailey. It was far more crowded than I had expected. But then, how many times is an inquest expected to rule on the death of an earl? Upon the stage sat the jury on one side, and on the other, a bench where sat a number of men whose faces were unknown to me. But among them the presence of Mr. Donnelly — surgeon, doctor, and medical examiner to the City of Westminster — assured me that these were the witnesses waiting to be called and sworn in, that they may give testimony. And there was something else about another of their number which seemed to tell me that I knew him from sometime before. But who was he, and what were the circumstances of our previous meetings? Between jury and witnesses was an elevated chair which now stood empty. That, doubtless, was intended for Thomas Trezavant; from it he would direct the proceedings.

I took a seat upon a chair quite close to the front of the audience. It afforded me a good view of both the stage and all those in the audience. As I waited, I began counting those present — from back to front. By the time I had counted up to fifty, with no more than a few more to go, I noted a woman dressed in widow's weeds and presumed her to be Lady Lammermoor. Yet in black, as she was, and wearing a heavy veil, there was no way to be certain. (I had also seen Annie in a dark, rear corner, removed from the rest.)

'All rise!'

An individual in some sort of special livery had appeared from behind the side curtain. 'Twas he who called out to the congregation: 'Mr. Thomas Trezavant, coroner of the City of Westminster, will now preside over an inquest into the death of Francis Talley, Lord Lammermoor.'

Mr. Trezavant did then make his entrance, marching across the stage in a manner most dignified. Truth to tell, he was much overweight, yet in this case, the slow and solemn gait forced upon him by the excess seemed altogether proper. He wore a robe of office (which Sir John had never done), and his feet tangled in it somewhat as he took his seat in the large chair in the center of the stage and behind a desk of sorts.

'All be seated.'

And as we returned to our chairs, he who had brought us to our feet also took his place at a small recording desk near the witness bench. He, I saw, would serve as a sort of court clerk.

Folding his hands before him, Mr. Trezavant leaned forward and began a sort of introduction to what lay ahead: 'As all of you must know, we are here to inquire into the death of Lord Lammermoor. It is, in many ways, a baffling case. We know *that* he died. We know *how* he died, yet in any true and final sense we do not know the *true* cause of his death. The purpose of this inquest is to examine, and in a few instances *re-examine* the known facts in hopes of turning up something new and pertinent that will help us understand the true cause of Lord Lammermoor's death. But enough of this. Let us proceed.'

All the time he had spoken he had not raised his voice. He gave emphasis in a few places where it was needed to make things clear, but it was clear that he had no wish to milk from the nobleman's death undue sentiment or sensation.

'Mr. Lawson,' said the coroner, 'call the first witness.'

'Michael Wilson, please rise.'

Michael Wilson, as it turned out, was Lord Lammermoor's Parliamentary assistant. Young and eager to be helpful, he misspoke a number of times in attempting to convey matters of a routine sort — his age, how long he had held the position he now held, that sort of thing.

'Mr. Wilson,' said Trezavant, 'would you please describe Lord Lammermoor's state the last time you were with him?'

'Oh, it was very good, sir,' said he. 'For months, you see, he's been troubled by the colonials, wanting to do something to put them in their place, and so on. And he'd come up with a plan, but the trick of it was to get the plan into a bill that would pass muster, as they say.'

At that point young Mr. Wilson began an attempt to explain the plan and the bill, but Mr. Trezavant stopped him. 'Has this bill been put before the House of Lords — or, for that matter, the House of Commons?'

'Uh, no, sir.'

'Then let us not discuss it. I think it improper to discuss Parliamentary matters before they have even been introduced in either House. And besides, that sort of thing is not really essential to the question I asked. I simply wanted you to describe Lord Lammermoor's state when last you saw him.'

'Oh, then, Mr. Trezavant, sir, I would say that he was in a very good state. We went over the bill together and talked it through right down to the last jot and tittle. Getting it ready to be printed up — that was what we were up to, so there'd be something to argue over. That's how it's done, you see.'

'I'd always wondered,' said Trezavant in a rather dry style.

'We spent well over an hour on it. And then he was satisfied, and so they left.'

The coroner gave him a long, hard look. 'Hold now. Just a moment. Did I hear you say *they* left?'

'Uh, well, yes, sir, you did.'

'Will you account for that, please?'

'Yes, sir, Lord Lammermoor had with him a young lady. His intention, I believe, was to see her home.'

'I see,' said Mr. Trezavant. 'Do you know her? Did you recognize her?'

'No, sir. I did not.'

'And were you introduced to her?'

'No, sir. I was not.'

'Then, Mr. Wilson, will you look round the audience and see if you recognize her among those seated here.'

'Yes,' said he, 'certainly, sir.'

And so saying, young Mr. Wilson turned and looked out into the audience. Scanning from his left to his right, he went through the fifty-odd who were present quite slowly row by row. There was approximately one woman for every two men there, and each looked anxiously at the others as Wilson made his survey. Most anxious of all was Lady Lammermoor. She turned this way and that, even raised her veil, that she might see better. She looked long and specially hard at Annie — or so it seemed. Perhaps — even probably — they had met before. But Annie, smart girl, did not return the woman's stare. Rather, she twisted about and looked all round her, as the rest were doing.

At last, Mr. Wilson turned back to the coroner. 'I don't see her,' said he.

Whether he had failed to recognize her, or simply, for whatever reason, chosen to overlook her, I could not say, but I was curious.

'You may step down,' said Mr. Trezavant. 'Call the next witness, Mr. Lawson.'

His name was Triplett, and he had evidently been chosen because he was the nearest to Lord Lammermoor when the latter dove into the Thames. Triplett himself cast a bit of doubt upon this in response to the questions of the coroner. He had been asked, as I recall, if he were the only one who might have had some chance of saving the Earl of Lammermoor.

'Now, that I couldn't rightly say,' said he. 'There was many on the bridge that night.'

'How many? Give us an estimate.'

'A dozen at least.'

'Where were you in relation to Lord Lammermoor? That is, were you back of him? Ahead? How far away?'

Mr. Triplett estimated that he was more than ten yards behind the nobleman but less than twenty. There was also a gentleman all bundled up who had just passed him and a young lady who was off to his left.

'When of a sudden,' Mr. Triplett said, 'Lord Lammermoor scrambled up on the handrail, we all ran for him to grab him so as to keep him from jumping. Wasn't a doubt in our minds but that was what he had got up there to do.'

Then, having said thus much, he stopped. 'It just came to me that what I just said, it ain't quite right.'

'Why? What do you mean?'

'Well, the young lady — she wasn't no whore, I'm just sure of that — she lets out a terrible scream, and it was that what got my attention. Then she run for him, and I run for him, and it was a close thing, but we both missed him. He got away from us, and he hit the river hard. 'Twould have knocked him out, I judge. But there was a strange thing about all this. Remember I said there was another one of us near the Lord?'

'Ah yes. You described him as a gentleman.'

'Just so. Well, he wasn't anywheres to be seen. Soonest thing as the Lord jumped there were people all around, leaning over to look for him in the river. The young lady was there, pulling away, getting ready to go. And I looked for that gentleman, and he wasn't anywheres to be seen. Then I caught sight of him just walking away at his own good time. He didn't even turn round to look. I looked round me again, and I saw that she was gone, too — only in the other direction, towards Southwark.'

'Tell me, Mr. Triplett, could this young lady who screamed and led the charge to Lord Lammermoor have been the same one mentioned by Mr. Wilson?'

'Well, I don't know, sir. I ain't really got any idea about that.'

'How could you be so sure that she was not a prostitute?'

'She was too well dressed for that, and she kept to herself, wasn't casting her eye about. But just one more thing, sir.'

46

'And what is that, Mr. Triplett?'

'When his lordship got up there, ready to jump, he made these funny movements with his arms. He kept it up right up to the time he hit the water.'

Mr. Trezevant frowned. 'What sort of movements?' he asked. 'Show me, please.'

And that is what he did, standing before one and all, flapping his arms foolishly. In response, there were giggles, snickers, and suppressed laughter from those in attendance.

'Just so, was it?'

'Just so, sir.'

'Hmmm.' A moment passed as the coroner mused upon Triplett's bizarre impersonation of the nobleman. At last: 'You may step down, sir.'

Then, rather quickly, Mr. Trezavant took Richard Porter, an elderly waterman, through his testimony. The coroner must have known in advance that the old fellow had one — and only one — thing of interest to contribute, for after getting a few routine matters (name, profession, etc.) out of the way, he went right to the point.

'Mr. Porter,' said he, 'over the years, how many bodies would you suppose you have taken from the Thames?'

The waterman hesitated, rubbing his chin

in thought. 'Well, just let me count up, sir. I'm near sixty. I got my first boat over forty years ago, and for a time. I'd get about one floater a year. Not near so many anymore, though.'

'And why is that?'

'Well, it ain't because there's fewer of them. It's just there's more watermen working the same stretch of river. Why, it used to be a man could make a tidy living but now you — '

'Before we get too far away from it, let me put the original question to you once more. How many bodies do you suppose you have pulled out of the river?'

'About twenty-five, sir.'

'All dead?'

'Yes sir, but not all by drowning.'

'Oh? How else would they have died?'

'Murder, sir.' Then, after hesitating a moment, he continued: 'There's accidental deaths, too, from drowning. And suicides, of course — they're by far the most. I'd say we get more suicides than anything.'

'How can you tell?'

'Well, the usual suicide loads his pockets with rocks, or cobblestones, or bricks — whatever he can find to weigh him down.'

'Now, you, sir, pulled Lord Lammermoor out of the river, did you not?'

'I did, sir. They were wavin' and shoutin' at me and pointin' down at the water when I caught sight of the body.'

'You were first to examine him?'

'I was.'

'Did you find any rocks or whatever in Lord Lammermoor's pockets?'

'No, sir.'

'Anything to make him heavier?'

'No, sir.'

'Would you say that the fact that you found no such objects proves that Lord Lammermoor had not intended his death? In other words, proves that he was not a suicide?'

Richard Porter puffed his cheeks, looked up and down, and he said at last, 'Proves it? No, sir, I would not say so. But I would say that it makes it more than likely that he was no suicide.'

'And you're basing that on your experience in examining the approximately twenty-five bodies you took from the Thames?'

'Yes, sir — that and my talk with the men I work with.'

'I'll accept your amendment,' said Mr. Trezavant. 'That will be all then, Mr. Porter. You may step down.'

Mr. Donnelly was at last called. He had not long before returned from Ireland a married man. His bride, Molly Sarton, had for a time been our guest at Number 4 Bow Street. And during the time she was with us, she cooked for us and taught Clarissa all the tricks in the culinary arts that she knew. And in the course of all this she had been introduced by Sir John to Mr. Donnelly. 'Twas not long thereafter that the two announced their intention to marry.

Mr. Donnelly, a doctor and formerly a naval surgeon, had much to occupy him, I was sure, what with establishing a new home and surgery. Yet he could in no wise neglect his duties as medical examiner, for his appointment to that position (arranged by Sir John) was that which had made all possible for him. It had given him position. In point of fact, he rather disliked Mr. Trezavant, as he later confessed, and it soon became easy to understand why.

Upon beginning and in answer to the coroner's questions, he gave his name, his profession, and his honors, such as they were. By the time he had done, all his listeners had a fair idea of his accomplishments.

'As medical examiner,' said Mr. Trezavant, 'you must have examined the body of Lord Lammermoor.'

'Indeed I did, sir. My report on the matter is on your desk at this moment.'

'Ah yes, so it is.'

'I have a copy, though.' He took it from his coat pocket and began reading from it aloud: 'Death by drowning was the immediate cause, but there are other — '

'Rather than read it to us,' said Mr. Trezavant, interrupting, 'perhaps it might be better if you answered a few questions.'

'As you wish.'

'In making your examination, I take it you first stripped the body, did you?'

'Of course.'

'Well, tell me then, did you find any marks upon Lord Lammermoor's body?'

'Marks, sir? Marks of what sort?'

'Oh . . . wounds, I suppose. Anything on his skin that might indicate that harm had been done — intentional harm, that is.'

Mr. Donnelly seemed for a moment to be slightly confused by Mr. Trezavant's explanation, though he made a quick recovery. 'No wounds on his skin,' said he quite firmly. 'But when I — '

'Good, good,' said he, again interrupting. 'But tell me, please, for I've no way of knowing since I've not been present at any one of them, do you actually cut into the bodies and examine the organs?'

'Oh yes, of course.'

A collective shudder ran through all who listened. The thought of such cruel treatment to a body after death was perhaps a little too much for them all. The ladies fanned their faces more vigorously than ladies are wont to do. The gentlemen fell to clearing their throats epidemically.

'And what did you find?' asked the coroner. 'Let's say in the stomach. What did you find there?'

'What did I find in his stomach?' A smile spread over his round face. 'Why, I found naught but the remains of his last meal — steak-and-kidney pie, by the look of it.'

A great round of deep, male laughter responded. The coroner made use of his gavel for the first and only time.

'Silence, please! I will have silence!' Mr. Trezavant seemed a bit flustered. 'Sir, I ask you to be serious.'

'I *am* serious. Just as I said, I found naught in Lord Lammermoor's stomach but the remains of his last meal.'

'No evidence of poison?'

'None at all.'

'Then, sir, considering the absence of marks or wounds upon the body, and the fact, as given by you, that there were no traces of venom in his stomach, is it not certain — or at least likely — that he was neither shot, stabbed, nor poisoned?'

'Well, I . . . .'

'Please, sir, the proposition seems simple enough.'

'Yes,' protested Mr. Donnelly, 'but there are other — '

'That will be *all*,' said Mr. Trezavant, interrupting once again. 'You may step down.'

And step down he did, having given up the fight before it did truly begin. I, for one, was quite disappointed.

'There is but one last witness, and we shall not detain him long, for he is the son of the subject of this inquest,' said the coroner. 'If I may invite Mr. Archibald Talley to stand I have but a few questions for him.'

Archibald Talley, of course! No wonder he had looked so familiar to me. Some four or five years ago I had brought him to meet Sir John, and young Mr. Talley had displeased Sir John greatly with his patronizing manner, his sense of privilege. He made no such display on this day as he stood and faced Mr. Trezavant. Rising unsteadily, he pulled himself erect, yet still his head was bowed as if pulled down by his heavy heart.

'You're bearing up quite marvelously well, Mr. Talley, but perhaps you could tell me, sir, was it you who identified the body as that of your father?'

'It was.' Spoken so quietly it seemed almost a whisper.

'And there was never a doubt in your mind?'

'None whatever.'

'And are you to become the next Lord Lammermoor?'

'Not I but my brother, who was Vicar of St. Swithen's Church in Liverpool. He has recently been made Bishop of the See of Liverpool. He could not wind up his affairs quickly enough to be here, and so he asked me by post to serve in his stead and represent the family.'

'None could have done it better. Your brother would be proud of you if he could see you.'

'Thank you, sir.'

'But one last question. To your knowledge, could your father swim?'

'To the best of my knowledge, he could not. Though we weren't on familiar terms, and I never had occasion to find out, it was generally known within the family that he could not.'

'Thank you, Mr. Talley. You may step down.'

'Thank you, sir.' Then did he retire with great dignity.

'In a sense, we should mourn all who pass through this rite of inquiry,' said Thomas Trezavant, as he began his summation. 'Still, it seems to me that Lord Lammermoor was specially worthy of our tears. Yet in this instance, our inquest into his death has proven worthwhile. It has answered a number of puzzling questions with which we began it — and answer them in such a way that they may bc of consolation to the grieving family.

'Mr. Richard Porter, a waterman of many long years of experiencc, cascd our minds on the first count — that of the possibility of death at Lord Lammermoor's own hand. Mr. Porter, who has taken twenty-five or more bodies from the Thames, introduced to us a most interesting fact: that those who intend suicide load their pockets with rocks, bricks — anything, in short, that will weigh them down and hasten drowning. Since no such objects were found in Lord Lammermoor's pockets, we could rightfully conclude that it was not his intention to drown himself. And for that, of course, we are all most grateful.'

(Let me interject here, reader, that even I, who have had no formal training in logic or rhetoric, found something wrong with *that*.)

'Secondly,' he continued, 'the testimony of our medical examiner, Mr. Donnelly, revealed that there were no marks or wounds upon Lord Lammermoor's body and no internal evidence that poison had been administered.

Therefore we may conclude that Lord Lammermoor was not murdered. And this, too, offers comfort to us and to the family.

'If, by elimination, we have dispensed with suicide and murder as the possible cause of death, we are left with naught but 'death by misadventure' — and that will be the finding of this inquest.'

With that, Mr. Trezavant turned to the jury and asked that the foreman stand. He then addressed him as follows: 'Mr. Foreman, I direct you and the jury to return a verdict in the matter of Lord Lammermoor of 'death by misadventure.'' The jury huddled for hardly more than a minute (and perhaps less). Then did the foreman of the jury return to the coroner with the verdict in virtually the same words in which it had been given him. Mr. Trezavant then struggled to his feet.

'And that,' said he, 'is the opinion of this inquest into the death of Francis Talley, Lord Lammermoor.'

'All rise,' shouted the clerk.

And indeed we all rose to our feet as the coroner made his slow exit at stage left. Once he had disappeared, I made my way as quick as ever I could to the stage.

★　★　★

56

As Mr. Donnelly and I walked swiftly down the Strand we talked of nothing else but what had to come to pass within the ballroom of the Crown and Anchor. I fear that I was partly to blame for the hostile nature of our talk, for I provided the flame which sent the Irishman's short fuse sputtering to life. It all began, you see, when, just as we had left the Crown and Anchor, I made what I thought to be an innocent enough comment. I remember telling the good doctor that I had never before been to a coroner's inquest, and that under the circumstances, I thought that Mr. Trezavant had conducted himself rather well — much better, in any case, than I had expected.

That was the flame, reader, and then, almost simultaneous, came the explosion.

'Never been to a coroner's inquest before, have you not? Well, let me tell you something, Jeremy my lad, you haven't been to one yet — not in any proper sense!'

'Did he not follow proper procedure? I thought that — '

'You'll find nothing wrong with the *form* of his little dramas — ah! But the *matter* of it, that's something else again. In his hands — and I admit he does it all rather cleverly — an inquest is simply a device for advancing his career, each one of them providing an opportunity to curry the favor of those in power. It is all mapped out in advance.'

'Oh?' said I. 'Well, surely he couldn't have intended to reveal the presence of a young lady. That caused quite a stir — and will no doubt cause an even greater one.' (Poor Annie!)

'What is that Sir John keeps telling you? 'Think like a lawyer!' Well, I believe he has finally done it.'

'Done what?'

'Gotten you to think like a lawyer. You went right to the weakest point in my argument. You're right. He had neither intention nor wish to introduce her — whoever she may be — into the inquest. But once he had asked that young fellow — the legislative assistant — to explain his use of 'they,' then the cat was out of the bag, as they say. He had to carry on. None, I'm sure, was more relieved than he that the young fellow could neither name her, nor spy her amongst the onlookers. And so I must allow that Trezavant simply made a mistake and was forced to recover as best he could. But what about his interview with the waterman? That went all his way, didn't it?'

'Why . . . yes,' I admitted, and 'I must say that provides an instance in which his logic was employed quite illogically.'

'Well put, Jeremy, well put indeed! The idea of accepting the notion that to separate the suicides from the rest it is necessary only to go through their pockets for stones — that is surely one of the most outrageous suggestions ever heard in an inquest of this sort. Stones fall out of the pockets. Suicides often act on impulse and may not feel the need to go about searching for stones of the proper size and weight.'

'Or,' said I, joining in, 'they may be new to suicide and simply never heard of the time-honored practice of hastening the process of drowning in just such a way.'

'Exactly! And his treatment of me!'

'I call that downright rude, to say the least.'

'I have naught but contempt for the man,' said he. 'And a good thing Molly had not attended. She would have attacked that lump of midden right up there on the stage and given him a piece of rudeness he'd never forget.'

'Tell me, sir,' said I, 'what was it that our friend, the coroner, was so eager to keep you from saying?'

'It had little to do with the cause of death, nothing of the sort. Since he seemed determined to understand that the absence of wounds and the fact that there was no trace of poison in his stomach meant one thing only: that Lord Lammermoor had not been murdered. I simply wished to point out and have it on the inquest record that there are other ways to die besides murder, suicide, and death by misadventure.'

★　★　★

I was prepared to part with Mr. Donnelly when we arrived at Number 4 Bow Street. Yet he entered with me, asking only if this were a good time to visit Sir John.

'As good as any,' said I.

And so we entered together — I off to interview the prisoners in the strong room, and my companion continuing down the long corridor to Sir John's chambers. Watching him go, I found myself wondering idly just what it was he had to discuss with the magistrate. I was not to discover the answer to that until after Sir John had completed his noon court session. He invited me back with him that we might have — as he put it — 'a little talk.' That made me a bit uneasy. Could he have found fault with my work? Nothing of the kind. Nevertheless, when he asked me to shut the door after me, there could be no doubt in my mind that the little talk we were to have concerned a very serious matter.

'Sit down, Jeremy,' said he, as he sank into

the chair behind his desk. 'Mr. Donnelly has brought me some disturbing news. It is up to us to decide what, if anything, is to be done about it.'

'What is it, sir?' He had me worried.

'Perhaps I'm putting too dire a face on it, but you see he's talking of going back to Ireland. Well, more than that, really. It seems that he's been offered a practice in Dublin to share with a rather elderly doctor. The understanding, which the doctor is willing to put into writing, is that he will be retiring soon and wishes to leave the practice to Mr. Donnelly.'

'And how does Mr. Donnelly feel about this?'

'He feels that for a number of reasons it's a sensible thing to do. And I don't know but what I agree with him. It must be settled before he signs a lease on a house here certainly. One important reason he's given me for departing London is his position with Mr. Trezavant. He wants badly to leave him. He says his situation has become quite intolerable. What do you know of this, Jeremy? Is it as bad as he says?'

'Judging from what I saw today, I would say so, yes. Perhaps Mr. Trezavant's behavior today was an exception — though I doubt it. He seemed to be trying to humiliate Mr.

Donnelly — baiting him, cutting him off, et cetera. I know he is bothered aplenty by such treatment. We talked of it as we walked over here from the Crown and Anchor.'

'And did he threaten then to leave?'

'No, but looking back now, I can tell leaving was on his mind.'

'If he does stay, he'll lose half his patients. He'll have to start over again.'

'Oh? How so?' I asked.

'Well, he's sure to lose a good many, in any case, for he's now married. The hostesses of Bloomsbury will find him less attractive, less invite-able, now that he comes complete with a small family of his own. And Clarissa told me the other day that they're bruiting it about that Molly was no more than a cook in the kitchen of Sir John Fielding. All the gossips are having great fun with that! No, the more I think of it, the less likely it seems that the two together will ever impress London society.'

'Not favorably, in any case.'

'As you say.'

Together, we sighed.

'Do you know,' said I, 'if only Oliver Goldsmith were still with us, I do believe he could have steered us a course through these treacherous shoals.'

'Gabriel Donnelly and Oliver Goldsmith

— the two of them could liven any dinner party,' said Sir John.

'What about Molly?' I asked of a sudden. 'What's her attitude toward such a move?'

Sir John threw up his hands in desperation. 'Oh ... well ... Molly. She's for it completely. The Irish charmed her quite thoroughly.'

'Molly's quite the charmer herself.'

'Indeed, they recognized her as one of their own.' With a judicious shake of his head, he said, 'No, I fear that the move would be much to their advantage. There's no use for us to pretend otherwise. If we should try to dissuade him we would only be attempting to serve our own interests.'

'What shall we do without him?' said I.

'Ah well, cheer up, lad. He'll not be leaving tomorrow. In fact' — brightening a bit — 'he's invited us all to a medical demonstration of some sort tomorrow evening. He saw one quite like it in Vienna some time back and guarantees that we shall be entertained as well as enlightened.'

'A medical demonstration?'

'Yes, a medical demonstration of what they have taken to calling 'animal magnetism' — whatever that may mean.'

3

*In which Jeremy
escapes death at the
hands of Clarissa*

It had been agreed that since the so-called medical demonstration would not commence until ten in the evening, Mr. and Mrs. Donnelly would visit us for the first time as a wedded couple beforehand, and we would then sit down and break bread together. The burden fell upon Clarissa, whose responsibility it was to offer up another of her remarkable meals. It took a good part of the afternoon and early evening to produce it, yet Clarissa seemed to welcome the chance to show her teacher (Molly) how she had continued to advance her skill in the culinary arts — even in Molly's absence. I believe she looked upon the occasion as a kind of test; and if that was so, you may have my word that she passed it with distinction.

'Twas chicken provided the test. There were two of them — big, fat birds, dressed and ready to cook. But how? She later confided that it was specially taxing to think how to get them cooked through and through without burning them. She had no choice, it seemed, but to cook the birds in the old style: by mounting both on a spit and turning them over a low flame. You may guess, reader, who provided the power to keep it revolving. Indeed you have it right. It was none but I. And was it worth the trouble and effort we put into it? Our guests certainly thought so. If I am to credit their praise, then it was the best that either of them had ever tasted. Sir John and Lady Fielding were perhaps a little less generous — but then, they, as I, enjoyed her cooking each day of the week. To her credit, Clarissa attempted to deflect some of the praise in my direction, but the triumph was hers, as all well knew. Nevertheless, 'twas a day or two before my arm was fully recovered from all that slow turning.

Whilst we ate, we listened as Mr. Donnelly regaled us with tales of Anton Mesmer, his discovery of what was then dubbed 'animal magnetism,' and all the difficulties that discovery had caused him.

As I recall, it all began with a remark of Sir John's. A question, it was, and it betrayed a certain uneasiness in regard to the sort of presentation we were to see.

'Just what sort of evening have you planned for us, Mr. Donnelly? I recall that when you offered your invitation to us, you seemed a bit unsure about this fellow . . . what's his name?'

'Mesmer,' Mr. Donnelly offered.

'Just so — Mesmer. I recall that you said we'll be entertained as well as enlightened. That sounds to me as if you haven't quite decided which we should be — entertained or enlightened. Now, which will it be?'

'Both.'

At that he put upon his face an outrageous smile that set us all to laughing. Sir John, deprived of that sight, frowned in annoyance.

'Mr. Donnelly, you're quite impossible,' said he. Yet he did persist: 'Tell us a bit of what we might expect, won't you? Will it be offered by this man Mesmer himself? I do dislike listening to a German brutalize the King's English.'

'No, sir, the presenter is a disciple who has gone out to spread the word. Goldsworthy is his name, and he is a doctor right enough, but certainly not the originator of the treatment.' He paused, then added: 'Mesmer himself is a doctor. 'Tis he who discovered it — or perhaps better said, invented it. From what I have heard, though, the medical application is far more important than whatever he may claim preceded it.'

'Well, what does he claim preceded it?' asked Sir John most insistently. He would not be easily put off.

'What indeed?' replied Mr. Donnelly. 'It's years since I attended that earlier demonstration. I fear what I heard there has slipped my mind. *But*,' he added, 'there were some remarkable things we saw done in putting paid to aches and pains, the sort of thing which takes up most of any doctor's time.'

'Yet you cannot recall whence comes the power to effect these remarkable cures?'

'Sir John, 'twas naught to me, but the sort of metaphysical blather at which the Germans excel all others.'

'Come now, sir, let me be the judge of that.'

'All right then, as I recall, Anton Mesmer's theory was that there is a basic material, a liquid, which binds all together — moon, planets, stars, et cetera, holding all in their separate paths — and not large heavenly bodies alone, but all in the universe, all in our world are held by it. This material is invisible, intangible, though it is magnetic in nature. And it is through its magnetic properties that it has medicinal values.'

'Medicinal values of what sort?' put in Sir John.

'Ah, what sort indeed! This man Mesmer treats his patients with magnets. He concentrates the electricity from the magnet upon the place at which the pain resides — or upon the organ which fails in its function. All the while Mesmer holds the patient fixed in his powerful stare. As I recall, he presents a rather frightening figure: His jaw is set; his eyes bulge with intensity. I, for one, could not hold out long against him.'

'I'm sure that's true,' exclaimed Clarissa, quite unable to contain herself further. 'Fascinating, altogether fascinating!'

Though Mr. Donnelly had addressed Sir John throughout, he held the rest of us quite in thrall, as well. Unlike the magistrate, who was visibly impatient with such talk of mysterious substances which hold together the universe and treatment of human ills by magnetic electricity, we were, for the moment, quite taken.

'Well, Mr. Donnelly, you were right. What you have told me thus far of his doctrine would seem — how was it you put it? — like so much metaphysical blather to even the most dedicated lover of German thought. Or, putting it another way, it seems the sort of thing that could only excite one such as Benjamin Franklin.' At that, Sir John gave an abrupt laugh. 'Having heard this,' he continued, 'I wonder that you thought it of such importance that it should be brought to our attention. Why did you?'

Written thus, his comment and question may seem purposefully hurtful — and indeed I caught Molly blinking in surprise at what was said. Yet it was delivered in a bantering way, as was usual with just such good-natured challenges between friends. She had not yet grown used to this sort of play between the two.

Yet Mr. Donnelly was ready for him.

'Why do I bring this to your attention?' he asked rhetorically. 'For one reason only.'

'And what is that?'

'It seems to work — some of it in any case.'

Sir John did then sit up straight in his chair — 'twas as if he had, of a sudden, been pricked with a pin. 'Seems to work? How do you mean by that?'

'The man has had some success with this which seems could only be a quack cure. He has cured aches and pains in every part of the body, fits of all sorts, deafness, and — '

'Enough, Mr. Donnelly, please! Next thing I know, you'll be telling me that he has made the blind to see.'

'Well, he has done that, more or less, but it was *hysterical* blindness — and not your sort at all. And the treatment, for that matter, was not wholly successful. Her parents seized her and took her away.'

'Perhaps we'll speak of that later then.'

'Mesmer is by no means always successful,' said the medico.

'I should not suppose that he would be.'

'Yet his greatest error, it seems to me, is in hanging on to this theory of the magnetic liquid, the use of electric energy, et cetera. That is not the source of Mesmer's power.'

'Oh? What then?'

'Why, *he* is. It's the power of the man himself that accomplishes these wonders — that powerful personality, those staring eyes which seem so difficult for some, or most, to escape.'

'You speak now of this man Mesmer, of course.'

'Of course.'

'What about Dr. Goldsworthy?' Sir John asked. 'Has he the same sort of powerful personality? just such an overwhelming stare?'

'We shall see, sir, we shall see.'

★　★　★

The Covent Garden Theatre — otherwise known as the New Theatre Royal — is much larger than the Drury Lane; therefore, while Mr. Garrick could afford to allow his auditorium to go dark one or two nights a week, John Beard, manager of the Covent Garden, simply could not; but in lieu of theater seven nights of the week, Beard booked in a succession of lecturers, travelers, and musicians for Monday nights, so that those who attended might boast that they had not only filled the evening pleasurably, but had also added to their understanding of European culture — and boast they did.

There was thus a certain sense of intellectual pride among the many who were in attendance that evening. As we milled about with the rest, seeking to claim our seats in the second row, Clarissa and I heard naught but a jumble of names from Mondays past. Having heard what was said at dinner, we could scarce wait for the demonstration to begin. Clarissa seemed specially warmed to the occasion. I noted when she opened her bag that she had pencil and paper tucked away in it; she would take copious notes — and then transfer all to her 'Journal Book.' We two sat together at the far end of our group, Molly and Mr. Donnelly at the other end, with Sir John and Lady Fielding square in the middle.

We seemed to be awaiting the arrival of someone or something, though I had no idea what it might be. Ten o'clock came and went.

I noted Mr. Donnelly tug out his watch, open it, and shake his head as he might if one of his patients were late. Yet then, through the side door, where we ourselves had entered minutes before, came the reason for the delay: 'Twas none but Lady Lammermoor. How could I tell? (After all, one woman in widow's weeds looks much the same as another.) She was easily identified by the murmur that ran through the crowd — 'Lammermoor, Lammermoor, Lammermoor.' I heard it around us, muttered and whispered. And accompanying her, seeing her to their seats (as he had done the day before) was Archibald Talley, her younger son. As soon as they were settled in their seats, a gentleman strode on to the stage and, having reached its center, turned to the audience. A scattering of applause greeted him — but only that, for he had not yet proven himself, and Londoners were not to be taken in too quickly. He seemed to know that and wished not to claim too much — at least not at first. He began quite modestly by introducing himself.

'Thank you, ladies and gentlemen,' said he. 'Allow me to introduce myself. I am Henry Goldsworthy.' At that point, he dipped his head slightly in a gesture of humility before continuing: 'I am a native of Canterbury in the County of Kent, a doctor of medicine, and a graduate of the University of Vienna.' Hearing that, I bent forward and caught Mr. Donnelly's eye. He winked.

Having mentioned Vienna, Dr. Goldsworthy went on immediately to inform his audience of Anton Mesmer, who he was and how he had managed to cause such a stir in Austria, Germany, and throughout most of Middle Europe. Much of this we had already heard from Mr. Donnelly. It was the speaker's method not to tell all at once, but rather to intersperse tales of Mesmer's successes with demonstrations of his method. By the bye, I think it fair to say that Dr. Goldsworthy announced before beginning that whatever they might see, they were in no wise to think it magic or divine power granted to him to work miracles. 'I leave all that to the Lord above us,' said he. 'No, what you will see is based purely upon the scientific principles of Franz Anton Mesmer.'

Then, gesturing to one in the wings, a curtain behind him was opened to reveal two swarthy musicians, a player of the guitar and a violinist who began playing music of an eastern sort, slow and mysterious. Clarissa gave it as her guess that they were Gypsies.

Dr. Goldsworthy called for volunteers from the audience. Specifically, said he, he wished for those with complaints to come forward that he might choose a few for the demonstration, and at another signal from him, four chairs were brought out and placed in a row, spaced out widely facing the audience. And from the legion of sufferers that gathered at the foot of the stage, he chose but four. They were perhaps not the worst cases, nor were they the wealthiest, nor the poorest. I whispered to Clarissa that he had chosen those whose complaints were not physical, as Sir John's blindness was. According to what we had been told by Mr. Donnelly, we were not to see severed limbs restored, nor any such tampering with nature. Dr. Goldsworthy took only those whom he thought he could help — and how the rest did howl and complain that they had not also been chosen. Yet the doctor did simply dismiss them with a perfunctory apology and sent them on their way. Then did he begin his treatment of the four who now shared the stage with him.

From each he received a summary of the nature of his affliction — when it began, how it began, et cetera. For the most part, the patients he had chosen were unable to communicate their histories to the audience, unused as they were to addressing great numbers of people. And so the doctor passed on the specific complaints of those he had chosen to us all as the great hall went silent in anticipation of what we were about to witness.

The first to be treated was a man of about forty who suffered a most pronounced palsy, one which had spread, to a greater or lesser degree, all over the left side of his body. He twitched, he shook, he could scarce endure sitting, yet standing still was, alas, quite out of the question. It was, for me and for Clarissa — as well as for all in the theater — quite painful even to watch the poor fellow. It occurred to me that the doctor knew this as well, and therefore elected to treat him first.

Ah yes, the treatment! How strange it seemed to any and all who had never before seen it performed (and that included any and all of us but Mr. Donnelly). I described it all, sotto voce, to Sir John, and even he registered surprise once or twice at the rather outlandish carryings on. Was it the container of 'magnetized water' that Dr. Goldsworthy set down upon the stage between them that surprised him so that he burst into laughter? Or was it the picture that formed in his mind when I told him that the doctor was tying magnets all over the patient's left side? Well, it matters little what it was set him off, for the point is that his indiscreet giggles attracted a good deal of attention to us — particularly in our forward section of the audience. Lady Lammermoor turned, raised her black veil and gave Sir John the sort of glare meant to turn men to stone. Nor did he escape the attention of the good Dr. Goldsworthy: He turned a fierce eye to us, giving a hint of the power that Mr. Donnelly had said was in that gaze. But the moment was soon past. Doctor and patient returned to the task before them.

Mr. Patrick Ginder (which I now recall to be the name of the palsied gentleman) had informed us through the doctor that he had been afflicted in this manner for eight years, more or less — since the time that the widow he had courted so earnestly had chosen another suitor. It was perhaps a paltry thing when put against life's much greater disappointments, yet we know not the true and complete history of it. Sufficient it was to cause a great deal of physical disturbance in response. Oddly, Goldsworthy urged him to think upon it during all that followed — his humiliation, his bitterness, his frustration at having been forced to live ever after as a subject of ridicule. Then did the doctor properly begin his treatment.

First did he douse Mr. Ginder's clothing and exposed skin with 'magnetic water' from the container nearby — all those places, indeed, from which a magnet was not appended or tied. Then did the doctor begin to wave his hands and arms most mysteriously. Very slowly he moved them, exaggerating the grace till it be not grace but a contest merely to see how well and how completely he might hold the attention of his patient. Mr. Ginder could not, even for a moment, shift his view from Goldsworthy's slowly circling hands. And as those hands moved, so did the doctor's lips. He was saying something, whispering what could not be heard, not even by Ginder.

Yet what did it matter if he were heard or not? Those eyes of the doctor's, at once fierce and sympathetic, would have held him in any case. Thus minutes were spent, perhaps as many as five — though it seemed an eternity, a space of time to be measured in eons. The audience was so held by the picture of the two, one sitting and one standing, that all seemed almost to be breathing in concert — inhale, exhale, inhale, exhale, inhale . . .

So intent were they upon the scene on the stage that none seemed to notice that Patrick Ginder had ceased to twitch as he had done just a bit before (in real time). In truth, I *had* noticed, and what I saw was a gradual slowing down of hands and legs, fingers and facial features, so that before you knew it, all had slowed remarkably to a halt. And with that, Dr. Goldsworthy's hands and arms also ceased their slow, circular movements. Whereupon, the doctor snapped his fingers and, with a gesture, signaled to Ginder that he was to rise. That he did with a most peculiar look upon his face. He was like unto a sleeper of a sudden made awake. He blinked, rubbed his eyes, looked round him and out into the audience as if asking himself what he might be doing in such a strange place. Then, noticing for the first time that he had stopped twitching, he began to feel his face, to examine his left side with his right hand — all of this to make certain that what he had hoped for had actually happened.

'He has taken away my twitch,' said he, in a loud and confident bellow. 'Why, it's more than I thought, more than I ever expected.'

The audience, which until that moment had remained silent, did then burst into applause. Dr. Goldsworthy was plainly pleased by the spontaneous ovation, he made no bow and, with a bit of effort, managed to bring them to silence.

'Thank you . . . and thank you again,' said he, calling out to the crowd, 'but I must appeal to you all, not to applaud. This is a medical demonstration and *not* a show. So I must ask you to restrain yourselves. And on those same grounds, I now ask Mr. Ginder if he will honestly answer a few questions that I put to him.'

'Oh yes, sir, yes indeed I will. It's the very least I can do.'

'Very kind of you to say so,' said the doctor. 'First of all, tell me, do you know me? Are we personally acquainted?'

Ginder gave him an odd look, almost as if he had not quite understood the question. But he had: 'You mean, like, are we friends or some such?'

'Something like that, yes.'

'Why, no, sir. I never ever saw you before.'

'Another question. Are you an actor?'

'Oh no. Right here and now is the first time I ever was on a stage.'

'And what you told me before the treatment you just received is all true, is it not? Prior to coming here, you had suffered for eight years.'

'Oh yes, sir! Yes indeed!'

'Then go in peace,' said the doctor, 'and may you suffer no more.'

With that, another of the doctor's helpers appeared and ushered the good man off the stage. In spite of Dr. Goldsworthy's request, a few — nay, more than a few — in the audience applauded vigorously.

★   ★   ★

So it went, with one exception, through the remaining sufferers who were seated there upon the stage. (I experienced a growing suspicion — a mere hint — that this power of Dr. Goldsworthy's, for all its talk of magnets and magnetic water, bore a strong resemblance to the 'treatment' of Mr. Deekin's that we had heard described in Sir John's court.)

Next to be treated was a young man, hale and hearty to all appearances — except for the skin of his face, which was a mass of suppurating bumps and sores. The doctor took care in this case to bathe the young man's face in the magnetized water before beginning the treatment. And when he did, it seemed that he worked even longer and harder with his passes and gesticulations than he had before. But at the end of his labors, he was rewarded, for having taken the trouble to bathe his face a second time, he revealed it to the audience as free of draining pustules and blood. This time, rather than applause, they offered oohs and ahhs in appreciation of Dr. Goldsworthy's work. He assured the young man then that the bumps and dry pustules would vanish in a day or two, and there would be no trace of these blemishes in a month's time. He left the stage stroking his face, touching the places which, only minutes before, had been so sore.

The third cure was to me the most impressive of all, for it involved the help of one who was near completely deaf. You may wonder, reader, how he came to be chosen from those who crowded the foot of the stage. I recall that he wore a sign tied about his neck which said, simply, 'Deaf.' Put so by one of advanced years who wore an unspeakably doleful expression upon his face, the poor man must indeed have offered the good doctor an irresistible subject for his demonstration, except for the rude noises made by the subject. Nevertheless, Dr. Goldsworthy seemed to expect that there might be difficulties, and he sought to caution the audience of this.

'Ladies and gentlemen,' said he, 'though I have fortunately been able to help many, I cannot, I confess, help all. Since I put no blame for this upon Franz Anton Mesmer and his treatment, I must take all of it upon myself, if need for blame there be for what follows. You have been most appreciative so far, and so I ask you to bear with me now and give me your complete silence and attention.'

Without another word, the doctor set to work. First did he tie two small magnets round the subject's head just above the ear level. Then did he bathe the ears, both of them, in magnetized water. Having done this, he stepped round and attacked the problem from the rear. In this way, I received the best view I had yet been given of the strange motions he made with his hands and arms; they were slow and deliberate at first, yet they gained momentum until they reached a sort of climax and once again slowed. Ah, but his eyes! Never had I seen such! They bulged, whether from the emotional and physical effort demanded of him, or the exhaustion of his physical powers. So much, it seemed, must be put into this.

He could not have asked for a better audience — up to that point. Though tense, they remained silent. I could hear heavy breathing behind me, as if some or all wished to aid him with their own efforts. Still I dared not turn round and look, for fear I might break the spell of the moment.

Sweat stood out upon his face. He panted. He slowed his gyrations until, of a sudden, he stopped, took a breath, and clapped his hands over the deaf man's ears. The noise of it could not have been so great, yet it was as a thunder clap within the silent hall. All seemed to wonder what this meant; none seemed to know. He had never before touched his patients in the course of their treatment, only in preparation. What did this mean? His lips moved noiselessly. He — but then did the doctor jump back; exhausted — and near simultaneous, he who had exhausted Goldsworthy leapt from his chair and crowed loudly to all within the great theater: 'I CAN HEAR!' Or something a bit like it, for as deafness had till then not only blocked his hearing, it had also severely impeded his speech. All that one heard from him before the doctor administered the treatment were loud groans and other poorly articulated sounds. And now, though he could hear, his speech was not greatly improved — not immediately in any case. But once started, he was quite impossible to stop: he would let all know of his recovered faculty. He ran about the stage shouting it to one and all.

All was in a state of chaos there upon the stage. Yet in the audience, as well, disorder reigned. The ladies and gentlemen who had previously proven themselves well behaved by London standards were shouting and scream- ing one at the other. They shouted back at him who was previously deaf. Some were calling Dr. Goldsworthy a blasphemer, one who took God's power for his own. Others in the audience took exception to that and shouted back at his accusers. At last, given little choice, the doctor came forward on the stage and shouted in the loudest voice that he could muster that there would be a short intermission.

'Close the curtains,' said he.

And close them they did.

'Well,' said Sir John, 'what thought you of that?'

'What indeed,' said I. 'I've never seen the like.'

Out of the corner of my eye, I detected Lady Lammermoor and her son Archibald Talley making a hasty exit through the door through which they had entered. I called Sir John's attention to this, yet he seemed not overly concerned. 'Perhaps they left in embarrassment, hoping not to be recognized,' said he. Then was his attention seized by Mr. Donnelly, who had journeyed past the feet and legs of his wife and Lady Fielding to have a word with Sir John. What it was, I ne'er discovered, for I felt the familiar tug of Clarissa's hand upon my sleeve.

'Isn't this exciting, Jeremy?'

'Oh, indeed,' said I. 'I was just telling Sir John that — '

'Don't be a ninny,' said she, interrupting. 'Of course I heard what you said to Sir John. And I, too, agree. I've never seen the like. Never before such feats of healing. Never such an unruly audience. Never . . . ' She allowed her voice to trail off wistfully, and then did she exclaim: 'Ah, how I should like to have been chosen!'

'But you are in no wise ill,' I objected.

'I know,' said she. 'It is ever the same with me — good health when I need it least.'

She looked so unhappy at that moment that, unable to help myself, I burst out laughing — and that, of course, made her unhappier still. Yet she soon cheered up and admitted that barring the chance to have part in it all, watching the drama unfold before her came very close indeed.

'But, Jeremy?'

'Yes, Clarissa?'

'I've a question for you. Since deafness was the affliction of that poor man whose cure caused the row, how did it happen that it also affected his speech? I've known other deaf people, and they all seemed to talk in that same strange and incomprehensible manner. Why is that?'

'For the best of reasons,' said I. 'I did once put that same question to Mr. Donnelly, and he said it was simply because they could not hear themselves speak.'

'But now he *can* hear himself. Why does he not immediately change his manner of speech? Does he *prefer* speaking as he does? Surely not.'

'As you say, Clarissa — surely not. I believe

that the fellow must now teach himself to speak correctly all over again. Mr. Donnelly said as much.'

'Ah, we take so much for granted, do we not?'

'As you say, Clarissa, as you say.'

Thus did we prattle our way through the intermission. A bell was sounded to call members of the audience back to their seats. We resumed ours — and waited, for there was naught to do but that. The great hall filled, and in a few minutes all was silent.

Then did the curtains part to reveal a single tall female figure, clothed in black. Most there would have had no notion of her identity, but we in the second row certainly did. She was Lady Lammermoor — and she had come to have a few words with this potentially disorderly mob. She would, in a word, chastise them. Throwing back her dark veil, she took a firm step forward and shook her fist at the crowd.

'You have shamed yourselves again,' said she most angrily. 'If my late husband, Lord Lammermoor, were here, he would have you whipped like the naughty children you are. Some years ago he brought back from a diplomatic trip to Vienna tales of the remarkable theory of Franz Anton Mesmer, and the even more remarkable results Dr.

Mesmer had gotten by putting this theory into practical use. You have seen the results here this evening, and you — if you can behave yourselves — will see more of the same in the second half of the program.

'So impressed was my late husband that he insisted that I return with him to Vienna to see what he had seen. Though it was a grueling trip, I regret making it not in the least. I would not have missed the opportunity to see Dr. Mesmer, and to learn of animal magnetism, and, finally, to meet his assistant, Dr. Goldsworthy, whom, I discovered, to my surprise, was English born and English bred. We saw a great opportunity to acquaint all here with this great step forward in science. And do let me assure you — for he has assured you once already — that what he has presented to you this evening is science — pure science — and naught else. He is no blasphemer, nor is he a magician. He has no wish to take away God's power, nor to mimic it. He is content merely to heal a few so that he might show you that Dr. Mesmer's theory does really work. And it works in the most beneficial ways imaginable.

'Lord Lammermoor and I brought Dr. Goldsworthy here to England that he might demonstrate to you one of the miracles of modern science. As some of you may know, my husband died just a few days ago. I thought it so worthy of your attention to see him at work that I have broken my period of mourning to be here this evening. Now I shall leave you in his capable hands. I hope and pray that you will not disappoint me again.'

And, having said her piece, she turned and marched off the stage. A moment or two later Dr. Goldsworthy marched on to lengthy applause — not even he could silence them for a minute or two. But at last he persuaded them to silence and without a word of chastisement of the sort heard from Lady Lammermoor, he resumed where he had left off and began the second (shorter) part of the program.

'There is often some confusion of 'animal magnetism' with ordinary magnetism, or *mineral* magnetism, as I have called it. Though, as you may have noticed, I use ordinary mineral magnets in the experiments I have shown you thus far. That is because though they are different, there are, nevertheless, similarities between the two. The magnetic electricity generated by the ordinary, or mineral, magnet acts as a helper to the animal magnetism generated by us who deal direct with this fundamental element of the universe. I call this to your attention now because for the next experiment we shall not be using the small 'helper' magnets of the sort we have been employing. We shall, however, be making some use of the 'magnetized water' with which I have doused our subjects so liberally.

'Now,' said Dr. Goldsworthy, 'are you ready, Mr. Docker?'

A voice from offstage: 'Ready, Doctor.'

'Then come out, please.'

"Twas only when he did that that I recognized him as the fourth man upon the stage during the *first* part of the program. He had waited patiently through three experiments, yet when the third, though successful, caused a near riot, he was hurried off the stage. I, like most members of the audience, had forgotten about him completely.

I whispered into Sir John's ear just who Mr. Docker was.

He nodded in response. 'I had wondered,' said he, 'whether he had been completely forgotten.'

'I have learned all that need be told of his problem,' said the doctor. 'It is an easy one to solve for any who are adept in the uses of animal magnetism. Is that so, Mr. Docker?'

'Y-you s-s-said s-so.'

'And you believe what I told you?'

In response to that Mr. Docker nodded his head most emphatically.

Then did Mr. Goldsworthy address his audience. 'Mr. Docker is, as you heard just now, a stutterer. It is an altogether commonplace defect. All of you here must have known one at one time or another. It is treated as a nervous disorder, as indeed it should be. Which is to say, Mr. Docker's tongue, lips, and jaw are just as they should be. Yet for reasons we do not know, and he cannot tell us, his speaking equipment goes into a kind of spasm whenever he tries to speak. The result: He is a stutterer. We shall, if we are able, try to put an end to that.'

Then did the doctor make his preparations. He dabbed 'magnetized water' upon all the organs of speech (yes, even upon his tongue). That done, he began working very closely with Mr. Docker with circles and movements of the arms again. His eyes — what I could see of them — burned brightly. He presented an almost frightening figure; but not for long, for it seemed that in no time at all the stutterer had passed out of wakefulness into a deep slumber. At this point, Dr. Goldsworthy turned to the audience.

'He cannot hear us now,' he said to us. 'While he is in this state, I shall give him special instructions.'

He bent over the sleeping form in the chair and whispered in his ear. 'I have told him,' said the doctor, 'that when he hears a certain phrase, he is to react in a certain way.' For the first time a look of sly amusement crossed his face. 'I shall wake him now.'

And he did, snapping his fingers sharply and signaling Mr. Docker that he should rise. Yet again, though his eyes were open, he appeared somewhat fuddled by sleep, as if having wakened at just that moment — which, of course, he had.

'Well, tell me, Mr. Docker, did you have a good sleep?'

'I did, sir. Oh, yes indeed I did.' He yawned.

'Do you notice something different about yourself?'

'Why, no, but let me see.' He scratched his head, as some will to stimulate thought. Then, of a sudden, did his eyes widen. He clapped a hand to his check in astonishment. 'Oh, dear God in heaven, I can speak proper now! I can talk as any other! You've cured me, so you have. How can I thank you?'

He did not speak quite as I have it here, for though the stuttering had vanished, the hesitations remained. Like the deaf man before him, he would have to learn speech once again. Dr. Goldsworthy informed him of this, but in a week's time, he assured him, he would indeed speak as any other.

And that, bless him, was what Mr. Docker hoped to hear. 'Well, I shall practice, sir, as no other. Just see if I don't!'

The audience was growing restless in anticipation.

'And you have every expectation that you will retain this power?'

'Indeed, sir.'

'Will it be with you tomorrow, say, when the *cock crows?*'

Just as I was wondering why the doctor had so emphasized the last two words, reader, Mr. Docker jumped up upon his chair and let loose with a full-throated 'cock-a-doodle-do.' Then did he climb down from his perch and resume his place beside Dr. Goldsworthy, while all the while the audience shook with the merriest round of laughter that I, for one, had ever heard. For his part, Mr. Docker simply appeared puzzled, yet not by the laughter alone.

'Why did I do that?' he asked the doctor.

'Do what, Mr. Docker?'

'Why did I just now jump up on that chair and make a fool of myself?' He seemed a bit out of humor.

'You mean 'cock-a-doodle-do'? I told you to do it.'

'When did you do that?'

'Whilst you were sleeping.'

'But . . . why?'

Taken somewhat aback by that response, Dr. Goldsworthy adjusted his face into a somewhat more solemn set. And, when he spoke, he assumed a more lofty tone. 'Why? You ask me why. It was for the amusement of these good people in the audience.'

The laughter now came a bit uncertainly from those good people in the audience. Where but a moment before, laughter had welled from them as from a fountain, I now heard only giggles and cackles. Were I asked to guess the reason for this, I should have said that they were wondering if this sudden change was planned for or not. And the answer to that came swiftly.

Mr. Docker (I never did hear the man's Christian name, and I'm not sure that it was ever spoken) drew himself up to his full height, looked the doctor in the eye, and said, 'Well, I'm not sure that I like that. No, I'm not sure I like that at all.' Then did he turn and walk off the stage and into the wings. There was but silence as he made his way.

Thus failed the doctor's attempt to play the crowd. Still he resolved to win them back — and one way or another he did just that. Putting a smile upon his face, he rubbed his hands together and called out to the half-filled house, 'Are there any questions?'

In mounting panic, he scanned the audience and saw not a single uplifted hand. As many a speaker before him, he must have asked himself just how he would fill the remaining minutes of the demonstration. Perhaps if he were to summarize what had been told them as he went along. Yes, that would: If only there were a question to propel him into such a summing up. If only . . . ah, saved by a single hand raised toward the rear of the auditorium.

'Yes, sir. You, sir. What is your question?'

'I was wonderin' if you wouldn't mind telling us just how it was that you done that last trick.'

'Trick, sir, trick? It was no trick but a valid demonstration of the workings of Mesmer's theory of animal magnetism.' Then did his expression alter and with that his tone. He seemed consciously to be restraining himself. 'Ah, but I know that it can be difficult with these scientific matters. They can seem to one such as yourself most confusing. Let me review the principles of animal magnetism for you, so that you may see how such 'tricks,' as you call them, can be accomplished.'

And so saying, he launched into just such a review, keeping a smile upon his face, and making little witticisms as he went. This effort must have taken him a full fifteen minutes, or perhaps longer. In any case, once he had finished it, there seemed an even greater danger than before that he might be losing his audience. A few individuals and couples sitting near the doors had already made a quiet exit. How many would follow?

Yet who should save the day for Dr. Goldsworthy but Sir John Fielding, Magistrate of the Bow Street Court! When the call came from the doctor for further questions, Sir John pulled himself to his feet and spoke out loud and clear in his court voice.

'Dr. Goldsworthy?'

'Yes, sir?'

'I have a question for you. Can you tell me just how the things that you have revealed and shown us this evening might affect or be affected by crime?'

'Could you be more specific?'

'Could *you*? That is to say, your last demonstration, as it was described to me by my assistant, frightened me a little.'

'Oh? How so?'

'It seemed to me that if a man could be induced to make a fool of himself in front of a large body of people such as this, then he could be made to do things other than crowing like a rooster — things against his will, things which are against the law, things which are criminal in nature.'

'A very reasonable question,' said Dr. Goldsworthy. 'Yet what you suggest is really quite impossible.'

'And why is that?'

'Because what you suggest would be an imbalance in the magnetic fluid. But rather than state the matter, would it not be better if I were to offer you a demonstration?'

Sir John appeared slightly skeptical. 'Perhaps it might.'

'Then I shall need some volunteers.'

Those words had barely left his lips when Clarissa was up on her feet, jumping up and down and waving her hands.

'All right,' said the doctor, 'already we have one, yet we shall need another.' He swept the auditorium with his eyes where others stood waving — yet he ignored them all. 'You, young sir, why not you? If you are acquainted with the young lady, why, so much the better! Come up here, both of you.'

I turned to Sir John for guidance. I asked him most direct what I should do.

'Go, by all means,' he whispered. 'You're the only one who might possibly be able to restrain her.'

And so up the stairs we went, Clarissa and I. Then, briefly through the wings, and we came out upon the stage.

'What have you got us into now, Clarissa?'

'Oh, hush, Jeremy.'

'What are your names?' Dr. Goldsworthy asked. We told him, and he introduced us to the audience.

'Now, Clarissa, Jeremy, I wish you to know what to expect, so I shall tell you now that before anything else, I shall have to put you to sleep as I have done with all the rest. If you have any objections to that, now is the time to make them.'

I glanced over at Sir John, and he gave a reluctant nod. I wondered at that. How was I to watch over Clarissa if I, like her, had been reduced to naught but a dozing lump of midden? What was I doing up here, anyway?

The doctor took our silence for assent and called into the wings for chairs. When they arrived, he took aside one of those who had brought them onto the stage and held a whispered conference with him. Then was he ready to begin. At his instruction, he took Clarissa aside and sat her in one of the chairs.

'Now,' said he to her, 'you must keep silence and look deep into my eyes.' He said that in a deep, quiet tone, repeating it over and over again in a lulling manner as he moved hands and arms about in that manner which had become quite familiar to me by that time. I think she must have gone into that sleeping state in less than a minute.

Never could there have been a more willing subject than she.

Then did he come to me. The chair in which I sat was about ten or twelve feet from Clarissa's. He came direct to me and stood with his back to the audience. Waving his hands about, he began that same chant, 'Look into my eyes . . . Keep silent and look into my eyes.' A full minute of this passed without affecting me in any way. He seemed to speed up and become more commanding, yet that worked even less well than the earlier manner. What was happening — or, rather, *not* happening? I was not consciously resisting him. Yet what had worked so well upon Clarissa was not working at all with me.

'Drop your head and feign sleep,' said he to me in the same rhythm and tone he had been using only moments before. 'All will be well. Trust me . . . trust me . . . trust me.'

Having little choice in the matter, and feeling some responsibility to the audience, I did precisely as he directed. He then left me and went into the wings to conduct a little business with the fellow he had sent off on an errand of some sort. I wondered what it might be, yet I could not discover that without moving my head. I could keep Clarissa within my sight from where I sat by opening my two eyes, each to a slit, and nevertheless keeping my head down. Keeping her within my view seemed to me to be my first responsibility.

Dr. Goldsworthy returned from the wings, pulled up a chair beside Clarissa's, and sat down in it.

'Well,' said he to her, 'are you comfortable, Clarissa?'

'Yes . . . comfortable,' said she in a voice not quite her own.

'Would you prefer to lie down? Would you be *more* comfortable in a bed?'

'No bed.'

'Well, I can make one for you out of two chairs. Let us try, eh?' He jumped up and moved his own chair to a more advantageous spot. Then did he doff his coat, fold it, and place it upon his chair. 'You may make this coat your pillow,' said he. 'Put your head right here, and keep your feet on your chair.'

She managed to do as he said but did not appear specially comfortable doing it. She shifted one way and then another.

'Would you like to stretch out, Clarissa?' asked the ever solicitous Dr. Goldsworthy. 'You do not appear to be completely comfortable.'

She raised herself and nodded her head. 'Stretch out.'

And so he began pulling the chair — his

chair, on which she had rested her head — farther and farther from her chair — the one on which she rested her feet — until she presented a very strange picture.

Though I had not such a clear view as members of the audience, I could tell that Clarissa was now suspended rigidly between the two chairs — the upper part of her head upon the doctor's coat, her heels upon her own chair. The rest — that is, the entire seven-eighths of her — was stretched out so stiff that it was as if she were supported by some invisible board. In fact, but for the muscle in her back, she had no support. Whispers came from the audience. There were fears expressed that she might fall and hurt herself. There was speculation that this was naught but a conjuror's trick. Of a sudden, there was doubt in the air.

'Clarissa?'

'Yes?'

'Are you comfortable?'

'Oh yes, very.'

'Well rested?'

'I certainly am well rested.'

'Well then, perhaps you would allow me to assist you to your feet so that we may get on with the demonstration.'

'All right.'

He took her two hands in his, thus

supporting her and allowing her to rise gracefully from her quite impossible posture. There was applause once again. The doctor held up a hand in a halfhearted gesture to end it, yet he said naught in reproof and allowed it to continue, obviously pleased.

He put his coat back on and went offstage for a moment. As he returned, I noticed for the first time that there was something heavy and large in his right coat pocket — though what it was, I could not say. With Clarissa then safely seated, he stood behind her chair and lectured the audience.

'My friends,' said he, 'though animal magnetism may make it possible for the subject to do some things and assume positions that he would not ordinarily be capable of — as you have seen — it can do nothing to alter the moral code of him who is under its influence. May I demonstrate?'

More applause. He seemed now to dote upon it.

'Ah, thank you. Let me caution you, however, that the exercise you are about to witness should give you no true cause for alarm. I ask you to put yourselves in my hands as completely as Clarissa here has done. In short, trust me.

'Now, Clarissa, tell me, have you ever shot a pistol?'

'No, never.'

'As I shall show you, it is very easy.'

'Very easy,' she echoed.

Then did he reach into his pocket and hold up for viewing a dueling pistol in the French style, a little smaller than military ordnance but quite large enough for Clarissa. There was considerable response from the audience at the appearance of the pistol — intense discussion, cries of surprise, even a suppressed scream.

'Here,' said the doctor, 'take this pistol by the handle.' Indeed she did take it. Yet she found it quite literally too hot to hold. When she sought to wrap her hand round it, she dropped the pistol into her lap, then attempted a second time to get a grip on it — without success. It clattered to the floor.

'What have you done, Clarissa?' He came round her chair and shook his finger at her, now playing the roll of the angry schoolmaster. He picked up the pistol and ordered her gruffly to stand. She rose and stood stiffly.

'And you, Jeremy,' said Dr. Goldsworthy. 'I want you to stand, as well.'

I got to my feet, as he had ordered, imitating, as I did, Clarissa's mechanical movements.

'All right, do as I say now,' said he to her. 'Take the pistol into your hand — and hold on to it this time!'

She did as he said, though it took a considerable effort.

'Now you pull back the hammer — this piece right here. No, don't touch the trigger yet. You must aim the pistol first.'

(Reader, I did sweat as I had never before done. How I managed to stay rooted in the same spot, I shall never know.)

'Clarissa,' said the doctor, 'I want you to aim at Jeremy. I want you to shoot him and kill him.'

There came but one syllable from Clarissa in response. She let out a howl, a scream, a sound more animal than human:

'NO!' Then did she throw down the pistol to the floor and seemed set to kick it away, but Goldsworthy managed to rescue it before she could do that.

'I believe,' said the doctor to the audience, 'that I have proven my case.' Then did he snap his fingers, bringing Clarissa out of her state, all teary and yet smiling. She seemed quite as ever, except for the tears. She ran to me, threw her arms about me, and gave me a most public kiss. 'Oh, Jeremy, tell me what happened. I feel very strangely.'

'I'll tell you soon, but you must tell me first.'

'It was wonderful, really. I've never known

quite anything like it.'

'Nor have I,' I volunteered, 'nor have I.'

All this we shouted each at the other, for the audience had of a sudden gone quite mad with applauding.

★ ★ ★

We were all quite fortunate in having Mr. Benjamin Bailey, captain of the Bow Street Runners, along to show us our way home. He met us at the theater entrance, a lighted torch in his hand. We walked in good order behind him, and all the while the two friends argued over what they had just seen.

'I still say that what we witnessed tonight had some value as a scientific demonstration,' declared Mr. Donnelly.

'I do admit that it may have some value in the treatment of imagined illness. As for the rest, I must think upon it,' said Sir John.

'First of all, these illnesses, which you call imaginary, are indeed more than that. Secondly, I'm glad you admit then there is something to think about. When you put such heavy matter before an audience as Mesmer's animal magnetism, then you must buoy it with laughter and thrills — as you would admit yourself if you were not so stubborn.'

'Laughter and thrills, is it? There were

plenty of those this evening, were there not? Yet I wonder, could it have been the *tone* of his presentation that angered Lady Lammermoor? When we went backstage to speak with him, the two of them were screaming one at the other like a pair of newlyweds. Could you make anything of that through the door?'

'No. Just enough to tell me that this was no time to press our congratulations upon him.' Mr. Donnelly offered an ironic smile, which was lost on Sir John. 'Besides,' he added, 'if we'd waited till they quietened down and then knocked and entered, you might well have subjected Dr. Goldsworthy to abuse of the sort I have often endured from you.'

'Oh, come now, Mr. Donnelly, you cannot be serious, surely. Why, I — '

At that, the medico quite lost control and began to laugh as uncontrollably as one with a feather to his foot.

'Well and good, well and good,' said Sir John, chuckling in spite of himself. 'I'll never again be persuaded to take seriously one of you Irish. I've learned my lesson, I have. I'll never . . . '

It was not given us to learn what it was that Sir John would never do, for it took but an instant for laughter to overcome him completely.

They laughed together, laughed in concert,

until all eyes in Drury Lane turned upon them. I had seen them before in such a state. They were as men of a sudden become boys.

For their part, Lady Fielding and Molly Donnelly, who walked just ahead of Clarissa and me, clucked and shook their heads and gave every sign of appearing mortally embarrassed by their husbands' conduct.

At last of course, the laughter died, and perhaps the reason for that became quite evident when Sir John managed at last to speak.

'Ah, Mr. Donnelly,' said he, 'how I'll miss you when you are gone.'

'Well,' sighed the surgeon, 'we've not left yet, though I feel I must confess that this very morning I wrote to him who made the offer, and I accepted it.'

4

*In which Clarissa
meets Joseph Deekin
and his companion*

Next morning, Sir John dictated to me a
letter for David Garrick, wherein he urgently
requested the presence of Annie Oakum in
Bow Street. Then, having dictated it, he
appointed me to deliver it — with instructions that I was to wait for her until Mr.
Garrick released her, and then was I to
accompany her direct to Bow Street.

'Good God, sir, are you charging her with
. . . what?'

'No, nothing so grim as that.'

'What then?'

'I want the girl to understand that she is a
witness to a crime — and an important
witness at that. I'll not be fobbed off with
some excuse, or special pleading simply
because she can claim our friendship. Setting
conditions, asking you to promise not to tell
me whence this juicy bit of information had

come, that sort of thing — it simply won't do. Impress that upon her, will you?'

He had my promise of it, and so having my usual busy morning before me, I set out straightaway for the Drury Lane Theatre. Sir John assured me that Garrick's company would already be at work, rehearsing the next play upon the boards, which was, as we had heard, *The Prince of Denmark*. How strange it was to walk up Drury Lane of a Tuesday morn — how empty the street, how full of foul traces of last night's drunken revelry. And how strange it seemed to enter the empty theater. 'Empty' did I say? Well, not quite. There were, first of all, a good many people onstage; they included, by the bye, Mr. David Garrick and Mistress Annie Oakum. Also, there was another — a gruff, rough individual who stopped me at the door and attempted to bar my way.

'Here you,' said he, 'this here is a closed rehearsal. You'll just have to turn round and go back where you come from.'

'Afraid not,' said I. 'I've a letter to Mr. Garrick from Sir John Fielding, magistrate of the Bow Street Court.' I said it rather loudly, hoping to be heard.

'Well then,' said he, 'give it me, and I'll see he gets it.'

Behind him, on the stage, action had

ceased. The familiar figure of David Garrick stepped forward and peered out into the darkened theater. 'Who is there, please?'

''Tis I from the Bow Street Court,' I called in return. 'I've a letter for you, Mr. Garrick.'

'From Sir John?'

'Just so.'

'Let him through then, Joe.'

Reluctantly the guard stepped aside and allowed me passage to the stage. I noted a rather nasty look upon his face — though he spoke not a word to me.

I handed up the letter to Mr. Garrick and waited as he read it through. As I did, my eyes scanned those on the stage, all of whom wore their street clothes. With some difficulty I found Annie among them. She had shrunk back until she was all but obscured by two tall cast members. Her eyes were visible, however, and the look in them seemed to express something between fear and consternation.

Mr. Garrick knelt down close to me and lowered his voice: 'Sir John says 'urgently' here. Does that mean 'immediately'?'

'Not necessarily. What had you in mind?'

'Well, we're rehearsing *Hamlet*, and we've just begun Act Four, Scene Five. I'd like to finish the scene. Annie won't be needed after that. It will take only about ten minutes, no more.'

I nodded and gave my consent.

'One more question,' said he. 'She's not in trouble, is she?'

'No, not really. She was but a witness, though an important one — but don't tell her that. Treat it seriously, if you would, sir.'

Nodding, he rose and appeared relieved. Then he returned to his company and called out the place at which they were to resume. As I hurried Annie back to Bow Street, I kept her hand tight in mine and pulled her along at a pace to which she soon objected.

'Jeremy, will you stop — or at least *please slow down?*'

I had waited patiently — perhaps too patiently — for I soon understood why Mr. Garrick was eager to have done with this scene before Annie was snatched away: She played Ophelia; the whole scene was hers — and most of her speeches were sung! The ten minutes that he had promised me stretched soon into fifteen, and the fifteen into twenty. What with his promptings and corrections, there was no telling how long it would have continued had I not seized the first opportunity and called out to him my intention to leave and take Annie with me, no matter what.

He signaled to her with a wave of his hand that she was to leave with me, which was well enough, yet he stopped us when I had her nearly out the door and warned her that she was to be prepared with those song lines when next she came — or she was not to bother coming at all.

Foolishly, I gave in to her pleas and did slow down sufficiently for her to catch her breath. Yet she used that breath to upbraid me for pulling her out of a rehearsal.

'Jeremy,' said she, once out in Drury Lane, 'why must you treat me so?'

I could only sputter in reply: 'Why? Why? Well, I . . . I . . . '

'Explain to me just what is so terribly important that you take it upon yourself to interrupt one of Mr. Garrick's rehearsals and pull me away as you've done. Don't you realize that I'm no longer a kitchen slavey, no longer your cook? I am an *artist*, Jeremy! Do you have any idea what that means?'

'Yes,' said I, ready with a proper response at last, 'it means that you had better be prepared with those songs at next rehearsal or not bother to come at all.'

She gave me the most hateful look. Yet as I watched her face, her expression changed somewhat to one of doubt and suspicion.

'Jeremy, did you break your promise to me?'

'Promise? What promise?'

'What promise indeed! The one you made to me not to tell Sir John whence came my account of Lord Lammermoor's death.'

'I made no such promise!' said I, stoutly. 'You wished me to, yet I promised naught. Can you believe that I would keep anything from him? I told him of your desire to keep your role in it quiet, and he indicated he would not bruit it about needlessly. And that, dear Annie, is as much as you could expect from him. He is, after all, an officer of the court.'

Though it may not have satisfied her, it did at least silence her, so that by the time I handed her over to Sir John she seemed resigned to relating her story to him at least once, probably twice, and even perhaps a third time (which was his way).

He met her at the door to his chambers, a smile upon his face, putting her at ease in spite of herself.

'Ah, my dear, come in, come in,' said he. 'So happy to see you again.'

She gave him a proper buss upon his cheek in the French style and went directly into the room. In response to his urging that she sit anywhere she liked, she chose a chair quite near his desk, that they might be eye to eye during his interrogation, or nearly so.

Excusing himself, he took me out into the hall.

'You may stay, if you like, Jeremy, and listen in.'

I had given some thought to this and came to a conclusion that surprised even me: 'I think not, sir. Though I know I often clamor to be included, on this occasion I believe she would say more to you alone than if I were present.'

'Some difficulty between you two?'

'A little. Besides, I must get on with the preparations for this day's court session.' I had noticed quite a group of them tucked in behind the bars of the strong room. 'Duty calls.'

'As you will then.'

* * *

Thus it was that Sir John managed without me — and managed quite well, if I'm to judge by the results. He found out a good many things about the length and nature of her attachment to Lord Lammermoor. Sir John was surprised, as was I, at her estimate of the number of those in London who knew of the liaison. ('Half of London, I should suppose,' she estimated — and that number would have included David Garrick.) Most surprising of

113

all was Annie's encounter with Lady Lammermoor. It had taken place after she had made her report to Clarissa and me, so it had not been withheld from us; nevertheless, I had the feeling that if I had been present when she told Sir John of what had happened, the tale might not have been told at all.

It seems that when Mr. Trezavant ended the hearing and made his departure, Lady Lammermoor took a post near the door so that Annie would have to pass her by to make an exit. I heard nothing of what then happened, for I was up on stage, taking names and addresses of the witnesses called that day so that Sir John might proceed with his own investigation.

Though Annie tried her best, she could not evade the clutch of Lady Lammermoor. She tried, in fact, to slip by whilst one woman was between her and the noblewoman — to no avail. Lady Lammermoor simply reached round the interposing figure and grasped Annie by the wrist. Nor would she let go. Nevertheless, not wishing to make a scene, Annie gave in and allowed herself to be led away.

She asked Annie if she knew who she was. Annie looked her up and down, widow's weeds, veil, and all, and she said that she supposed the woman was Lady Lammermoor (though she was obviously much younger than Annie had expected and showed no signs whatever of any sort of illness). 'Well,' said the woman, 'I know who you are, as well, and I'll settle with you soon. Just be careful.' And then she left her where she stood, making for the street door in spritely style, where she was joined by her son Archibald. Annie told Sir John that she had the awfulest feeling that she had just been visited by a witch.

'And now, Jeremy,' Sir John said to me, 'you can just suppose that she feels doubly betrayed. She was obviously betrayed by whoever it was pointed her out to Lady Lammermoor as the husband's lover. But Lord Lammermoor betrayed her as well in depicting his dame as old and infirm — near to death even. I've made inquiries, and it seems that she is not yet forty and is his second wife. His first died in childbirth.'

'The present Lady Lammermoor then is *not* the mother of the next Lord L.?'

'No, she is not.'

'Well, considering all that you have told me, I may have been a bit hard on her, dragging her out of the rehearsal.'

'Ah well, I'm sure she forgives you. But make no mistake. In most situations Annie is quite capable of taking care of herself. She knows the wrong side of London quite well, unfortunately. Nevertheless, I intend to assign one of the constables to accompany her to and from the theater. Can you suggest anyone?'

I put forward the name of Benjamin Bailey. But Sir John objected that Mr. Bailey, competent though he was, had never even seen a play and would not appreciate the boon he had been given. What about Constable Patley, my companion on our (mostly unsuccessful) trip to Newmarket? Sir John had nothing against him, and so it was settled.

★   ★   ★

All this had taken place during the morning and early afternoon. It had been a light day in court and not much to do afterward, and so I climbed up the stairs, thinking I might find a snack of some sort in the kitchen, one that would last me through the day till dinner.

Instead, I found Clarissa — and glad I was for it, for we had not had the chance to talk of last night's astonishing happenings. In a sense, I had been disappointed in that I had been rightly judged a bad subject for animal magnetism — yet only in a sense. Though I

116

was deeply curious of Clarissa's experience, it had been so extreme, so far beyond anything I had previously seen or heard, that I was (I must confess) a bit fearful of the entire experience. I would not wish to repeat it for the world. I would much rather hear about it from her. She had, in an odd way, evaded my questions till now. How best to approach it? I considered the matter as I munched upon the bread and sipped the tea she had given me.

'Clarissa,' said I, 'would you tell me something?'

'I would tell you anything — or almost anything.'

'Very well then, when you were under the influence, shall we say, of Dr. Goldsworthy . . . '

'Yes?'

'Well, do you remember anything of your state? Were you happy? sad? Taken all in all, would you say that it was for you an unpleasant experience?'

'Oh, some of it was. When he told me to shoot you — he did do that, didn't he? — I began to shudder. It was terrible, really it was.'

'And you threw the pistol down.'

'Did I?'

'All right, put it like this then — was it *all* an unpleasant experience?'

'Oh, by no means,' said she. 'I had the most remarkable visions.'

This was indeed something new to me. 'Visions?' I asked. 'Visions of what sort?'

'All sorts of things — pictures, colors, shapes. I've been trying to describe it in my 'journal book.''

'Could I read what you've written?'

'You could if I could just get down on paper what I remember. The more I write, the more I despair of ever recapturing the beauty of those visions in writing. If I could only repeat the experience!'

'You mean you wish to be put into a trance once again?'

'Oh, if only I could be!'

I thought about that for a moment or two. After all, why not? If I could but secure his address we might pay him a visit and ask him to put her once again in a trance. Of course he would remember us — Clarissa especially. And it should not take long. Last night, it took but a minute or less. But who would know where Dr. Goldsworthy had taken refuge? Was it with Lady Lammermoor? Was that not what she said — or at least implied? Who could give a definitive answer? Not Sir John. He would question the wisdom of such an expedition. But if not he — then who? Why, Mr. Donnelly, of course! The two medicos had Vienna in common. They would have a good deal to talk about. Perhaps Gabriel Donnelly would be so excited by my plan that he would accompany us.

For her part, Clarissa was delightcd, so much so that she insisted on going with me to Mr. Donnelly's surgery. There were matters she wished to discuss with Molly before she left for Dublin. And so, stopping by at Sir John's chambers to make certain he had no more for me to do, we hurried forth to Drury Lane on our adventure.

Mr. Donnelly's surgery and living quarters were just down the street from the place I had been earlier that day to collect Annie. He would have been the first to admit that all in these few rooms was too crowded together for any degree of comfort. Even if he had decided to remain in London, they would have found it necessary to find larger space; a house of some sort would be the best — perhaps the only — solution to the problem. Yet all that was aside now, for Mr. Donnelly had made his decision and written off an acceptance to the doctor in Dublin. This, as I recall, weighed heavily upon me as I knocked upon his door.

After a slight delay, Molly answered my knock.

'Ah, it's you two, is it?' said she, sounding

far more Irish than she had ever done before. 'Did you come to help?'

'Help?' Clarissa managed at last. 'Help at what?'

'Why, help at packing, of course. Surely you didn't suppose that all these things you see round you would be conducted through the air by magic to our new home?'

Clarissa was speechless. I was nearly so myself. 'You're not leaving already, are you?' said I.

Then, saving the day, Mr. Donnelly appeared, wiping his hands upon a towel and laughing at our wondering and fearful faces. In another instant Molly joined in his laughter. Then did Clarissa also give herself to the general merriment. Only I, being perhaps a bit more literal minded than the rest, failed to respond till almost the very end when I managed a few low chuckles.

'One of your Irish jokes,' said I, doing my best to smile it through.

'Well, I'm just acquainting Molly here with the form,' said Mr. Donnelly. 'I'd say she's doing rather well, wouldn't you?'

'Yes,' said I, 'I suppose she is.'

'But no, Jeremy, it will be awhile yet till you see the last of us. We're certainly planning on being here for your wedding.'

'Well, good, I'd wondered about that.'

'I, too,' said Clarissa quite simply.

'Don't worry. Don't give it a thought.'

'But what can we do for you?' asked Molly. 'I'd invite you to sit — and you may, if you like — but when I opened the door to you, you seemed so excited, full of purpose, like you were off on an adventure.'

'Well, we were, more or less,' said I.

'No, that's it exactly — an adventure,' said Clarissa. 'I want to be put once again into a trance.'

'And we thought you might be able to tell us where to find Dr. Goldsworthy. Do you know where he is staying? From what Lady Lammermoor said, it seemed likely he was at their house in Bloomsbury.'

'Exactly my thought,' said Mr. Donnelly. 'I had a few very specific questions I wished to ask him with regard to my theory that the trance state had little or nothing to do with magnets or magnetizing or a liquid substance that holds together the universe; and it has everything to do with the personal power of the individual who gives the treatment.'

'Oh yes, I remember you mentioned that before we went off to the demonstration. What did Goldsworthy have to say about that?'

'Nothing at all. I went to the house in Bloomsbury — you were right about that

— made inquiries at the door and was told by the butler that indeed the good doctor had been there for a number of days, but he had left only a little over an hour ago, started off on a tour through all of Great Britain.'

'When was that?'

'About eleven o'clock, I should judge. All I could do was leave my card and hope that he will write me when he returns, and that they will forward his letter to me in Ireland.'

'Where might he be going first?'

'To Liverpool, as it happens. Yet that does me no good because I know not where or with whom he will be staying. The butler could not help me there.'

'This is indeed unfortunate,' said I, commiserating. I looked at Clarissa then and shrugged. 'Perhaps we've done all we can,' said I to her.

'Perhaps we have.'

At that low point of dejection we said our good-byes, wished them well through the rest of the day, and departed. We said little as we shuffled along Drury Lane. Clarissa did mention, however, that we might cut through Covent Garden, for there were a few things she might pick up for dinner. I, with the rest of the afternoon free before me, had no objection to that, and so at the earliest opportunity we set off in the direction of the Garden.

We were not far, of course, and as we approached the great marketplace, the noise of it grew louder and louder. One voice, it seemed, rose above the general hubbub of selling and buying. What was it about that voice? Something familiar, certainly — but more than that, it was a voice I had heard in the last few days. But where? Whose was it?

Only then did it begin to come clear to me. First, I recalled that I had heard the voice in court — the Bow Street Court — though not from an accused felon but rather from a disputant. Ah, there it was! His name was . . . Joseph Deekin, a quack of some sort — or so he had been labeled by the other party in the dispute, a Dr. Grenfell, who —

It all flooded back upon me now: I had liked Deekin far better than Grenfell; he claimed that he could cure some — but not all. He knew not whence his power had come and offered no elaborate metaphysical explanation to account for it. Grenfell's complaint was that Deekin claimed so little, yet with some, his mysterious cure worked demonstrably well. And once cured, those few were quite vocal in their praise of Deekin and his ministrations; such praise could be heard by

Dr. Grenfell's patients as they awaited their chance to buy his pills and nostrums. They began to wonder if, by chance, they had gone to the wrong man for treatment. In short, Mr. Deekin's success was bad for Dr. Grenfell's business.

Having remembered all this, I also recalled that I had been appointed by Sir John to witness the effectiveness of Mr. Deekin's treatment and report back to him on this matter. I had not yet done so. Now was my chance. And come to think of it, there was another reason . . .

A number of times during Dr. Goldsworthy's 'medical demonstration' I had been struck by the similarity of what I then watched to . . . well . . . something. And *this* was the something of which I had been reminded — Mr. Deekin's own description of his 'treatment.' First of all, there was the admission that it did not work upon all (as indeed it had not worked on me). There was also the therapeutic use to which it had been put by both men. And thirdly, there was — oh, what did it matter? Let us see for ourselves and make our own decision.

'Come along, Clarissa, I do believe I have the answer to your problem . . . '

★　★　★

It later struck me as ironic to a remarkable degree that Joseph Deekin's presentation seemed more 'scientific' than that of Dr. Goldsworthy. After all, Sir John had been right: there was perhaps a bit too much of the 'show,' the 'entertainment,' for the audience to take the matter entirely seriously. And most there seemed to know that. They applauded him as if he were pulling rabbits out of a hat. Mr. Deekin, on the other hand, seemed as he had in Sir John's courtroom — a simple man who has found a way to alleviate or remove some sorts of pain. (Some sorts, though not all.) He knows not whence comes this power, though he is certain it has no diabolical source. Et cetera.

Mr. Deekin's method of demonstration was similar, too. From those he had gathered with his own strong voice, he selected a group — not a great many — who were invited up to the makeshift stage for treatment.

I was taken somewhat by surprise when Mr. Deekin chose Clarissa so quickly. She was perhaps the third of nine taken. She made it easy for him. It was evident that she had come with me, and from the nod he had given me, I knew that I had been recognized by him. Thus did he show great confidence in his powers by choosing my companion. Not that she had made it difficult for him. She clamored and waved along with the rest, and though she could display no outward sign of disability, not even a tic, she must have seemed to him, somehow, a likely candidate for treatment. Once up on the stage, she conducted herself with dignity and decorum, and left little doubt that she belonged there. But what did she seek from Deekin? The crowd round me seemed to wonder at it — nor could I have answered if the question had been put to me.

It was a good harvest for Mr. Deekin. Of the nine he had invited to the stage, four were given help of some sort. Or perhaps better said, there were five, for Clarissa, always a special case, would have to wait a bit to see if her request would finally be granted.

And where, by the bye, was Deekin's friend Hannah through all of this? She busied herself bustling about the stage, setting out chairs for the volunteers and then taking them away again when and if Mr. Deekin should find himself unable to put them into a trance state. This sort of preparation was done very swiftly. It seemed that all that Deekin needed to do was stare purposefully into the eyes of a volunteer, and he would have sent him or her into a trance; or if not, Deekin was off to the next, and Hannah was whispering into his ear an urgent request to leave the stage. In this way, there were soon but five seated upon the stage, glassy-eyed, in a trance state, ready and waiting to be called upon by Mr. Deekin. Three men and two women there were. Deekin conferred with each one before beginning his 'treatment.' With most, it was not difficult to tell why they had come. One of them, the man farthest to the left, had an eye that blinked so rapidly that it seemed likely that it might fly out of his head at any moment. Another, his neighbor, had a great twitch in his leg. Clarissa's companion female had a pain in her side so constant and severe that she was forced to walk in a manner which favored that side and bent her nearly double. And of course there was, perhaps inevitably, a stutterer, one who seemed even more miserably afflicted than the man cured by Dr. Goldsworthy the night before.

It was worth mentioning that Mr. Deekin's treatment included a physical act which had great purpose and meaning. At what proved to be the climactic moment in the treatment of the volunteers, Deekin directed each to grasp the offending organ or part of the body and cast from it that which had caused trouble. And as each did this, he was instructed to cry out, loud as could be, 'Begone! And never return!' So that it seemed to me that there was something to this ritual of exorcism. This I found strange and quite fascinating.

But what of Clarissa? What had he to say of her — or to her? Through it all, she had sat, indifferent to the rest, a distant, smiling expression upon her face. She wasn't like the rest of them there on the little stage. They, even in the trance state, watched Mr. Deekin perform his separate miracles upon one and then another with some vacant interest. Clarissa, however, sat back, eyes open and focused just ahead of her and slightly above. What was most arresting and plain to see was the pleasure which she took in what she saw. Every now and then some exclamation of delight would escape her — an 'oooh' or an 'aaah.'

At last Mr. Deekin came to her. A hush fell on the crowd as all strained to hear just what he would say.

'Clarissa?'

'Yes, Mr. Deekin?'

I thought it important that though she responded to him, her eyes did not shift in his direction. She continued to watch what had held her complete attention for the past quarter hour or more.

'Do you hear me well?'

'Oh, very well!'

'And do you see what you hoped to see?'

'Yes sir. It was very plain indeed.'

'And would you describe what you see?'

'That's very difficult to do — but I shall try,' said she. 'I see colors and shapes.'

'Only that?'

'Oh no, sir, for the colors and shapes are constantly moving, flowing one into the other. Oh, it's quite beautiful. I wish that I could do a better job of describing it. Perhaps I can, once I have a pen in hand.'

'Ah, you are a writer then!'

'Oh no, sir. I am a cook. I would be a writer, though.'

'What then prevents you?'

'Again, it's difficult to say. I am given the time and opportunity, but somehow my hands are tied. I simply cannot do what I want most to do. I cannot write. I fear that I am to become a laughing-stock, a figure of fun.'

'Do you want for ideas?'

'Oh no, sir. I have many ideas — or perhaps too many. Perhaps that is my trouble.'

'Do you believe that?'

'No.'

With that, she put a full stop to the interrogation for a long moment. There seemed nowhere to go. But then did Mr. Deekin brighten.

'You used an expression but a short time ago. You said, 'my hands are tied.' Do you recall?'

'Oh yes.'

'Show me how you mean. How are they tied?'

She did then make fists of her hands and put them together at the wrists, as if bound together there.

'Like this. You see?'

'Keep them together just so,' he told her. 'But now tell me, what is it binds together your two hands?'

'Rope,' said she, 'very strong rope.'

'Well then, you must be rid of it. You cannot use your fingers to untie the knot. What *can* you do?'

Now she understood. She joined in most eagerly. 'I can bite it through!'

'Well, do it, my girl, do it!'

Then did she show her teeth and growl. Yet the sound that issued from her as she ground her teeth at the imaginary ropes was, in a way, quite frightening. Yet to hear it so from one so dignified and otherwise so proper must have struck many in the audience as comical, at least to some degree, for laughter broke out among them. But Clarissa paid it no attention whatever. She kept right on gnawing — until she had done what she set out to do.

'There! Look!' said she. 'I've bitten through them.'

And indeed she had! She pulled her two hands apart and opened her fingers to demonstrate that she might show them all.

'Good, good, you've done wonderfully well, Clarissa. But where's now the rope with which your hands were bound?'

'Down here,' said she. 'Down on the floor.'

'Well, get it. Pick it up.'

She bent low and felt round on the floor before her. Then did she hold them aloft and wave them about proudly for all to see. (Though of course there was naught for any to see — more laughter ensued.)

'Now, you have it?'

'I do. I have it.'

'Now throw it away. Throw it as far from you as ever you can, and as you do, you must shout loud and clear: Begone! And never return!'

And that she did, so that her own voice drowned out all the many and diverse sounds of Covent Garden. At that they cheered her and applauded. I'd no idea that Clarissa could shout so loud.

*　*　*

After that there was little for Mr. Deekin to do but make a speech of support of his tonic

131

water. ('It will ease your pain, if not cure it complete,' said he.) A few bottles were sold — enough, apparently, to satisfy him. He then called after the departing crowd that he would make the final presentation of the day at five o'clock, and they were all welcome to come back. Then did he wave me up to join Clarissa upon the small stage. On my way to her, I saw that the coins in the collection plate did not amount to much, and so I contributed a shilling in Clarissa's name, looked up, and found her by my side.

'Ah,' said I to her, 'you're with us now, are you?'

'Yes, oh yes,' said she. 'I'm back, yet with no memory of where I've been. Perhaps you can help me remember.'

'Perhaps,' said I — and only that.

Mr. Deekin approached us with a smile. He swept up the coins in the collection plate in a single motion and asked if we would care to join him and Hannah for a cup of tea.

'You might have some questions need answering,' said he.

We agreed and followed him behind the back curtain to a small space wherein Hannah fussed and fidgeted at a kettle on a small outdoor stove. From it (remarkably enough) she soon brought forth boiling water sufficient to provide four small cups of tea.

'What have we more to offer them, Hannah?' said Mr. Deekin to her.

'Naught but bread and butter and a fine, big apple.'

'Well then, butter the bread and slice the apple, and we'll make a snack of it, eh?'

As she proceeded to do just that, he turned to me and said, 'I hope you did not judge it forward of me, inviting your young lady friend up on the stage.'

'Oh no,' said I. 'It was her wish.'

'She seemed ever so eager to come,' Hannah put in.

'Oh, I was indeed,' Clarissa put in. 'That much I recall, if little else.'

'You remember nothing at all, eh? Ain't that always the way of it, Hannah?'

She agreed, nodding firm, yet she said nothing.

'Won't someone please tell me what it was happened whilst I was away — or asleep — or whatever was my state during that period which I cannot remember?'

Looking troubled, Mr. Deekin gave a negative shake of his head. 'It ain't really our practice to do it that way. And it's specially sort of a problem with you because it may take a while — a real, long while — before we know if it worked with you.'

'What worked? What do you mean?'

'Your 'treatment.' That's what we call it. Y'see, your problem wasn't the usual one. It's mostly, can I relieve this pain or that, can I get them talking right. And I know right away if it worked out proper — or if it didn't.' Mr. Deekin took a good-sized bite from the quarter apple Hannah had passed to him; he chewed upon it thoughtfully. Then, after a bit, he resumed: 'Even as I'm talking about it here, I'm thinking back to that poor woman who was all bent over, like. I couldn't help her at all, it seemed. Maybe if I'd stayed with her longer.'

'That ain't so,' Hannah said sharply. 'You helped her considerable. She said so herself. She said you took away her pain, or most of it.'

'Maybe that's all I'm good for — takin' pain away.'

'Oh, stop, Joe. None of that. Wasn't it you who said that the minute you start doubting your powers, that's when you'll start losing them?'

He said nothing for a long moment. Then, grudgingly: 'It was me, all right.' He turned to Clarissa and me. 'You see how your particular problem doesn't fit in with my usual, don't you, miss?'

'Accepting your vague description of it, yes, I suppose I do see that much, anyway.'

'So, p'rhaps you, young sir, will tell her of

what was said and done upon this stage here if ever her life should change in a significant way.'

As I nodded my agreement, Clarissa interrupted in a most exasperated manner. 'For heaven's sake, my life is certain to change in many significant ways in the next few months, for we're to be married soon.'

Predictably, there was a great chorus of 'congratulations' and 'best wishes,' et cetera. But Clarissa was not to be put off by it.

'My question is simply this,' said she, raising her voice to a shout — or quite near it. 'How shall I know which of these many changes is the 'right' one?'

'You won't,' said Mr. Deekin. '*He* will.' Pointing at me. 'And if he will then be so good as to inform me, just as soon as he has told you, I should then be ever so grateful.'

★   ★   ★

We two left not long after that. I cannot now recall what, if anything, we discussed on the short walk back to Number 4 Bow Street. All that I remember is that somewhere along the way, she said with a vehemence that seemed quite surprising, 'I hate surprises!'

5

*In which Sir John
learns more of
Lord Lammermoor's
secret life*

For the next few days Sir John interrogated
the witnesses who had appeared before the
coroner, Thomas Trezavant, in the course of
the inquest into the death of Lord Lammermoor. Having heard the little they had to say
to Trezavant in response to his questions, I
was amazed, and ever again amazed, at how
much more Sir John drew from those same
witnesses when he put questions to them.

It was the magistrate's philosophy of
interrogation that the interrogator discover as
much about the man or woman answering
the questions as might be possible in the
allotted time (and often beyond it). His
intention was to gather overmuch and then
go through it at his leisure, looking for
inconsistencies, interesting details, et cetera.
He often found them.

For instance, in his interrogation of Michael Wilson, Lord Lammermoor's parliamentary assistant, Sir John discovered that Wilson himself had political ambitions and that he intended to run for a seat in the House of Commons at the next opportunity. Was he then being a bit *too* discreet in not telling us earlier and more about Annie's presence there? That led to what was really a rather curious question on the part of the coroner. What was it he had asked? Ah yes, he had asked if Wilson would take a look round the audience to see if that unknown young lady were there. What had given Trezavant the idea that she *might* be there? Why would anyone suppose such? And that leads to the even stranger question of how Wilson could have missed Annie there. Perhaps he hadn't missed her. Indeed, the more I considered the matter, the more certain it seemed that he hadn't missed her at all. Of course she had looked on either side of her — left and right — and turned round in her chair for a better look behind — a cunning bit of improvisation, that. It was as if she were as ignorant of who the mystery woman might be as any around her. It was possible that this had thrown Wilson off her track — but not likely. Yet Wilson stuck to his story. No, he had *not* recognized any female in that small crowd of onlookers. Sir John pressed him, pointing out that, after all, Lady Lammermoor was in that 'small crowd,' and he must have met her a time or two previous to the inquest. But he insisted he had never had contact with the woman, before or after the inquest. Reluctantly, Sir John accepted that and let the matter go — at least so far as his interrogation of Wilson went.

Yet in a sense the matter came up again when he talked with Mr. Triplett. He, if you'll recall, was the walker on the bridge who happened along at the moment that Lord Lammermoor jumped from the railing and into the river. He saw the man who had passed some brief message or other on to Lord Lammermoor and set the mad chain of events into motion. More to the point, he saw Annie, as well: He said that the two of them had reached Lord L. at about the same moment, but they were too late to prevent him from jumping. Then, when he had left their grasp and fallen to the cold waters below, she ran off in search of help — and never came back. But at the moment they reached Lord Lammermoor and attempted to hold him back, she and Triplett could only have been about two or three feet apart, at most. He must have had a good look at her then. Yet Mr. Trezavant never asked Triplett if there were anyone present who resembled the young lady in question. I wondered at that and conveyed my doubts on to Sir John. He took them and put a few questions to him. As I remember, this is how it went:

Sir John: Sir, as you and the young lady struggled to keep your grasp on Lord Lammermoor, you must have been very close to her.

Triplett: Yes, very close, I s'pose.

Sir John: Would you recognize her again?

Triplett: I doubt it. We was just holding on to him. I wasn't thinking about her — just saving him. Then he was gone, and so was she.

Sir John: Then you could not have done what Mr. Trezavant asked Mr. Wilson to do?

Triplett: You mean look over the women there in the room and pick one of them out as that particular girl?

Sir John: That's right.

Triplett: (shaking his head) No, sir — and for just the reason I said. All happened too fast.

Then did Sir John move on to another point entirely.

Afterward, he said to me, 'I hope that you were not disappointed that I did not press the matter further, Jeremy. Yours was an interesting point, but his response was most natural and logical — or so it seemed to me.' I was satisfied.

And finally, as Sir John and I sat together in his darkened study, he broke a silence of a few minutes' duration when, apropos of nothing at all, he said: 'You know, it's quite interesting that Mr. Trezavant failed to ask Triplett to look round the room for Lord Lammermoor's female companion. Why should he have held back?'

I considered that a moment. 'Mr. Donnelly says that Mr. Trezavant's purpose in life is to curry the favor of those in power.'

'No doubt true,' said Sir John. Then, after a moment's hesitation: 'He must have received a signal of some sort not to continue down that road.'

'Lady Lammermoor sat in the front row. And I do recall the coroner stealing glances in her direction.'

'Well, there you have it.' Silence reigned for a good, long stretch of time. Then: 'Would you drop by Mr. Donnelly's surgery sometime tomorrow and pick up his copy of the report to the coroner on Lord Lammermoor's death? There may be something in it of value.'

'Certainly, sir.'

'You've had no luck finding the waterman, have you? What was his name?'

'Richard Porter, sir. Well no, he proves quite difficult to contact. I return again and again to the Whitehall Stairs, which is where he ties up — yet I always seem to miss him.'

'Is he avoiding you? Is he in hiding?'

'No, I don't think so. It's just a matter of stopping by at the right time.'

'Well, keep after him then.'

'I shall indeed.'

★ ★ ★

Taking Sir John's advice, I went early the next day to the Whitehall Stairs in search of Richard Porter. It was the fifth or sixth time I had visited the place — I had lost count, truth to tell — so I had a good notion of who and how many I was likely to find there. I had done no more than start down the stairs when a glance to the foot of them told me that there were more present than was usual. Could this then be the day? In a word, reader, it was.

'Well, wouldja look who's here!'

'Hey, Dicky, it's the boy from Bow Street, and it's you he's after. Better mind what you say to him now.'

They continued with their bullyragging and teasing for minutes longer. Mr. Porter didn't seem to mind.

There were, by my recollection, about four or five there on that little island in the Thames. Perhaps it was the four to whom I'd made my inquiries on earlier visits, and the addition of Richard Porter made it five. In any case, I was here, and so was he. I had found him at last. I beckoned to him and led him up the stairs out of earshot of the rest.

'Mr. Porter,' said I, 'Sir John Fielding, Magistrate of the Bow Street Court, would like the opportunity to speak with you at Bow Street.'

'Right now?'

'No, not necessarily. It can be at anytime during the day. You fix the time, but don't be late.'

'Am I in trouble? I tried to do everything just the way we're supposed to.'

'And I'm sure you did. No, you're not in trouble. Sir John simply wants to take you through your testimony at the coroner's inquest and ask you a few more questions.'

'That's all?'

'That's all.'

'Oh, well, that's nothin' to be afeared of.'

'Just as I said.'

'Awright then, let's say about two o'clock this afternoon, if that suits you.'

'It suits me fine, as I'm sure it will Sir John, as well. We'll see you then.'

As I marched back up the stairs I heard Mr. Porter's mates asking to know what all this was about. He dismissed their questions as 'just more foolishness 'bout that floater I pulled out of the river the other night.'

★ ★ ★

When I knocked upon Mr. Donnelly's door, I thought it likely that the two of them might yet be in bed. They seemed to be spending more and more time there, rising later and later, since their return from Dublin.

The medico came promptly to the door, dabbing dry the excess shaving soap upon his face with a towel.

'Ah, Jeremy,' said he, 'what can I do for you this fine morning?'

'What but the usual sort of request? I'm here on an errand for Sir John. I mentioned to him that you had prepared a report upon the corpus of Lord Lammermoor for the coroner's inquest.'

'Right — and given no opportunity to read

from by said coroner.'

'That must have hastened you on your way to Dublin.'

'Indeed it has had that effect.'

'Is there a copy of that report about?'

'As a matter of fact, no, there is not.'

'Really? But I thought it was from that copy that you attempted to read.'

'It was, but let me explain.'

Prevented from reading from the report, Mr. Donnelly folded it up and tucked it away in his coat pocket. And there it stayed until two days past when none but Archibald Talley, the younger son of Lord Lammermoor, came to the door and asked if he might have it. In a way, it seemed an odd request, for after all, what use would he have for it? Yet Mr. Donnelly kept silent, for what reason could there be to withhold it? Mr. Trezavant had his copy, had he not? And that is the one which would go into the inquest file.

'My copy,' said Mr. Donnelly, 'was hardly the sort of thing I would take with me to Ireland. In short, I let him take it away.' He chuckled. 'I had to search some to find it, though. But what use would it be to anyone now?'

I shrugged. 'Sir John seemed to place some value upon it.'

'Well, if that's the case, he can ask me

about it. After all, I wrote it. I know what's in it.'

With that, he went to fetch his hat and coat and tell his dear Molly that he would be off to Bow Street but would soon be back.

'I hope she heard me,' said he to me upon his return. 'At least she grunted as if she understood.'

★　★　★

The way to Bow Street was short, and we took it at a brisk pace. There was time enough for Mr. Donnelly to ask no more than a few questions. Yet he, being a man of considerable curiosity, managed to ask them.

As I recall, the first of them concerned the specific authority of Sir John's interest. 'Is it merely academic? Has he had orders from above to conduct his own sort of investigation? By what authority?' Et cetera. I assured him that as magistrate, he had the power to open or reopen any case that he might choose.

Mr. Donnelly wanted to know the particular nature of Sir John's interest in this one. 'Has he told you anything that would indicate what part of my report interests him?' I reminded him that he had not yet seen Mr. Donnelly's report, so how could he know which part or parts interested him most?

And finally, he asked quite bluntly if this investigation might mean the downfall of Mr. Trezavant. On that one, I did inject some of my own feelings in response. 'Mr. Donnelly,' said I, 'Mr. Trezavant has so many friends in very high places that I doubt that he will ever suffer any sort of 'downfall.'' At that he sighed. 'I have heard that view stated by others,' said he, 'yet even now it is difficult for me to accept it.'

Thus came we to Bow Street Number 4.

Sir John was quite unsurprised that Gabriel Donnelly had chosen to accompany me, and he seemed naught but delighted to hear his step down the long hall accompanying my own.

'Is that you, Gabriel?' said he as he came forth from his chambers with hand outstretched.

Mr. Donnelly took that hand and pumped vigorously. 'It is,' said he, 'though each time I visit now, I question that I have made the right decision.'

'Well, you have made it and that's an end to it. You've argued it all so well to me that I am convinced, so whilst you are yet here in London, let us enjoy such occasions as this. Come, sit down in my chambers, and we shall talk over this report to the coroner. You have it with you, I assume?'

Mr. Donnelly, of course, was forced to admit that he had not. Yet when he told the magistrate who had come asking for it and came away with it, Sir John was left speechless for a moment or two.

'Archibald Talley, you say? Lord Lammermoor's second son?' He sputtered and stuttered. 'But . . . but . . . well, I never heard of such a thing.'

'Nor had I. Still, I couldn't withhold it.'

'Why not?'

He gave to him the same reasons he had given me.

Sir John sat behind his desk stroking his chin, thinking this business through. 'Yes, I can see that if you had no reason to hold on to it . . . '

'Exactly.'

'But the question remains, why should young Talley want it? What would it be but a reminder of his father's death under what I would consider very questionable circumstances.'

'Well, there was something perhaps that they might wish to keep quiet.'

'Who do you mean by 'they'?'

'The family, Lord Lammermoor's people. Just at the entry of the small intestine into the large, there was a tumor — a malignant growth. It was new. It was not, certainly not, the cause of death — but it was there and no doubt would eventually have killed him.'

'How long would that have taken?' asked Sir John.

'Oh, a year, at the earliest, probably much longer.'

'But Mr. Trezavant asked if there had been anything in his stomach,' I put in, ' — any wounds, et cetera.'

'Yes, Jeremy, his *stomach*. This was his lower intestine, in which I spied the growth. That is what I was trying to tell the coroner and his jury when the coroner kept interrupting me. You'll recall I was trying to tell him that there were other causes of death besides murder, suicide, and misadventure?'

'But why did you not just say so?' I asked it in a manner rather naive, I fear, but then it was a rather naive question.

'Well,' said Mr. Donnelly, 'there is among the members of the public — be they high or low — a most peculiar attitude toward cancer. It's as if it were agreed that a tumor was a sign of some moral failing, something reprehensible on the order of the pox.'

'Ah, 'tis true, Jeremy,' said Sir John. 'When you were but a boy, the first Lady Fielding, God rest her soul, had what was termed by doctor after doctor a 'mysterious female ailment.''

'Oh, I remember, sir. Indeed I do.'

'Do you? Yes, of course you would. Well, there was nothing mysterious about it. She had a cancerous growth upon her ovary. But none of them would tell me that until Mr. Donnelly came along.'

'And by that time all that could be done for her was prescribe opiates,' said Mr. Donnelly. 'The cancer had spread all through her body.'

'What a sad tale,' said I.

'I could tell you others — but there's no need. I'm sure you understand now why I attempted to call attention to the fact that there are *other* causes of death to be considered. That might also explain why Mr. Trezavant kept interrupting me and not allowing me to speak out. The hint of a cancer of any sort might move some men to suicide.'

'And anything which suggested suicide would not be acceptable to the widow and her sons. Nor therefore to Mr. Trezavant.'

'Exactly.'

'It might actually be interpreted as a motive for suicide — nor would that have been acceptable to Mr. Trezavant.'

'Why, in all truth, I had not thought of that,' said Mr. Donnelly.

Just then Sir John gave forth a mighty clearing of the throat. He caught our attention and reestablished his authority with one great *harumphh*. He fixed his face in a frown and thrust out his jaw.

'Must I break up this discussion before you two take this investigation out of my hands completely and prove me quite superfluous? Jeremy, if I am not mistaken, you have a number of interviews to conduct before the court session begins. And you, Mr. Donnelly, you must tell me what else, besides news of a dead man's tumor, is contained in your report to the coroner.'

★ ★ ★

I interviewed two brawlers arrested at one of the dives in Bedford Street rather quickly; so drunk were they that neither could remember what it was he fought about. There was a light-fingered moll accused of picking the pocket of a journeyman carpenter. The purse in question contained less than a pound, which was lucky for her, for had it exceeded that amount by much, she would, by necessity, have been passed on to felony court for trial. There were two more who had been picked up in the Covent Garden area for public drunkenness.

There was naught of an unusual nature in this group of offenders. Nor did they prove in any way difficult for Sir John to deal with. He considered it a good day when he sent none on to Old Bailey for trial, since all too often a guilty verdict there meant a certain trip to Tyburn Hill in a tumbrel.

Grenfell and Deekin were another matter entirely. As with the last time they made an appearance in Sir John's court 'twas those two who caused the most difficulty. They argued, each with the other, as I attempted to interview them. Yet in all truth, there was little interviewing to be done. All that had changed since last they met in this courtroom was that I had gone (in Clarissa's company) to see Joseph Deekin's presentation, which I have already described in these pages. I told Sir John of it in some detail when I returned; he asked a few questions but offered no comments of his own, except to say that he would be happy to see them in court again. I wondered just how happy he would truly be if he saw them in his court as I saw them beforehand. They chattered as angrily as a pair of magpies, making threats, shaking their fingers, offering their fists. I warned the two that they had best not show such rude behavior before Sir John, or they would finish the day behind bars on a contempt charge.

Oddly, 'twas only Mr. Deekin who took my advice to heart.

As the complainant, Grenfell spoke first, laying before the court the separate damages done him by Deekin's presence in a place so near to his surgery. 'My patients,' said he, 'must pass close by this man's show tent on their way to my office. They hear his patients praise his methods.'

'What is the harm in that?' Sir John asked.

'Why, he makes claims for what he calls his 'treatment,' yet it is no true treatment at all. What medicine does he sell? He makes no assertion that he is a doctor of medicine. Why not? Would no school of medicine enroll him? Would no doctor apprentice him?'

On and on he went with his tirade again Joseph Deekin. The only remedy he could see to the situation was for Deekin to move out of the area of Covent Garden — though out of London would have been preferable. But as Sir John frequently interrupted him with the sort of questions which would trouble any reasonable man, he became more short-tempered and openly angry at the magistrate. It was at last when Grenfell heard him say that in the report he had received upon Mr. Deekin's activities, 'there was nothing of the bad character which you ascribe to him,' that the doctor became reckless. 'If that is what your report says, then your report lies.'

'*Sit down*, sir,' said Sir John. (Did he say it? Nay, he roared it.) 'I will not have you impugning the veracity of an officer of this court. All you have done in framing your complaint is to attack the character and practices of Mr. Deekin. He shall now have his say in response. And I promise you, sir, if you interrupt him or me, it will be off with you to Newgate for the next ninety days. Have I made myself clear?'

It was evident that he had done so, for Grenfell simply nodded his reply. Which Sir John, of course, could not see.

'You may speak sufficient to make it clear you understand and agree,' said Sir John.

'I understand and agree.'

'That is enough. Now, take your seat and remain silent.'

That he did, his eyes wide with shock.

'Mr. Deekin, now you have the opportunity to defend yourself. Come forward, please.'

Joseph Deekin delivered his defense with greater style and rough eloquence than would ever have been expected from him. It was a prepared statement, and it was plain that he had practiced it so that it offered rebuttal to Grenfell on nearly all the complaints made against him.

Among the points that he made: True, he

had no formal education in medicine, but there was none better versed than he in the uses of plants, roots, and herbs: yes indeed, he also sold bottles of medicine, but he made no special claims for their contents. 'You see,' said he, 'not all takes to my treatment, only about half, but for that other half that don't, what's in my medicine may be just the thing. It has a good taste to it, and it does no harm. The main thing is, sir' — speaking to Sir John — 'it's what people believe and expect decides what's going to work for them.' Finally, Mr. Deekin made it clear that he knew not whence came this power — not from the devil for as he said, he was as good a Christian as most, and he did no harm with it.

His response to Grenfell could only have taken not much more than five minutes, yet it was so thorough and precise that I, who had actually witnessed one of Mr. Deekin's demonstrations, could have added very little to it. I scanned the crowded courtroom once again, searching for Clarissa. She had said — pledged, actually — that she would be here for the hearing of the complaint that she might lend moral support to Mr. Deekin. Still, she was nowhere to be seen.

Sir John had a question or two. 'Mr. Deekin, tell me, if you will, how and when

154

you first became aware of this power that you have.'

'Gladly, sir,' said he. 'I am a farm boy, and it was my responsibility to care for the farm animals — all of them. And like all who work with such, I began to wonder what they understood and how much. I talked to them and gave them commands and such, but I began wondering if I could tell them this or that without actually speakin'. What was most important, though, was giving them a special sort of look — real powerful, but not threatening — and concentrating real hard. And what do you know, sir — it worked! With some it worked better than others. Best of all was the pigs, which surprised me, then the horses, then the cows. Anything smaller — from sheep on down to chickens — was just too small brained to understand.

'So I went from animals to people, and with my younger sisters and older brother, I got the same sort of results. But that was when I found out that some just wouldn't be touched by my *special* look. One of my sisters told my parents what I was up to — and that was all it took. Oh, but I played it like a game with all my mates and got a reputation for it, of course. By the time I was out of school I was sort of notorious for the tricks I'd play on people. The parents never liked it much,

155

though. And the vicar! He was just sure I was one of the devil's own — that's why I'm always making that little speech about not knowing where the power comes from but being absolutely sure it ain't from the devil. Anyway, when I got a little older, I was smart enough to see that I'd never inherit the farm, nor no piece of it, so I decided to see if I could make a living at my tricks and with my special look. Only by that time, I'd found out I could help people get rid of certain kinds of aches and pains and whatnot. I liked that better.'

'And you've been at this how long?' Sir John asked.

'Three years now, going on four.'

'And one last question. Have you seen any medical demonstrations of 'animal magnetism' by Dr. Goldsworthy?'

'No, but I've heard a lot about him in the past few days. From what is said, it seems like he and I are, what you might say, drinking from the same well.'

'Mr. Grenfell, I ask you now to stand and come forward. Take your place beside Mr. Deekin.'

He did as he was bade, yet as he did, he silently made plain the disgust that he felt for Deekin. He wrinkled his nose and edged away from his opponent.

'Here is the decision of this court. I charge you, Mr. Deekin, to make an effort in good faith to find a new place to park the wagon whereon you have pitched your tent and made a stage. If you find such a place, with willing neighbors, et cetera, then Mr. Grenfell is to bear the cost of the move. If not, then Mr. Deekin may remain in the place he has chosen for as long as he wishes to do so. Both of you are to return here a week from today and inform me of the final disposition of this complaint.'

With that, Sir John picked up his gavel and beat a sharp tattoo upon the tabletop. 'This session is ended.'

First there was a round of applause, which Sir John must have thought quite unseemly. He rose, found his way to the door leading to his chambers, and exited the courtroom. Out of the crowd two women rushed forward — Hannah and Clarissa — filled with the excitement of the moment.

'You've won, Joe, you've won!' Hannah sang it forth and made a kind of chant of it as she jumped up and down. Deekin tried to quiet her, yet his efforts went for naught.

Haply, I caught sight of Dr. Grenfell, and the look I spied upon his face was frightening to see. Dark and threatening was it, the very

157

face of Lucifer himself. Then did he speak loud and clear.

'You must remember this moment,' said he to Deekin, 'and enjoy it whilst you can, for there will come a time not too distant from now when you will rue and regret it.'

In response, Deekin wisely said nothing, but from his appearance it was evident that he took the threat just made with the utmost seriousness. If only Hannah had followed his example! Though she, too, said nothing, she stuck out her tongue at the medico and fluttered it at him, making a low, farting sound. And if that weren't bad enough, Clarissa began to laugh at her. She clapped a hand over her mouth and attempted to stop — all to no avail, for she laughed all the harder. Dr. Grenfell stamped away toward the street door, as the remnants of the crowd jeered at him. Fearful that she might occasion an even more aggressive demonstration by the crowd, I took Clarissa by the elbow and rushed through the door to the backstage area.

'Now, Jeremy, stop this, please.' I swept her up the stairs to our living quarters. 'I didn't even have the chance to congratulate Mr. Deekin,' she declared.

'I am less concerned about that than the possibility of heaping even greater ridicule upon Dr. Grenfell.'

'Well, he deserves it.'

'Perhaps he does, but that is no sign that he should be made so bitter that he will seek revenge. Did you not hear him? He has already threatened it.'

'Revenge? Of what sort? Against whom?'

'Against me, you, Sir John, and above all, Mr. Deekin and Hannah.'

'Are you sure?'

'No, I'm not sure, but would you wish to chance it with any I've named?'

She took a considerable time to answer, and when at last she did, she had, of a sudden, grown more somber in her manner. 'Of course I would not,' said she.

We were by that time in the kitchen. I thought it best to strike off in some new direction, rather than lecture her further. Who was I to lecture anyone? Had I not made errors aplenty myself?

'I looked for you earlier,' said I. 'You nearly missed the hearing of the complaint.'

'Oh . . . oh yes,' said she, somewhat abstracted. 'I've been writing the past few days.'

'A new idea?'

'Oh, no, I've so many old ideas . . . '

'Is that what all this is?' I gestured to the tabletop, which was littered with manuscript and notes, all in great disarray. 'I hope it's not your old notion to write a romance about *us*?'

'Well . . . ' She seemed reluctant to say a word. Could she truly be writing something, rather than talking about writing something? She began gathering up the sheets of paper from the table, putting them into some sort of order — perhaps one known only to her. 'Perhaps,' said she, 'you'll see it when I have finished.'

'That may be never,' said I, attempting to make a joke of it with a little ha-ha at the end. Still, it must have sounded a bit unkind.

Ever the realist, Clarissa nodded obligingly. 'You may be right,' said she. Nevertheless, after giving the matter a moment's thought, she added, 'But I don't think so — not this time.'

★　★　★

Richard Porter, the waterman, came promptly at two, as he had promised. There was no surprise in that. Everything about him indicated that he was a man who could be depended upon. Grizzled and wrinkled, he nevertheless had a steady eye and the strength in his arms and back of a much younger man. When Sir John offered the man his hand in greeting, Mr. Porter looked upon

160

it oddly for a moment as if he knew not quite what to do with it. Then, just as the magistrate seemed ready to withdraw the hand, Porter seized it and pumped it vigorously. All this made for a rather awkward beginning.

'Sit down, Mr. Porter. This need not take long.'

And indeed it did not. Sir John explained that he wished him to repeat his testimony during the coroner's request. He might interrupt him from time to time with questions and would likely have a few more questions when he had done. And thus it proceeded.

Inevitably, in the course of the interrogation, many more details were drawn from Porter than before, most of them insignificant, and only one or two of them of any real significance. Only Sir John had thought to ask him, as an instance, whence he had come when he had been hailed from the Westminster Bridge and told of the body in the Thames.

After a bit of thought, he came up with this information:

'I remember it as a churchman — some bishop or other — down from the north to take up residence in Lambeth Palace. He was there with his retinue, and they had to be moved with all their baggage quite some distance downstream. It took many trips and damn near wore me out, but I collected a fair price of silver for it. Anyways, that's what I was doin' out there so late.'

'Very good, sir,' put in Sir John. 'Now, tell me, do you recall this bishop's name? His age? His appearance?'

'Well, he was awful young to be a bishop. I can tell you that. Which is to say, that's what you noticed about his appearance — looked about thirty, still had the blond in his hair.'

'But you're sure he was a bishop?'

'That's what they called him — but I can't remember his name.'

'You're sure?'

'I'm sure.'

'Then how can you be sure he was a bishop?'

'Because *that's what they called him* — either that or 'my Lord.''

Sir John rubbed his chin thoughtfully. 'Hmmm,' said he — that and nothing more.

They continued through the testimony that Porter had given before Mr. Trezavant. Though they stopped a number of times, it was for naught but matters of detail or clarification. When he had done and had told all that he had said to the coroner, Mr. Porter did the intelligent thing: He stopped.

Yet Sir John, thinking he had merely paused, leaned forward in his chair quite eagerly. 'Yes, yes?' said he. 'Go on, please.'

'That's all I have to tell.'

'What do you say to me? You mean that this last matter of the stones in the pocket was all that Mr. Trezavant was interested in?'

'Seemed to be.'

'But there's something missing here. How did Lord Lammermoor's body get from your boat to Mr. Donnelly's surgery? You didn't take it upon yourself to deliver the body, did you?'

'Oh no, not I, sir.'

'How then?'

'Well, sir, that is easily told, yet not so easily explained.'

'What do you mean by that?'

'Well, I'll tell it,' said Mr. Porter, 'then maybe you can explain it to your own satisfaction. Now, when those people on the bridge started shouting down at me, pointing where the body was last seen and all, I saw I was practically right under Westminster Bridge. I know this stretch of the river as well as I know my way home because Whitehall Stairs, where I tie up my boat is the next one down from it. So as soon as I got the body and tied him up to the boat, I shouted back at them that I'd take him to Whitehall Stairs. They waved back that they understood, and I set off for that little island on the north bank of the river.

'It didn't take long for them to find me. I had tied up my boat and pulled the body out of the Thames onto the riverbank when up on the stairs I heard a racket of footsteps hurrying down to me there. I looked up and saw three figures, yet when they arrived, there were but two. Now that, I'll tell you, was a bit confusing.'

'I should think so,' said Sir John.

'But I took another peek up the stairs, and I saw that the third man was waiting 'bout halfway up. I couldn't see him well because of the distance and the darkness. Then, too, the others were upon me. One of them, the shortest one of the two, he asked me, was I the waterman who pulled the body out of the river. I said I was, and the fellow slips a coin into my hand, and he says to me, here's something for your trouble. I take a look, and I see that he's given me a sovereign and nothing less. 'Don't go telling this all over London now.' That's what he says to me. Then they pick him up between them and start back up the stairs.

''You know where to take him? Drury Lane? A doctor named Donnelly?'' I called after them.

''We know,' said the shorter one. 'We know all about it.''

164

'And from the look of them,' said Richard Porter, 'I'd say they were right about that.'

'And so you never got a proper look at the man up on the stairs?'

'Never did, for just after they disappeared, I heard a coach-and-four start up. It must have been theirs.'

Sir John nodded, though he said naught for what seemed an interminable length of time. We waited until at last he spoke:

'That will be all, Mr. Porter. I thank you for what you've told us. It may indeed prove important.'

Mr. Porter rose to take his leave. Sir John offered his hand again. This time it was readily accepted.

'Though I have no sovereign to give you, sir, I'll thank you to keep your visit here in confidence,' said he.

'You've my word on it, sir.'

I took him to the street door, and there I added my thanks to Sir John's.

'Think nothin' of it,' said Mr. Porter. ''Twas an honor meetin' the gent.'

★　★　★

I was properly excited by all that Mr. Porter had to tell us. So excited indeed that I quite forgot to tell Sir John what I had promised myself I would not forget: to inform him of the threat made against Mr. Deekin by Dr. Grenfell. That, in the coming days, would loom as quite important.

6

*In which I go afoot
to Lambeth Palace
to seek information*

As is well known to any who have looked upon a map of London, there is a great bend in the River Thames which begins just east of Bow Street. By Whitehall Stairs the bend is complete and for a time the course of the river runs south to north, rather than west to east.

I call attention to this simply to make the point that while I had walked many a mile on the western side, I had had no occasion to take me much beyond Westminster Bridge on the far side of the river. Yet even from the bridge it was possible to spy the watchtowers and banners of Lambeth Palace, my destination, there in the near distance; this august London residence of the Archbishop of Canterbury served him during the sessions of Parliament. The rest of the time visiting bishops were free to make use of it while in the great city. It was indeed an impressive structure. I recall that the first time I saw it I wondered at the need for such a fortress so near to the Tower of London, then was I told that its true purpose was not to house troops but to protect the Archbishop.

'Is he so unpopular?' I asked.

There was no response to my innocent question but raucous laughter from those about me. But a time would come when troops would certainly be needed to keep him from harm. They would not laugh quite so hard.

As I started across the bridge on that lovely May morning I was remembering the various versions of the death of Lord Lammermoor which I had heard in the past few days and attempting to put them together in some semblance of proper order.

Here, I told myself, when Annie and Lord Lammermoor were but a quarter of the way across, he must have seen and recognized the mysterious gentleman. Annie then moved away from him in the direction of Mr. Triplett. The two of them sprang to pull him back from the rail — yet they were too late. That was at a point about a third of the way across the bridge. Lord Lammermoor eluded their grasp and plunged into the dark waters of the Thames, and there he drowned. The mysterious gentleman, after delivering his brief message, then walked calmly away.

At that point, holding tight to the railing, I leaned far out and looked down at the river below. I had heard that it was relatively shallow here, and much shallower a bit farther back, within the shadow of Lambeth Palace, a hundred years ago and more, and that none other than Oliver Cromwell lost coach and horses while attempting to ford the Thames at that point. There are no proper fording places today. The river bottom has been dug and dredged to accommodate more and more boat traffic; and each year the rains are heavier.

Once on the far bank, I turned right and made for Lambeth Palace, which was in sight, perhaps a mile away. Behind me were the timber yards and wharves of Southwark and Bermondsey and ahead much greenery and even a corner of the Spring Gardens at Vauxhall. I soon found myself walking along a canal which ran the course of the river up to the palace — all quite picturesque it was, most specially on a clear day in May like this one.

Arriving at the fenced corner of the palace I halted and pondered at which of the buildings within the compound would it be best to make my inquiry. One was as good as another, it seemed to me, so I turned in at the nearest and approached the guard at the gate. He wore outlandish ceremonial garb from a few centuries back. Nevertheless, he held a musket at his side and looked properly menacing. I approached him with caution.

'Beg pardon, sir,' said I. 'I am the clerk of the Bow Street Court, and I am come at the direction of Sir John Fielding, magistrate of that court, to find the answer to a question.'

The fellow remained glassy-eyed through my little speech, staring at some distant point above and far beyond my left shoulder.

'What is the question, *sah!*'

'A bishop arrived here at Lambeth Palace six nights past. Could you inform me as to the name of that bishop and his see?'

In response, he said naught to me, but rather bellowed forth at his loudest, '*Corporal of the guard!*' Still, he did not move his eyes from that spot above and far beyond my left shoulder. He did a sharp right-face and marched half the distance to the gate. Then did he about-face and begin his return.

But at that moment the corporal of the guard appeared, waved me through the gate and offered the guard a nod of approval. He, I noted, was dressed in the sort of uniform that might be seen worn on any parade ground or drill yard from Aldershot to Zim-Zim.

The corporal of the guard looked me up and down. 'I b'lieve I heard your question from the guards shelter,' said he. 'You wanted to know the name of the bishop who presented himself six nights past. Is that correct?'

'Well, yes, more or less,' said I.

'It so happens, young sir, that there was three bishops come in that night you're speakin' of. That's not to mention the three that's come in since then, nor even givin' a thought to all the auxiliary bishops, secretaries, nor whatnot who're travelin' with the bishops. Just to let you know, young sir, we been workin' damn hard just finding places for all these churchmen to lay their heads of a night.'

'Well, if you — '

'No, now, you let me finish, will you? I don't know who told you to go at this arse-backwards, holdin' back the name of the bishop you're seekin', but if you'd just tell me that, it would be a good deal easier for both of us.'

It was Sir John, of course, who instructed me to go at this in just such a way. ''Be casual,' said he to me: 'Do not seem overly eager to know just who it was arrived at such

171

an odd hour.'' As you can see, reader, I had a good notion of how it *should* go. It was just that in dealings with others, things seldom go as they are supposed to. Ah well, I had tried my best, had I not?

'Talley,' said I. 'His name is Talley.'

Hearing that, he fetched out a notebook from some inner pocket of his coat and quickly found the right page.

'Bishop John Talley of Liverpool, arrived six nights past at approximately midnight. He brought with him his secretary and the newly appointed Auxiliary Bishop of Liverpool, Alastir Stubbs, and they are quartered in the South Tower. If you'll just follow me . . . ' And with that he took off at a quick march in the direction of the far tower.

This fitted together almost too neatly! I was not at all sure that this was what I wanted. Had I been sent here for that? No. Had Sir John armed me with questions for Bishop Talley? Indeed he had not. I was, for the moment, in quite a quandary; and so, I chose the path of least resistance — as I did so often in those days — and hurried to catch up with the corporal of the guard. And catch up with him I did.

'Where are we headed?' I asked.

'Where indeed but to the South Tower. Ain't that what you wanted?'

I said nothing, which in this case seemed to signal my assent. On our way, we passed a large building hidden behind even larger ones. They seemed to be joined together with connecting gardens of flowers, all of them in full bloom. Just ahead was the structure I had correctly identified as the South Tower. He took me to a door, more than half hidden by bushes and plants.

'Just down here,' said he. 'We'll save a step or two.'

We descended a short stairway. He took from his pocket an impressive ring of keys and opened the door with one. Entering, he waited till I was safely inside, then locked the door behind me.

In the dim light I found myself quite amazed by our surroundings. 'Twas as if in passing through that door we had gone back some centuries to the period which they now call 'medieval.' The low ceiling was in the 'vaulted' style of that time — columns branching into arches, connected each to each in support of the floor above.

''Course you never been down here, have you?' said my guide. ''Course you never. But this is how they used to build them — strong and made to last. Something to see, ain't it?'

It was indeed — yet he would not linger: In another moment or two he was leading me up

173

another set of stairs and we were on the main floor, where a wide staircase led us up to the floors above. I thought he might leave there — but no. We went up a section of the stairway to the first floor, then down a long hall to a great door. Behind it, I heard voices raised loud in argument.

'This is where they meet,' said he to me, 'and when they meet, they argue — and your Bishop Talley, he's the loudest arguer of them all. The youngest, too.'

'What do they argue about?'

He threw his hands into the air in a despairing gesture. 'Ah, who could say? Church matters, I suppose — naught that concerns ordinary folk such as you and me, young sir. You should've heard them last night! Does them good to take a break now and again.' So saying, he raised a fist and battered the door with it.

All shouting did then instantly cease.

'They think we're spyin' upon them. Ain't that silly?'

Just then, the door opened slowly and cautiously, exposing half of a face and a single eye.

'Yes?' said the speaking part of the face. 'What will you?'

'This young man beside me wishes an immediate and private audience with Bishop Talley.'

'Bishop Talley is not available. He is in conference.'

'That's as may be, but this young man represents the law. He is here on a mission from the Bow Street Court. Sir John Fielding sent him.'

'I shall pass the message on to the — '

'Here I am!' There could be no doubt who spoke in that roaring tone. 'Twas that 'loudest arguer of them all,' Bishop Talley. And he proved it by pushing aside that nameless face and throwing open the door. Indeed, here he was: John Talley, formerly vicar of St. Swithen's Church and now Bishop of the See of Liverpool. He was not tall, nor was he, at approximately eight inches above five feet, terribly short. Yet he was portly and substantial, which gives any man of such dimension a sense of solidity. Nevertheless, he appeared young as few Londoners of his age ever do. He had even managed to retain much of the youthful blond in his hair, which gave him an almost boyish look. He was over thirty — but not by much.

'What will you, lad?'

'A word with you,' said I, refusing to be intimidated, 'alone.'

'I have no secrets from my fellow bishops.'

'I believe you would wish to hold this conversation apart from them.'

He frowned in such a way as to make it plain he had no firm notion of just what it was that I was talking about. He seemed not near so sure of himself as he was when he first presented himself. 'All right,' said he in a much quieter voice. 'I suggest we go to my rooms above.' And we set off together.

The corporal of the guard bade me farewell and returned in the direction we had come. I was led up the wide staircase by the Bishop, who spoke not a word.

Then, at last in the modest room which was his, he wasted no time with me. He swung the door shut behind him, turned to me, and said, 'Well, what is it? I feel I've already given you more time than you deserve.'

I ignored the intended slight and proceeded aggressively: 'You arrived six nights past at about midnight, did you not?'

Taken slightly aback, he gave a lengthier and more considered response than ever I expected: 'Yes,' said he, 'there were but three of us — I, my auxiliary, and my secretary. The fog was such that we could not see the bridge from where we were. I had been informed that there was a ford at some point near Lambeth Palace, but the driver of our coach refused utterly to make any attempt at fording — and with good reason, as it seems now. In any case, having no other choice, we hailed a passing waterman, and 'twas he who took us cross the river — but in three separate trips. It must have been one o'clock, at least, before we were settled in our separate rooms.'

'And since then? You've been working here, have you?'

'Yes I have — in preparation for the next session of the House of Lords — and that's all I can say about that. My presence here is rather a secret — and I would ask you to keep it so.'

'You've seen none of your family here in London since your arrival?'

'What family have I here? A rapscallion father? A stepmother who presses for her son's advantage at every opportunity? A half brother who spends his time plotting against me? No, I've met with none of my family. The only one I am likely even to see is my father, whom I shall view across the divide in the House of Lords.'

'Well, Your Grace, I have news for you of a sort which I am loath to deliver.' I paused, but he said nothing. He seemed merely puzzled at what I might have to impart.

'You'll not see your father there in the House of Lords,' I continued, 'for he died in a leap from Westminster Bridge six nights past.'

'Westminster Bridge? Six nights? But then . . . ?' He seemed almost dazed by what I had told him.

'What this means is that your father died not much more than a mile away — an oddity, certainly, but there are others.'

'Such as?'

'The same waterman who ferried you cross the river continued on afterward and was called upon to pull Lord Lammermoor's body from the Thames. And the — '

'No,' said he, 'that's quite enough. I fear I'm not taking this in as well as I should. This is a good deal more than I supposed. It's — well, it's very difficult.'

'I'm sure that it is, Your Grace, but I must ask you to come to visit Sir John Fielding, magistrate of the Bow Street Court at any time between two and six this afternoon. He will have some questions for you.'

'I see. Is this a . . . criminal investigation?'

'It is, yes. The coroner's inquest found death by misadventure, but for his own reasons Sir John has decided to conduct his own investigation. I shall probably be present.'

With that, I bowed sharply and made for the door.

'I do thank you. Please forgive me for my manner earlier. I was, I fear, rather brusque in my manner.'

'Nothing to forgive,' said I. 'But you do realize, do you not, that but for a few formalities you are to be the next Lord Lammermoor!'

'Well do I realize it,' said he. 'It is that which has me so worried and confused.'

On my way out the gate I ducked in at the guard shelter to thank the corporal of the guard for his help and to confirm the details of Bishop Talley's arrival.

'Get what you wanted from him?' he asked.

'That remains to be seen,' said I.

★ ★ ★

Back at Bow Street, I had time aplenty to tend to my duties as court clerk; indeed, having given Sir John what I learned interviewing those in the strong room, I was able to describe to him at length what I had learned during my visit to Lambeth Palace.

Sir John was plainly pleased at my report and did not hesitate to say so. 'But,' said he, 'what did *you* think of him? What was your estimate of the man?'

'Well, he's a bit taken with himself, as I suppose all Bishops must be. But once his guard was down, he seemed quite sincere.' I hesitated, but then did I plunge on. 'It

179

seemed almost too good to be true, did it not, sir?'

'What is it you mean, Jeremy?'

'Why, this coincidence of time and place — him being just a mile away when his father dove into the river. The fact that Mr. Porter, the waterman, went on from Lambeth to pull Lord Lammermoor's body from the water. All of that.'

'I see what you mean, yet all I can say is that, remarkably enough, things sometimes turn out neatly in just such a way.'

'What then do you do?'

'At such times I believe a bit more fervently in God.'

★ ★ ★

The Bishop arrived shortly after two. It was evident, at least to me, that he had come with the intention of asking as many questions as he answered. Sir John made it plain that this was not to be by meeting him with a barrage of interrogatives the moment he set foot in the magistrate's chambers.

Sir John: What was the time of your arrival at Lambeth?

Talley: Approximately midnight. It took an hour for the waterman to get us across the river and for the soldiers to get us up the stairs with our baggage. But let me ask you, sir, if I may —

Sir John: (interrupting) Why so late? You could not have planned such an arrival time.

Talley: Why no, of course not. The driver, a man local to Liverpool, is an employee of the diocese and knows nothing of London. He became helplessly lost in the outskirts of the city — the narrow streets of Clerkenwell, and so on. You understand, of course. But if I may ask, sir, how did you learn not only that I had come to London, but also *when* I had come?

Sir John: (making a dismissive motion) I ask the questions hereabouts. Let that be understood between us. Now, why did you come to London? Why are you here?

Talley: Why, sir, because I am a bishop.

Sir John: Because you are a bishop? That explains nothing. Why have you come at this particular time?

Talley: Because Parliament goes into

session next week. I am come to claim my rightful place in the House of Lords on the Bench of the Bishops.

Sir John: Bit early, aren't you? After all, it's the better part of two weeks between your arrival and the opening session.

Talley: Well, if you must know, we're planning our strategy. We do not wish to be caught unprepared.

Sir John: Strategy? Caught unprepared? You sound to me — if you will pardon my saying so — as if you're getting ready for war. Are you?

Talley: In a sense, I suppose we are. I realize that's not much of an answer, but I fear you must be content with it.

Sir John: What is it you say? May I remind you that though you may be a Bishop and are soon to be made an earl, you are nevertheless a subject of the Crown. And in such matters as criminal investigations, *I represent the Crown.*

He kept at the Bishop in just such a way until he had broken down his defenses and his resolve to say nothing. Sir John had an answer for every one of the Bishop's objections; and, without once resorting to the sort of loud badgering that is so commonly heard in the courts today, managed to drag from him the nature of the preparations which were then being made for the opening session of the House of Lords.

Word had come to the Archbishop of Canterbury that a group of Whig lords had banded together and planned to introduce revisions to the Act of Tolerance wherein the advantages enjoyed by the Church of England in so many areas would be removed altogether or reduced in number. Roman Catholic clergy would thus be able to minister to the spiritual needs of their flocks, marrying and burying, hearing confession, though they might not appear in clerical garb on the streets of the town, nor could they seek to add to their number by conversion. And, oh yes, the voting privileges enjoyed by the Bench of Bishops in the House of Lords would also be removed.

'Well, you see, of course,' said Bishop Talley, 'that this could never be. Before you knew it, it would lead to equality. Or considering how those Irish multiply, they would doubtless be in the majority before we knew. We would then be halfway down the road to Rome.'

'You, I'm sure, would know a good deal more about such things than I,' said the magistrate.

'Oh, indeed I know a great deal about them,' said the Bishop, nodding wisely. 'When you see the Irish pour into Liverpool, you realize the extent of the problem. I've talked to the clergy — *our* clergy — all through the diocese, telling all who would listen about the problem. It was this, I'm sure, that won me my bishopric. I know it was. The Archbishop told me so himself. After all, a man so young as myself . . . '

Bishop Talley then went into the plans laid by this secret committee of bishops to counter the drastic revisions to be proposed by the Whigs. To sum them up, friendly Tories had offered to put forward a bill of their own, which in fact would be written for them by the Bishops. In its own way, this bill would be far more extreme than that sponsored by the Whigs — reaching back to Elizabethan practices of priest hunting, public executions of the more spectacular sort, et cetera. There was now, however, some difficulty in actually writing the bill: as to how far they should go; disagreements on just how strongly the case against the Roman Catholics should be put. After all, the idea was just to get the Whigs to negotiate, for in that lay the genius of the clergy. The bishops might well come up with a compromise which would satisfy both parties — in other words, one quite like the situation that existed at that moment. And that, of course, would have been quite acceptable.

By the time he had revealed all this, the Bishop's manner began to change. It was as if, having survived an hour or more of Sir John's interrogation, he had got it into his head that this would be all that would be required of him. He was like a man set free, until:

'I shall probably need to talk to you again,' said Sir John. 'Would this time tomorrow fit your schedule?'

'Uh, well enough, I suppose.'

'Good. And if you would not mind, bring along the other two who are in your party. The two who traveled with you from Liverpool.'

'Will that be necessary?'

'I think so.'

At that, Bishop Talley rose and made a little speech about how he did indeed look forward to seeing him again on the morrow, bade him good day, and turned to leave.

'Your Grace, I did have one more question to ask, now that I think of it.'

'And what is that?'

'Your father — what was your situation with him? Were you on friendly terms with him?'

'Hardly that. I believe that I referred to him as a 'rapscallion' to your clerk here. He was all of that, but as they say, *De mortuis nibil nisi bonum*. He was a conscientious legislator and a — '

'You used some Latin there,' said Sir John, 'something about the dead and the good.'

'What? Oh yes. 'Of the dead, speak only well.''

'I had a little Latin and retained less — just enough to get me past the bar. What about your stepmother and half brother?'

'How was that?' He seemed no little confused. 'What about them?'

'How do you get on with them?'

'Well enough — when I see them. Yet I confess I have not laid eyes upon either one for years.'

'You did not authorize your half brother to speak for you at the coroner's inquest into your father's death?'

'Why, no.'

'You've had no contact with them since you came here to London?'

'No — but then again, that's not strictly true. A day or two after my arrival I sent my secretary with my card and a note upon it to the effect that I was staying at the Lambeth Palace for the coming term of Parliament. Yet my secretary returned with news that both were out of town. He heard naught from their butler, however, of my father's death.'

At that, Sir John burst out laughing, thus confusing the Bishop even further. 'Forgive me,' said the magistrate. 'I laugh merely at the confusion of intentions. I've no doubt that your stepmother and half brother were on their way to Liverpool when your secretary called upon them in your stead.'

'Do you think so?'

'Have I not just said it?' Sir John's patience with the man seemed to be growing thin.

Nevertheless, Bishop Talley had not done with him. 'I hesitate to mention it,' said he, 'but as we talked just now I was reminded of a matter which perhaps needs a bit of explaining.'

'Oh? And what is that?'

'You would eventually hear, so I might as well tell you now.'

'Might as well tell me what?'

'Well, you see, when we arrived cross the river from the palace and had secured the aid of the waterman, I rode cross with him on his first trip. Then did I remain to instruct the soldiers on moving the baggage up to our apartment of rooms. Once I had instructed them I felt I could leave them to follow my orders, and so I went for a walk.'

'A walk?'

'That's correct. I was so battered and bent by the long ride cross England that I felt that I must get out and stretch my legs a bit. You understand.'

'I believe I do. You took a walk, did you?'

'Yes, yes I did.'

'And how long were you gone?'

'Quite some time, actually. It must have been near an hour. When I returned, the soldiers informed me that all were moved in, safe and sound. One of their number accompanied me and showed me to my quarters.'

'In which direction did you go? Upstream or down?'

'Truth to tell, I know not. I did, however walk within sight of that bridge — the one we searched for that same night. It was hidden in the fog.'

'Ah yes, the fog,' said Sir John. Then did he lean forward in a manner most keen, as if peering deep inside the man. 'Did you go to the bridge and actually walk upon it?'

'No, I did not. I should say that the closest

I came to it was fifty yards or so. I turned round and returned to Lambeth.'

Thus did the magistrate let forth a great sigh. 'Better I should hear this from you first, Bishop.' He gave him a sharp nod. 'You may go now,' said he.

★ ★ ★

Clarissa was, at the moment of my return, just disposing of the scattered papers upon the kitchen table. Make no mistake: These were her papers, right enough, all of them well filled with sentences and paragraphs in her neat, strong hand. By the time she had put them all together they did indeed make quite a pile. I'd no idea what the size of a book should be, yet this was, by any measure, a considerable and growing pile — something near half an inch, or so it seemed to me.

My presence in the room seemed to embarrass her. She looked up at me and forced a smile. I thought I ought to say something.

'Don't stop on my account,' I told her. 'I'm going right up to read a bit of law.'

'Do as you like,' said she, 'but I must begin dinner.'

Something more seemed to be called for. 'Been hard at work, I see.'

'Yes, I have.' That was said almost defiantly. 'Well then, off I go.'

And so saying, I made for the stairway, thinking dark thoughts of the fickleness of women and the changeableness of fortune. We seemed to be getting on so well till she began writing away with such a sense of dedication. All this since Mr. Joseph Deekin tried his treatment upon her. Should I tell her the source of this great infusion of literary energy? How would she take it?

But then, quite of a sudden and most unexpectedly, Clarissa left the table and ran to me. She called my name as she came and threw her arms round me when she arrived.

'Ah, Jeremy, try to understand me. It is just that I feel that now that I have the energy and the time alone, I must give myself to this work that I've talked of so often. If I don't do it now, then I fear I never shall.'

'You mean it's now or never?'

'Yes, I suppose I do. It's true that I'm working hard, terribly hard, but at the same time I'm having such a grand time of it, Jeremy. I love my characters. I want only the best for them. But this doesn't mean that I love you any less. I just have to do this. You do understand, don't you?'

Looking into her eyes, which were at that moment rimmed with tears, I believe I understood more than she knew. 'Of course I do,' said I and gave her a kiss upon the cheek. 'I'm *for* you, Clarissa, really I am.'

'I know you are,' said she, 'else I would not have given a thought to marrying you.'

Then did she turn and run back to the table, thus giving me ample opportunity to start up the stairs. As I climbed them, it came to me that I might never tell her of the part Joseph Deekin played in her literary beginning. It might be best so.

★ ★ ★

'Twas after our dinner of a savory stew, and indeed well past that, for I was then bound and promised to do the washing up afterward. That I did, till the pots, pans, and plates did shine. At last, having done all, I scaled the steps to the floor above and went straight to that small room to which he repairs each night after dinner, the small room which Sir John calls his study.

I tapped upon the door and was invited in. Sir John urged me to seat myself, which I did, and I wasted no time pointing out to him that we had not yet discussed the visit of Bishop Talley this afternoon.

'Do you think it worth discussing?' Sir John asked.

'You mean because you have not yet done with him?' I suggested. 'He returns tomorrow, after all.'

'No, that is not my meaning. Though I shall squeeze him a bit more — I do so enjoy putting the screws on these pompous fellows — my own instinctive feeling is that he does not have it in him to commit patricide, which is a very grave crime, after all. He does not hold the earlship to be of such value as to justify the risk. No, he would much rather spend time and energy scheming against the Church of Rome. What is most interesting about him is that he should appear in London, unbidden by us, at the moment that he did.'

'You mean at almost the exact moment of his father's death?'

'Precisely — and with the addition of that last detail in his story . . . '

'And now you refer to the walk taken by him along the Thames whilst his fellow churchmen struggled with the baggage?'

'Of course. It is almost as if he — or fate — were daring us to consider him a proper suspect, whereas, having met the man, all that we perceive about him urges us that he could not be the murderer of his father.'

'To simplify what you're saying then, while the Bishop may just barely have had the opportunity, he seems to have lacked the motive.'

'Hmmm,' said Sir John, 'that may be simplifying it more than I would wish to do, but I suppose you have the basic idea there.'

We sat in silence. Sir John gave no sign that he wished me to leave, nor indeed did I make a move to go. The question, as we both saw it, was what to do next. Speaking for myself, I must say that the coincidence which brought the Bishop to Lambeth in the hour of his father's death seemed such a gift that I was for a while convinced that it must be the key to everything. At that moment, however, it seemed the key to nothing at all.

'Perhaps now . . . ' I began, then did I find myself unwilling to continue.

'Perhaps now . . . what?' said Sir John.

'Oh, nothing. It's so obvious.'

'Though likely not so obvious as you suppose. What is it?'

'Well, shouldn't Lady Lammermoor be interrogated? Not to mention her son. She did, after all, threaten Annie, did she not? You thought the matter serious enough that you assigned Constable Patley to go to and from the theater with her. That he has done for nearly a week — without event of any sort. Might it not be better, now that Lady Lammermoor has presumably returned from

Liverpool, to give the widow a proper interrogation — and inform her that we know of her threat to Annie. Should anything happen to Annie, we shall hold Lady Lammermoor and none else responsible.'

Sir John laughed abruptly. 'You seem to feel that the only effective threat against a threat is another threat.'

'Perhaps I do.'

'Well, in this case, you may be right.' Yet still he considered the matter and considered it closely. 'Their town residence is in Bloomsbury Square, is it not?'

'That's correct, sir.'

'How convenient,' said he. 'We may stop off for a visit to the Lord Chief Justice beforehand. It is time, Jeremy, that we settled with him the rules of engagement.'

7

In which we pay
visits to residents
of Bloomsbury Square

As a consequence of his early days as a midshipman, Sir John Fielding often resorted to naval or military terminology in describing a course of action. Thus it was that I was not so much surprised that he had used such a phrase as I was at the strength of it. The 'rules of engagement' were those orders passed to the captain of a ship or the colonel of a regiment which, in very precise terms, set forth the circumstances under which a potential enemy could be met with hostile action. For example, in an incursion or an invasion, or, on neutral seas or territory, should warnings be issued before presenting fire? Should parley be sought? Should fire be held till fired upon? If so, how long? Et cetera. These were important matters in the complex game of modern warfare.

And when, by analogy, the phrase was

applied to such matters as, say, interrogation, you can well suppose its uses. Sir John wished to know from the Lord Chief Justice himself (since he had ordered the investigation) just how far he might go in attempting to intimidate, or even plainly threatening the subject of an inquiry. With titled members of the nobility, it could be a matter of some delicacy. If there were to be outright prohibitions, or areas in which he would be urged to tread lightly, then the magistrate wished to know of them in advance.

★ ★ ★

We two were quite early enough to catch Lord Mansfield before his departure for Old Bailey. That much was evident from the presence of his coach-and-four waiting at the door. We mounted the few steps till Sir John, assured he was properly placed, took his walking stick and beat briskly upon the oaken portal.

Lord Mansfield's butler answered the summons and seemed specially eager to bring us inside. Alone, I never was given such treatment, yet the mere presence of Sir John was sufficient to send the fellow into a sudden dither.

'Right this way,' said he, 'Lord Mansfield

has been expecting you, more or less, these past few days. I thought to install you in his study whilst he finishes readying himself for the day.'

He threw open the third door in the long hall and bowed us inside. 'Sit anywhere you like. I'll tell him you're here.'

It was near as generous an offer as it sounded, for there were but two or three chairs in the room, apart from that which stood at the desk; we took the two opposite it.

The door remained open. We talked quietly as we waited.

'This bodes ill,' said Sir John.

'Oh?' said I. 'How so?'

'Why, if I have been eagerly awaited these past few days, then it is because the Lord Chief Justice expects me to give him the solution to this puzzle with which he presented us. We must begin by disappointing him — never a good way to start.'

'I suppose not,' said I. 'But if we — '

He held up a hand and silenced me. His sharper ears had picked up the sound of footsteps on the stairs which I heard moments later. I knew that rapid step quite well. It was William Murray, Earl of Mansfield, Lord Chief Justice of the King's Bench.

Lord Mansfield burst into the room,

smiling and all but rubbing his hands in anticipation.

'Ah, Sir John,' said he. 'I'm delighted to see you. I knew you wouldn't let me down.'

'Perhaps you anticipate too much from my appearance here this morning. I'm here, truth be told, to seek your help in this Lord Lammermoor matter.'

'*My* help? I'll do what I can, of course, but it's *your* skill as an investigator — *your* intellect — that I hoped to engage in this enterprise. I know my own limitations, after all.'

'Be assured you have my skill and my intellect completely engaged in this problem. Nevertheless, there are parts you know far better than I. And as I stand before one such, trembling with ignorance, I asked myself who might best give me advice as to how to proceed. Quite naturally I thought of you.'

The Lord Chief Justice had upon his face an expression which was a bit difficult to describe. It was, sure enough, a smile, yet it was, if such can be pictured, a smile of a remarkable sort; the corners of his mouth drooped down in disbelief; the expression conveyed in his eyes was one of doubt. There was naught of pleasure in that smile.

'I take it,' said Lord Mansfield, 'that this space through which you seek my guidance is not one that has much to do with the colonies in North America?'

'You refer now to your theory that the Adams brothers are at bottom to blame for Lord Lammermoor's death?' Sir John shook his head regretfully. 'No,' said he, 'I fear not. Nothing that we have found thus far points in that direction.'

'What have you found thus far?'

'Quite a lot, actually. First of all, we found that you were correct in saying that no matter what is said to the contrary, and no matter who says it, Lord Lammermoor did not die a suicide.'

'Well, thank God that's been laid to rest! How did he die then?'

'According to the coroner's inquest, your friend died a death by misadventure.'

'*Misadventure?*' He frowned, unable quite to grasp the reasoning behind such a verdict. 'How did they come to that conclusion?'

'They came to it because Lord Lammermoor did not have rocks or cobblestones in his pocket.'

'*What!*'

'I know, I know. That was Mr. Trezavant's notion. It was a directed verdict.'

'Why, that's near as bad as suicide — death by stupidity. After all, taking a precarious perch upon the bridge while knowing you can't swim. That's stupid, isn't it? What is your view of the cause of death?'

'I have interviewed all those that Mr. Trezavant did and at much greater length — as well as another one or two — and from what I have learned so far, I have concluded that Lord Lammermoor was murdered. But it was done in a manner so ingenious that it would not appear as murder to anyone.'

The Lord Chief Justice mused for a moment, then asked: 'What is this 'manner so ingenious'?'

'I have not yet got the straight of it myself.'

'Hmmm. Well,' said he. 'Perhaps if we got together in a few days you will have it.'

'Perhaps.' He did not sound optimistic.

'Anything else?'

'Oh, a number of things. I can mention a few, though I must warn you that I'll not go into detail on any of them. First of all, I have discovered that Lord Lammermoor was *not* alone there on Westminster Bridge. He was with a young lady, who was his mistress. Secondly, unknown to any of his family, Bishop Talley — the heir to the Lammermoor title and lands — was in London at the time of his father's death. And thirdly, because his family did not know that he was in London, his stepmother and half brother journeyed to

Liverpool to inform him that Lord Lammermoor had died.'

'All that?' crowed Lord Mansfield. 'Then I can tell that you're well on the way to a solution.'

'I wish I were as confident as you. But by the bye, I've not yet fixed that last bit about Lady Lammermoor and her son in Liverpool. And that is why I have come here to you.'

'That is why . . . *what?* I don't quite understand.'

'I need advice from you, Lord Mansfield, on dealing with Lady L. I had always heard that she was a difficult woman, and I have gotten close enough to her in the course of this investigation to know that this is so. From what I know about her, and have observed, I would say that she certainly has it within her power to make a shambles of this investigation.'

'Oh, come now, Sir John,' said the Lord Chief Justice, 'you exaggerate, I'm sure. What have you seen that would lead you to such an extreme conclusion?'

'Yes, well, she has threatened one of my witnesses, perhaps the most trustworthy of them all.'

'Threatened? In what way?'

'Well, in a nonspecific way, if you must. Still, I take what Lady Lammermoor said

201

with sufficient seriousness that I have assigned a man to accompany her husband's mistress whenever she ventures out of doors.'

'Come now, don't you think you're overemphasizing her — threat to this undertaking?'

'No, Lord Mansfield, I do not.' He was as firm in that as I have ever seen him.

'She is, I quite admit, a willful woman, but — '

'A willful woman?' Sir John groaned at that. 'That's not the half of it from what I hear. Obstreperous would be more truly descriptive.'

'Willful? Obstreperous? What does it matter, after all? Do you truly believe that it is essential to your investigation that she give testimony?'

'Yes.'

'But she's from a good west country family and not the sort to kill her husband.'

'That may be,' said the magistrate, 'but we shall never know unless we interview her. Besides, it may well be that she knows something about another that would help us on our way — perhaps something she does not even know she knows.'

The air between them seemed to have become almost heated with emotion. It seemed unlikely to me that the two would ever come to any sort of agreement on the matter, so deeply entrenched were they in their separate positions. Briefly, silence fell between them, a silence in the nature of a truce, wherein they might catch their breath and think of new arguments. I had no doubt that it would be Sir John who would break the truce — and it was.

'Lord Mansfield,' said he, 'when a witness or potential witness refuses to answer my questions, I have it in my power as magistrate to make him so uncomfortable that he will gladly give forth in interrogation. A short sentence of up to three months in Newgate for impeding an investigation always seems to have the effect I wish. Even the threat of it seems to work — for such is Newgate's reputation. Could I make that threat to Lady Lammermoor? Not with any hope that it would bend her vaunted will to my own, for she would appeal to you or any other high-court judge, and would not be forced even to glimpse the interior of that awful place. Am I right in that, Lord Mansfield?'

He hesitated, cleared his throat, and in a low, muttering voice, he said, 'More or less, I suppose.'

'I interrogated Bishop Talley, who is heir to your great friend's title and lands,' continued Sir John, 'and when he declined to answer one of my questions, what did I do? I browbeat him, blustered at him loudly and arrogantly. Yes, I was reduced to that! Of course the poor fellow had not a chance against me once I began roaring, though mind you, we parted on good terms. But now, tell me, m'Lord, do you believe that I should employ the same devices with Lady Lammermoor?'

'No, I do not,' said he in a most forthright manner.

'Well, that would be all that would be left me in dealing with her should *she* refuse to answer any of my questions.'

'Sir John, let me propose something, if I may.'

'Propose whatever you wish, by all means.'

'Just this,' said the Lord Chief Justice. 'I would have you go cross the square, knock upon the door of Number Nine and ask for Lady Lammermoor. Question her. Ask her whatever you like. At her first refusal to answer any that you put to her, tell her that she has the choice of answering your questions today or mine tomorrow. If she is steadfast in her refusal, thank her politely and leave. I shall be responsible for all that happens after that. Do you agree?'

'I fear that I am forced to do so — but never mind that. Yes, I agree.'

He accompanied us outside as far as the coach. And, whilst the footman held the door for him, he offered a few last words as a sop to Sir John.

'I hope,' said Lord Mansfield, 'that you are happy with this arrangement between us, as it stands now.'

'Happy? Well, that might be overstating it somewhat. Let us say now that for the time being I am satisfied.'

At that Lord Mansfield let out an abrupt cackle, and said, 'Then am I also satisfied.' He gave a wave and heaved himself up into the coach.

We stood waiting on the walkway until they had pulled away, when, at a nod from Sir John, we started cross the street and then cross the square. I knew not what awaited us, nor did I suppose that Sir John was any better armed with foreknowledge of the events ahead than I. His face was very near expressionless. Quite frankly, the Lord Chief Justice had frightened me somewhat, for what he seemed to be advocating to Sir John was one law for the common folk (was this what was meant by common law?) and another, more permissive code for the nobility. This I knew to be in direct contradiction to all that

Sir John had taught me. I said not a word of that to him, however, nor would I until this whole affair be ended.

We stood at Number 9 before a door that seemed even larger, thicker, and heavier than that of Lord Mansfield's across the way. The magistrate made no move to knock upon it. Instead, he said, 'Go ahead, Jeremy, you have at it, will you? And make a proper racket of it, eh?'

That I did, grasping the hand-shaped knocker and banging it down upon the plate a half dozen times, at least.

'Why, Jeremy, I'd no idea!' exclaimed Sir John. 'There lurks within you the soul of a nasty little noise-making ragamuffin. Give them another of the same.'

Again I did as directed, yet only managed two or three slams at the plate before the door, all of a sudden, did swing open, and I fell into the arms of the butler. But for supporting me in my effort to regain my balance, he was utterly indifferent to me. 'Twas Sir John who received his attention.

'What do you wish, sir?' he asked.

'I wish to speak with Lady Lammermoor.'

I was now standing squarely upon my two feet; once out of the butler's arms, I was able to get a much clearer view of him. He was not tall — no more than I — and could not have been more than forty years of age. And he looked very determined.

'Quite impossible, I fear. Who are you, if I may ask?'

'I am Sir John Fielding, magistrate of the City of London and the City of Westminster. No door in those environs can be closed to me!'

'Nevertheless, sir, it is quite impossible for you to see her, for she has not yet risen. Now, if you might care to leave your card, I shall call it to her attention and you could return at another hour — or even another day.'

So saying, he gestured toward a silver bowl placed upon a table near the door; it was filled to overflowing with cards of callers come to express their sympathy for Lady Lammermoor's loss.

'I have no card,' said Sir John. 'I need none. I am known to one and all in the precincts of this city.'

'Nevertheless, sir, you are not known to me. So if you would repeat your name and your office, I shall pass them on to Lady Lammermoor at my earliest opportunity. She will be happy to receive your condolences, I'm sure.'

'I'm not here to offer them.' It was a bit difficult to understand him, so tightly was his jaw clenched. I had not often seen him so angry. I was fearful that in the next moment or two he might set out to thrash the fellow with his walking stick. I tugged at his sleeve and began to mutter in his ear something about leaving while we could and coming back later. But he paid no attention to me — even to me.

'I'm here,' he continued at a shout, 'to pursue an investigation of *murder!*'

'Ah, well, you've come to the wrong place then. There's been no murder — '

The butler did not finish that sentence. The reason was a third voice at a near distance coming from behind the butler — a voice that seemed to me oddly familiar.

'No, Henry, no, no, no! All that this gentleman says is true, I'm sure. And if he says he is come to pursue an investigation of murder, then indeed that must also be true.'

The door swung open wider, revealing Archibald Talley, the half brother of the heir apparent and an acquaintance of mine from years past when I frequented the courts of Old Bailey.

'Oh, Mr. Talley, is it?'

'Why, yes, sir, it is. And you have just proven what I once heard of you, Sir John.'

'And what is that, Mr. Talley?'

'That you have the power to recognize any and all by the sound of their voice alone.'

Sir John chuckled at that. 'Well, perhaps not any and all . . . '

(In faithfully reproducing this conversation between Sir John and Archibald Talley, I touch upon a fault of Sir John's, perhaps his only one: He was given somewhat to vanity. Flattery, when used cleverly upon him, could be quite effective.)

'Henry, I have just come from my mother, and she is now awake. I shall tell her that Sir John has come, and she should be ready to receive him shortly. Take these two gentlemen to the library, if you will. They should be more comfortable waiting there.'

Yet he did not immediately depart. He stepped aside to allow Sir John and me passage. To Sir John he murmured his apologies for the misunderstanding. And to me: 'Jeremy, is it not? So good to see you again. How I do miss our days at the Old Bailey!' He grasped my hand as I passed by and gave it a wiggle. Then was he away and up the stairs.

The library was as grand as any I had seen in a private dwelling. There were two chairs of a kind and a small serving table between, all of which were tucked off in a corner. Henry, the butler, led us to them and promised us coffee before he left. He also surprised me by offering Sir John an apology.

'I do hope you will forgive me for my confusion at the door,' said he. 'It's just, sir, that so many have come by to offer sympathy in one way or another during the past few days that I quite naturally put you among them.'

'Oh, think nothing of it,' said Sir John in a great show of magnanimity. 'I've forgotten it already.'

Knowing Sir John, I doubted that greatly. And my doubts were confirmed when, alone at last, he leaned across the serving table and whispered to me: 'What a terrible fellow. If I were master of this house, I would discharge him most immediate!'

Quite unable to help myself, I burst out laughing at that.

'Oh? Think it's funny, do you? Why, I'll have you know I came ever so close to giving that fellow a sound thrashing right there as he stood in the doorway.'

Still laughing, I gasped out, 'I know,' and then managed to calm myself.

'But I daresay that young fellow, Archibald, handled things rather well, did he not?' said Sir John.

'Very well indeed,' said I.

'I met him some years past. You brought him to me, as I recall, though I also recall that he did not make near as good an impression upon me then as he did just now.'

'True enough. You asked me never to bring him to Bow Street again.'

'I did, did I?' He cackled at that. 'Well, he certainly seems to have improved himself between that meeting and this one.'

'It would seem so,' I agreed.

'Or perhaps I was a bit hasty in my judgement of him. That does happen from time to time, you know?'

Just then the door opened quietly and Archibald Talley entered the room. He closed it just as quietly and hastened to us.

'Sir John,' said he, 'I looked in on my mother. I told her of your arrival. She's quite pleased you've come, and will be down shortly to greet you herself. In the meantime, sir, I'll be happy to answer any questions you might have.'

'Good,' said the magistrate. 'I do have a few questions specifically for you. Why don't you pull up a chair, and we'll get them out of the way before she comes.'

'I'm all for that — all except the part about pulling up a chair. We've just returned from Liverpool, mother and I, and I fear that my backside is so sore that, well, I'd really rather stand.'

Sir John chuckled at that. 'Yes, certainly. But you've answered one of my questions already. I was going to ask if you accompanied your mother to Liverpool. You've made it plain you did.'

'Indeed. I left with her early in the morning following — oh, a sort of demonstration of something most popular in Austria called 'animal magnetism.' My mother is quite interested in it.'

'Say not another word,' said Sir John. 'We attended the demonstration, as it happens, and in point of fact, our party sat direct behind you and your mother. Remarkable, eh?'

'Oh, quite.'

'And we have information that your brother — half brother, I suppose — was not there in Liverpool to greet you when you arrived. That must have been terribly disappointing.'

'Well, it was, of course, most specially for my mother. She was determined that he get the news from us — the family, you see.'

'He has only lately received the news, you know. He's staying at the Lambeth Palace, you know.'

'Yes, we're going to see him this afternoon so that we may offer our tardy congratulations.'

'Dr. Goldsworthy was also in Liverpool, was he not? Did you see him while you were there?'

'No, I didn't. You'd have to ask my mother about that, though. She may have seen him while we were there.'

'When did you return?'

'Oh, just last night. She wanted — I daresay, *needed* — to rest up a couple of days before undertaking our return.'

There was a pause at this point as the butler entered, bearing a coffee service, complete with a steaming pot of coffee. As he served it up, I noted that there were four cups for the three of us. The additional cup I took to be for Lady Lammermoor. Ladies of the upper set were just then tasting coffee for the first time in the privacy of their homes — though never, of course, in coffeehouses open to the public. We sipped and commented upon the coffee, nibbled and praised the biscuits, until finally, the butler gone, Sir John returned to his questions.

'Mr. Talley,' he began, 'I have a few questions which have to do, more or less, with the coroner's inquest. If you will indulge me, sir, I shall put them to you.'

'Of course.'

'You yourself made an appearance at that inquest, representing the family, did you not?'

Mr. Talley sighed. 'Yes, I did — and I fear I know already what you're about to ask.'

'I shall ask it nevertheless. You said in your

testimony to the coroner that you had communicated the fact of your father's death to your brother, John, heir apparent to title and property, and that he *asked you* to appear in his stead. Yet we know from what you told us earlier that you had had no such communication with your brother, and therefore that he could not have asked you to appear in his stead. How then do you account for this . . . discrepancy?'

'Not, I fear, in any way that does me credit. As I indicated to you when you mentioned the coroner's inquest, I was immediately fearful that you would fix upon this misstatement of mine. Having just reached the age of majority, I am quite sensitive as to the matter of age. And so you might say that I exaggerated my right to speak for brother John because I wanted to be taken more seriously. After all, I said nothing to the coroner that John would not have said.'

'What you say now about that is no doubt true, yet we cannot know that with absolute certainty because earlier you lied under oath. And if you lied then how much more likely are you to lie in a simple interrogation such as this.'

Through all this and what followed Archibald Talley said nothing. He wore a contrite expression and nodded from time to time. He was most attentive to Sir John as the magistrate continued:

'It is a very grave thing to lie under oath. Even if you do not pay a price in prison for your perjury, you pay an even greater one outside it. To be known as one who has perjured himself is never to be believed completely again. Now, I am quite willing to keep to myself your misstatement, as you call it, if you answer my remaining questions in all truth. Have I your word on that?'

'Oh, yes, sir. Believe me, you do.'

'Then I accept it, and I put this to you: Was it your idea to appear for your half brother and say that he had asked you to do so?'

'No, sir, it was not.'

'Whose idea was it then?'

His voice had, by that time, thickened, so that it became necessary for him to clear his throat deeply and at length if he were to answer that question at all. At last he managed to bring forth a response.

'It was my mother's.'

'Well, all right. Thank you, Mr. Talley. And did she give you her reasons?'

'She pointed out to me that I had, after all, identified the corpus of my father and spoken for the family in that matter. Why should this be so much different? And if I spoke for all, we would appear a properly close family.'

'And you are not?'

'Not really, no. We go our separate ways.'

'Just one more matter, sir, and that has to do with the copy of Mr. Donnelly's autopsy report on your father. You asked him for it, and he gave it to you. Again, whose idea was this?'

'And again, it was my mother's.'

Frown lines appeared above the black silk band which covered his blind eyes. 'But . . . why? That is to say . . . I don't — '

At precisely that moment (so well timed was it that I later suspected that she had been listening at the door) Lady Lammermoor made her entrance. The door flew open, and she blew across the library as she might with a strong west wind behind her. She talked loudly and with great animation. She was one of those people who generates a sense of excitement wherever she goes. She had certainly stirred things up a few nights past when she lashed the crowd at the Covent Garden Theatre for their misbehavior at Dr. Goldsworthy's demonstration of animal magnetism. Now, the fury she had shown them became excitement of a different sort as she bubbled and gushed at the magistrate.

'Ah, Sir John Fielding! It is you, is it not?' she cried out to us from the door. 'You are the one man in London I've wished most to meet.' Then, rushing forward: 'It's so sad that your visit is occasioned by my dear husband's sad death. Or perhaps not? My son informs me that you are conducting your own investigation. Could it be?'

'Yes, Lady Lammermoor, it could be and it is.'

'How thrilling! Do you truly believe that there is sufficient reason to suppose that it might have been murder? I thought the verdict handed down at the coroner's inquest might have ended matters.'

'I am in no position to answer your question at this point, Lady Lammermoor, for I am still gathering evidence and testimony.'

'Ah yes, of course.'

'And that is why I am here.'

'Oh?' She, who had been so loquacious up to then, did stop so abruptly that it was as if she had come up against some invisible wall. 'Whatever could you mean, Sir John?'

'Why, it is my intention to put a few questions to you. Your son has already obliged me by answering the few I've put to him. I have but one or two more to ask him.'

'I see,' said she. 'Well, of course we shall be more than happy to help in any way we can, but . . . '

'But what, Lady Lammermoor?'

'Oh, nothing. It's just that I've never been questioned before — not in the formal way which I'm sure you must mean.' She hesitated a moment, and then she brightened quite of a sudden. 'I have an idea,' said she.

'And what is that, pray tell?'

'Why do you not continue with Archibald, and I shall learn how it is done by listening to his answers. Would that satisfy you?'

'So long as he has no objections, certainly. Archibald?'

'Oh, I have no objections. None at all.' So he said, yet I could not but notice the look of woeful uneasiness that came over him as he glanced over at his mother.

'Excellent then. Let us proceed. Now, as I recall, we came to a halt as I was trying to form a question on the matter of the medical report prepared by Mr. Donnelly for the coroner. I was unable to suppose just *why* you should want such a document. Why did you want it?'

What happened just then was something altogether remarkable: Just as young Mr. Talley was opening his mouth to respond to Sir John's question, his mother spoke up, saying, 'Oh, I can answer that, Sir John.' But quite by accident, it was all so perfectly timed that there was an illusion, lasting only a long moment, that Lady Lammermoor's voice was issuing from the lips of her son. Taken aback suddenly as I was, I was unable to help myself: I laughed.

Archibald Talley gave me an odd look; his mother fixed me with one of scorn; and Sir John, lacking sight, could only frown.

'How then do you account for it? — since you have volunteered, m'lady.'

'Well, perhaps I shouldn't have intruded,' she began, 'still, my dear son might have been too embarrassed to make plain the true reason. First of all, 'twas my idea. Did he tell you that? Perhaps not. You see, Lord Lammermoor was given to little affairs of the heart with women — or perhaps better said, girls — of the lower classes. Oh, I know the tradition of saying only good things of the dead, but this is an investigation, is it not? I am therefore bound to tell all, am I not?'

She halted then, as if waiting for Sir John to give permission to continue. And yes, when it came, it was evident that he would play her game — but only up to a point.

'Yes, yes, of course, Lady Lammermoor,' said he impatiently. 'But please get on with your story.'

I was by then sufficiently well acquainted with his method of interrogation to know that whatever emotion he showed in such situations, he showed quite purposefully. He probably intended to demonstrate to her that he was in charge of the interrogation — and not she.

'Certainly, if you wish me to get on with my story — as you put it — then I shall.' She tossed her head and pouted, parading her hurt feelings. '*Well*, it had come to my attention that the latest of these affairs, one with an actress, was taking entirely too much of his time and attention. Usually, you see, these have been no more than impulsive pursuits — seductions, if you will. Yet this time it was altogether different. Where earlier episodes were brief, this one had gone on well over a month before I found out about it — more likely two months. He had even installed her in a location more convenient just across the Westminster Bridge from his office in Whitehall.'

(May I interject at this point that there was no longer any possibility that Lady Lammermoor could be speaking of anyone but Annie Oakum, 'our' Annie. This, I knew, would make for unforeseen complications, yet I knew not then how many, nor how great they would turn out to be. If Sir John was thinking also in just such a way, his face did naught to betray this.)

'After his death by a leap from that very bridge,' Lady Lammermoor continued, 'when there was such a to-do between the Irish doctor and the coroner over the postmortem report, I began to wonder if there weren't something else in it that the coroner wished to keep quiet. To be quite frank, I feared my husband might have contracted some disease of venery and passed it on to me. They can be quite virulent, you know.'

'Oh, indeed, I do know.'

She seemed to be searching his face for some reaction to what she had said. She found none. Was she annoyed at that? I think she was.

'As it happened, we were not too far off the mark. In fact, my husband did have a most terrible condition, though not one of the sort I had feared.'

'What was the condition, if I may ask?'

'Cancer,' said she. 'It seems he had within him a tumor in his intestine. He would have died, it seems, in a year's time.'

'How sad,' said Sir John, sounding as if he meant it.

'Yes, isn't it?' said Lady Lammermoor, sounding as if she did not.

Turning abruptly in the direction of Archibald Talley, the magistrate spoke sharply to her son. 'Now you, young sir, tell me where you were on the night when your father jumped from the bridge.'

'As it happens, I can answer that, too,' said his mother most helpfully.

'Then I must ask you to keep your answer to yourself.'

'What?' She was taken aback no little by Sir John's terse reply. 'But — '

'Mr. Talley, what have you to say for yourself?'

'Very little, I fear. I read a bit, had several hands of patience, and went to bed early.'

'You were at home then, I take it?'

'Oh yes.'

'When you say that you went to bed early, what does that mean, exactly? Nine o'clock? Ten o'clock? Midnight?'

'A little after midnight, I should say.'

'Some would not call that early, not at all.'

'I suppose I think of it as such because I was by then terribly bored.'

'Bored, were you? Are you often so?'

'Oftener than I would like.'

'Can anyone confirm that you were here as you describe?' He shrugged. 'The servants, of course.'

'I can,' said Lady Lammermoor. 'I was here with him all through the evening.'

'How convenient,' said Sir John, with just the hint of a sneer upon his face. 'You corroborate his story, and he, in turn, will corroborate yours.'

'Sir John Fielding, I resent your implication. I object most heartily to it.'

The mask was off. Of a sudden was all pretense of sweetness gone. Her face became twisted into such an expression of fury that she became as one of those harpies of ancient legend.

'You resent my implication, do you? What is it you take exception to, My Lady?' he demanded. 'I would say the same to any two who appeared before me at Bow Street Court and spoke each in support of the other.'

'That is precisely what I object to,' she screamed at him. 'You are treating us as common criminals, asking us to account to you for our time and to be prepared to prove it was spent as we say.'

'Certainly — as with any.'

'But do you not understand? We are not 'any.' We are of a noble family, one of the oldest in England. We came here with the Normans!'

'And mine were here to do you battle.'

'And lost! Don't you forget that.'

He sighed. 'Please, Lady Lammermoor, it seems to me that we're both being rather silly.'

She turned to her son. 'You see, Archibald? First we are accused of being common criminals. Now he implies that we conspired in your father's death.'

For his part, young Mr. Talley appeared to be quite miserable. He stared out the nearest window in the library and said nothing.

'But we know of a much more likely suspect. Don't we, Archibald?'

'Don't make me part of this, Mother.'

'Why, son, how you talk!' Then did she whirl round to Sir John. 'Not that I wish to do your work for you,' said she to him, 'but you and I both know that there is one other who has been described and all but named in testimony before the coroner. Well, *I* can name her: that actress I spoke of earlier — Annie Oakum. Oh, I know how you do your work, John Fielding. You would say that she lacked motive — and that I can supply. You see, when Lord Lammermoor's liaison with her was made known to me, I took him aside and told him what I had learned. I threatened to make the entire sordid affair known to all if he did not break with the girl most immediately. He bowed to me and promised to comply with my wishes.' Then, having said thus much, she bobbed her head with great finality, as if to declare that she had proven her point.

'I do not quite understand, Lady Lammermoor. Do you feel that what you have just told me significantly alters matters?'

'Why, of course it does! My husband must have revealed to her his promise to me and told her that she must look elsewhere for her patronage. This so infuriated the little trollop that she pushed him over the rail and into the river, knowing that he could not swim. In this way did she coldly murder him. I would bring that girl in and question her *now*.'

'Yet,' said Sir John, 'according to the testimony given at the inquest by Mr. Triplett, both he and the young lady were seeking to pull Lord Lammermoor in from danger.'

She moved her hand in a dismissive manner. 'Oh, pull or push, what does it matter? Both would appear much the same, would they not?'

'Why, I think it matters a great deal,' said he. 'After all, this was sworn testimony, and that carries considerable weight.'

At that, I glanced over at Archibald Talley and found him, in turn, looking sharply at Sir John. He had been taught a lesson, I believe.

'Besides,' the magistrate continued, 'with regard to your suggestion that I have Annie Oakum in for questioning, you may be interested to know I have already done that — twice. On the first occasion, she sought me out. It was the day after the tragic occurrence on Westminster Bridge. On the second interview, I brought her in for clarification on a few points, and it was on that occasion that I learned that you, Lady Lammermoor, had threatened her.'

'What of it?' said she rather nastily. 'I intended to do no more than frighten her.'

'I cannot say whether you did or did not frighten her, but I took your threat with sufficient seriousness that I have detailed one of my constables to accompany her until I see fit to remove the guard.'

'Well, you may remove him now,' said she. 'Nothing will come of it.'

'Nice of you to say so.' Again he sighed. 'Lady Lammermoor, I came to your residence in good faith, seeking to do no more than find the answers to some simple questions, yet you have been so uncooperative that I am now convinced that you will answer none of them, no matter how they be put to you. I had fears, based on your reputation, that this interview would end so, and for this reason I first visited Lord Mansfield and sought his counsel in dealing with you. He told me that if I should have difficulty with you, then I was to send you to him tomorrow. Now, I'm sure you must know where — '

'I know where he lives,' said she, interrupting. 'Just across the square.'

'Just so — and an early visit would be best.

He will interrogate you himself. Since he is the Lord Chief Justice of the King's Bench, I believe you may consider that a summons.' Then did he turn in my direction. 'Jeremy? Let us be off, shall we?'

★　★　★

As it was, we had little opportunity to prepare for that day's session of Sir John's court. I got for him the names, the charges, the conditions of arrest, et cetera. We left it up to the prisoners to do the rest.

Much more difficult was the work of drafting the letter to Lord Mansfield. We wanted to inform him of the difficulty we had had with her and explain that Sir John's belief now was that the woman was truly attempting to hide something. Sir John urged Lord Mansfield to get as much as he could out of her. 'Nevertheless,' said he, 'there are but two areas of questioning in which I am interested. The first is in getting her to tell just where she was from midnight to one o'clock on the evening her husband leaped to his death from the bridge. Insist that I be given permission to interview her staff of servants to confirm her response. Finally, find out if she saw Dr. Goldsworthy in Liverpool during their fruitless journey there. Get from her the next cities in the doctor's tour.'

That is, as I recall, the way that the final version of the letter to Lord Mansfield went out to him. I carried it back to Bloomsbury Square and presented it to Lord Mansfield's butler.

'No, there is no answer required. Therefore, I need not wait for his return,' I told him. 'Do give it to him soon as ever he returns. He's no doubt expecting some sort of report from Sir John.'

Upon my return, there was work of one kind or another to be done — report writing, filing, one thing or another. So it went until after dinner, when at last, done with washing up, I took myself up to the little room on the floor above which Sir John claims as his study.

'Is it you, Jeremy?' he asked, having heard my footsteps.

'It is, right enough,' said I. 'I wondered, sir, if you might perhaps feel some wish to discuss this case with me.'

'The Lammermoor case?'

'Yes sir.'

'Certainly. Sit you down, and let us consider matters.'

Where to begin, I asked myself. Perhaps by naming the suspects.

And so, suggesting that, I asked him how

many there might be. 'That perhaps is the best way to start,' said I.

'Perhaps. What would you say our first question should be?'

'The one to be asked of those in any group of suspects — *cui bono*.'

'To whom the good,' said he.

'Who gains?' said I. 'But . . . well . . . the two who seem to have the most to gain would then be Bishop Talley and, I suppose, Archibald Talley, as well. But somehow — '

'I know!' said he. 'Neither of them seems quite right. All good sense tells us that one of these two should be our murderer, yet there are other considerations.'

'Yes, of course. Our feelings count for something. Just because it's the first question we should ask doesn't mean it's the only question.'

'But there are so few likely suspects among the possible.'

'How many do you count?'

'Well, really only two.'

'So few?' said Sir John. 'It would seem to me that we have a superabundance of suspects.'

'So many? Really? Who then have you in mind?'

'Think back,' said he. 'Do you recall the demonstration of animal magnetism given by

Doctor Goldsworthy in all its particulars?'

'I think so.'

'Specifically, do you remember the stuttering Mr. Docker whose cure preceded the show put on by you and Clarissa?'

'I remember him very well indeed.'

'Well then, you remember that after he had been cured of stuttering, he became quite indignant when — simply for the amusement of the audience — he was made to jump up on a chair and crow as a rooster might. Mr. Docker had not willed it. He was simply acting upon a command that the doctor had given him whilst he was 'asleep' — that is, under the spell of animal magnetism.'

'Oh yes, I remember all that quite well.'

'Well, it is my belief that in just such a way Lord Lammermoor was murdered. How else? There were no wounds or marks upon his body, yet all who saw him describe him as having made strange motions with his arms just before jumping off the bridge. Two, I believe, said that he flapped his arms like unto a bird.'

'But,' said I, 'Dr. Goldsworthy demonstrated rather convincingly — with Clarissa's help, of course — that people could not be made to act against their moral principles or their deepest wishes.'

'Let us suppose then that someone in that

strange state produced by animal magnetism is told that he can fly. All that he needs to accomplish this miracle is to hear some secret word — code — a few words, nothing more — and he will be ready to flap his arms and fly. It sounds quite foolish, I know, but think of it, Jeremy: No moral principle is breached; and no law but nature's is broken. And what is more, the man who has been told that he can fly may want nothing more than that. He may have dreamed of nothing else — literally dreamed in his sleep of flying, of rising from the ground and passing with ease through the air as a bird does. Have you never dreamed such dreams?'

'Well, yes . . . when I was much younger. I recall the feeling of it still.'

'I, too, had such dreams.' For a moment his throat constricted; he attempted twice or thrice to clear it before he was able to continue: 'It was following my blindness, so it was — and how well I remember those dreams of flight!'

'But just suppose,' he continued, 'you're walking cross Westminster Bridge. Not the most convenient place, certainly. Nevertheless, when you hear those words which set you free to fly, how can you resist? You *can't* resist! You jump from the bridge, expecting to be carried along by the wind, but instead, you

231

drop into the river. You flounder about until you sink, and then you die.'

'I can see it,' said I. 'Truly I can! And now I understand. Dr. Goldsworthy is our villain, is he not?' It was all so plain to me at that moment.

'Perhaps,' said Sir John, 'for after all, someone had to prepare Lord Lammermoor for that great moment. But did Dr. Goldsworthy know that Lord L. could not swim? Did he intend that he should jump from the bridge? Was it the doctor who met him on the bridge and gave him the word or phrase that set him in motion? Or if not Goldsworthy, then who was it? It could have been Archibald Talley, but we agree it seems somehow unlikely. Who was that man who passed the Earl of Lammermoor on the bridge? It would seem that it had to be one in the family — or close to the family — who would know Lord Lammermoor could not swim. It could be one we don't yet know. It could be anyone.'

8

In which we attend a fire and comfort its near victims

As I recall, it was a specially warm night. I might have slept unaware through it all had I not thrown open the window just before retiring early. What time might it have been when I first smelled the smoke? Four o'clock, perhaps — yet no earlier, for when I pushed my head far out the window to search for the source of the smoke, I spied a band of faint light on the eastern horizon — first light it was. Near as I could tell, it was coming from some far corner of Covent Garden. There were selling stalls, carts, all manner of inflammable stuff.

Wasting no time in attempting to locate the fire more precisely, I dressed quickly and went running down the stairs to the floor below.

'Fire in Covent Garden!' I shouted the alarum, and then did I repeat it: 'Fire in Covent Garden!'

I heard someone stumbling about in the big bedroom. The door came open, and there stood Sir John in his nightshirt.

'Is it anywhere close?'

'No, sir, it doesn't seem to be so. It's off in a corner near King Street — or perhaps St. Paul's.'

'Well, go down and get Mr. Baker's opinion. We shall all dress and be ready to leave in the meantime.' (Owing to his blindness, there was naught which made him quite so uneasy as the threat of fire.) 'Oh dear, St. Paul's, is it?' he added. 'That could be quite disastrous.'

'Just a guess, Sir John,' said I as I made my way to the kitchen and pulled open the door to the downstairs area. Throwing myself recklessly at the stairs, I nearly collided with Mr. Baker at the bottom as he returned from Bow Street.

'Jeremy!' he exclaimed. 'You've come to see the show, have you?'

'Just a show, is it? Not much danger?'

'In truth, it don't look like it. I do believe they'll have it put out in just a few minutes.' I turned and started back up the stairs. But Mr. Baker called me back. 'Hi, Jeremy, not quite so fast. If you're going back up to report to Sir John, tell him that what's burnin' don't amount to much. 'Tis just a kind of a wagon that opened up into a patent medicine shop.'

Why, that sounded like Mr. Deekin's wagon! What rotten luck for him!

'But there's more,' Mr. Baker insisted. 'We got him who set the fire.'

'You do? So soon?'

'Aye! He was running away from it down King Street, carrying rock oil and all what's needed to start a nice big fire. He ran right into the arms of Constable Brede, and Brede brought him here. You can take a look at him if you want to, though he ain't much to see. He's right down there in the strong room.'

'No thanks, I must get upstairs and tell Sir John what you've told me.'

Which I did most immediate. All were up and awake and awaiting me. Sir John listened carefully to my report, which I repeated quite exact, much of it in Mr. Baker's own words. This is not to say or even imply that they did not respond. Clarissa, for instance, groaned to hear of Mr. Deekin's ill fortune. And when Sir John heard that the arsonist was in custody, he let forth a whoop and clapped his hands in delight.

'I shall go down and interrogate the fellow immediately,' said he.

'But, Jack,' said Lady Fielding, 'it's not yet morning. Why not come back to bed?'

'No, Kate, the Almighty had handed us this

one on a platter. This fire-setter will be more cooperative if we talk to him early. If I know my man, he's sitting in the strong room now, fearful and very unhappy. I'll present myself as his rescuer. That should loosen him up a bit, eh?' Then, without a pause, he turned to me: 'Jeremy, I want you to go to Mr. Deekin and see if he is all right — this we cannot know from what Mr. Baker did report. If he is, as we can only hope, discuss with him the extent of his loss.'

As I agreed and made ready to depart, Clarissa stepped forward and grasped me by the arm. 'I'm coming with you, Jeremy,' said she. 'Give me a moment whilst I fetch my cloak, will you?'

I protested vigorously, yet I could not dissuade her, but Sir John ended it all, saying, 'That will be quite enough, Jeremy. I believe you'll find her a considerable help.'

With that, Clarissa all but stuck out her tongue at me, so smug was the look she offered me. Then did she run back to her bedroom to fetch her cloak.

★   ★   ★

The walk cross the Covent Garden yard was never so short as it was that dawning morning in late May. We hurried cross the space,

236

matching stride for stride and step for step. Clarissa had always seemed exactly my height, and with her long legs she had no difficulty whatever in keeping up with me; 'twas I, rather, who was forced to push the pace just to keep up with her.

There was no difficulty finding our destination. The wagon — or what was left of it — glowed still, and around it milled a crowd of fifty or more. Where had they all come from? More than likely from Tom King's Coffeehouse, which could hold twice that number. Because of its loose clientele — whores, pimps, and criminals — it was considered a rather low sort of place. And now, with the sun just beginning to show his bright face to the world, there seemed to be even more of them than I had at first believed. There were evidently all sorts, from the concerned to the merely curious, pouring in from every street and alley with access to the great marketplace.

'Do you see them about?' Clarissa asked me.

'No, not really,' said I. 'Perhaps they're in the coffeehouse.'

In another minute or two we were milling with the rest of the crowd. I grabbed Clarissa's hand and held tight to it, not wishing us two to be parted in this disreputable mob. In all fairness, though, they didn't *seem* disreputable. They quite reminded me of children let out early from school, talking excitedly, laughing, enjoying their unexpected holiday.

We pushed in closer to the wagon, spent minutes searching all the while for Mr. Deekin and Hannah.

'You don't suppose that they were trapped inside and were burned alive, do you?' Clarissa asked.

'Do I? In a word, no.'

'Well, do you see them anywhere about?'

I had to admit that I did not. 'Shall I show you inside Tom King's infamous coffeehouse? You'll not see another like it in all of London.'

'Already seen it.'

'You have?' I must have sounded quite incredulous, for that is what I was. This woman — this girl — I was about to marry continued to surprise me. (And has done so ever after.)

'Of course,' said she quite dismissively. 'This was a regular stop for me on my searches for my father when he was out on one of his carousals. It was usually the place he would go last of all. He liked to drink his coffee in a cup with gin — 'coffee with a flash of lightning,' they called it. That was his way to soberize.'

'It probably didn't work very well,' I suggested.

'No, it didn't. But come along. Let's go inside. Oddly, I remember it as a rather jolly place. It never closes, you know.'

I took her arm at the elbow and guided her through the crowd to the doorway. I had noted that many of the men standing about held empty buckets. Thus I began to understand better how it was that the fire was so quickly brought under control.

Just then a bluff fellow, holding a bucket in each hand, walked toward me with a swagger and gave me a queer look. (He was tall, near a foot above me.) So I asked him his name:

''Tis Hobbes, and I ain't tellin' ya me Christian name. Why's ya askin' anyways? 'Tain't I who set the fire,' he said in a growl.

'Mr. Hobbes . . . sir,' said I, 'have you noticed or heard where the owner of that wagon might be?'

'Nay, ain't seen nobody but these me chums. 'Twere us who doused the flames. If they was in there, they cert'ny ain't among us no more!' Then pausing, he said: 'Get me gist?' And at that I turned to Clarissa, who stood with her mouth agape at this awful prouncement. I hesitated not a moment, for I knew what had to be done. And that was to search the smoldering rubble, grim as that might prove to be.

'No, Jeremy. You cannot!' said Clarissa as she grabbed my hand to pull me back as I turned to go. ''Tis not your duty!' she did shout.

'Unhand me, Clarissa. And stay back,' I ordered. 'The constables aren't here to do it.' But she would not let go of me so I pulled her forward in my march to the wagon, which still sparked with flames.

'Jeremy, can't you see there's no one alive in there!'

'Of course, I can see that — do you think me blind?' And truly I had never before been so angry with her, nor have I ever since that time past. Nevertheless, Clarissa finally released me and stood away, watching, as I did hoist myself onto the burning wagon, which emitted pulses of bursting flames. And as my legs were covered though my hands were not, I was careful not to touch the crackling timber that now surrounded me.

Once I was safely in, I searched for a plank on which to make my way across to the rear where the couple did bed at night. I continued onward with caution and took pains not to look back at Clarissa and to keep my arms tucked close to my body, though the effort did cause me to near lose my balance. By now, almost having reached the far end, I did hazard, with great relief, that the odors issuing forth were naught but the charred remains of wood and canvas. There was no odor so terrible, thought I, as that what might be the fate of Joseph Deekin and Hannah.

Thus relieved with what I had not found, and spying little danger to myself from what remained of the blaze, I stepped to a plank which I felt could sustain my weight enough so that I could balance upon as I leapt to the ground below. And then, of a sudden, as I paused to descend, I espied a look of horror on Clarissa's face. At that very moment, I lost all balance as the wagon floor did collapse in a great *swoosh*, carrying me with the falling wreckage unto the ground.

And there I lay, lulling in the crumble withal, my arms and legs atangle, as I beheld my rescuers pulling me from the rubble. Through this, however, I remained conscious. By the time I was helped to my feet by Mr. Hobbes, Clarissa, and others, to my great surprise, I did spy two smiling faces amongst the crowd gathered round me — and they were of Mr. Deekin and Hannah.

★   ★   ★

After all that had happened to me in that moment or two I was once again wishing for the strong taste of coffee to settle my nerves and awaken my dulled senses. And if it was that superior drink that I did crave, there was no better place at this hour to savor it than here at Tom King's Coffeehouse. And though tattered and light-headed, I was nonetheless feeling a sort of vigor at having escaped my 'downfall' with but mere scrapes and bruises. (At least, though I, Sir John could not see the disarray on my person. Nor would I tell him what had happened. Nor would Clarissa speak of it. Of that I was certain.)

'Jeremy!' Clarissa exclaimed. 'How could you frighten me near to death, playing with fire as a child might? And in front of my very eyes, put yourself into the gravest of danger! You do look such a fright! Please, do clean off that soot from your face!' (I took this pronouncement as pleading rather than admonishment. For I admit that she did speak the truth.)

'I would, Clarissa, if I could do so,' I said with a shrug and sigh.

Deekin and Hannah did chuckle at our banter though they looked away and did cover their smiles with a hand.

'Well, by the sound of it you two do seem to be already wedded!' announced Hannah as Clarissa disappeared into the crowd. The light from the candles in Tom King's Coffeehouse was so deficient that it did indeed seem that she had quite vanished — yet only for a moment or two or three. She reappeared from behind the stove, which was used to keep the coffee warm. Nodding, waving her thanks, Clarissa walked swiftly toward us. 'Here,' said she making a demand rather than an offer, as she thrust a wet towel at me for which the purpose was obvious. And such was also the embarrassment revealed in my expression; though I did wipe as much dirt as I could feel upon my face and see on my hands. I concluded my tidying up with an apology to Clarissa and put in also that I did indeed understand that she was most terribly worried for my safety and for that, too, I was grateful. I did even make a little bow, which did cause her to smile at me once again.

We then did all adjourn to a table somewhat away from the noise of the place, where we sat happily together at last drinking the coffee brought to our table by the same woman who'd given Clarissa a towel. Clarissa settled in beside Hannah, and they both gave each the other a reassuring squeeze. Deekin and I sat down, and immediately he began to tell the tale.

'"Twas but an hour ago or not much longer,' said he. 'I come awake all of a sudden, thinking I heard something. Had I?

Well, I guess I did, 'cause then I heard me a crackling sound — which was the fire, of course, and saw a strange sort of light, which was also the fire. And then this was the strangest part of all — there was a voice, somebody yelling in to us from the back of the wagon. 'Hi, inside,' says the voice, 'you're on fire. Better get out of there right now!' Then I stuck my head out the back, and I saw it was just so: We were on fire, and we better get out. I shook Hannah awake. Could you believe it? She slept real sound right up to then. And anyways, I told her to gather up what she could and get out of there fast. 'Why?' says she. ''Cause we're on fire,' says I. *Then* you should've seen how fast she moved!'

Then did Hannah speak in her own defense: 'Oh, he's always carryin' on about what a sleepyhead I am. But I got the most of our things, didn't I, Joe?'

'She did for a fact,' said he, 'and that's 'cause I jumped out and started giving the alarum for all I was worth. And that did some good, too, 'cause they heard me all the way here, and out they came. I guess they've had some fires here before, 'cause they knew just what to do. They formed a bucket line from that pump outside all the way out to our poor old blazing wreck of a wagon. As you could see, they put it out, all right. And it didn't take as long as you might s'pose.'

I had a question for Mr. Deekin when he had done: 'What about the man who told you the wagon was afire? A sort of Good Samaritan, was he? He may have saved your lives, you know. Who do you think he was?'

'Well, who indeed but the one who started the fire?' said Mr. Deekin with great conviction.

'You're as certain as all that?'

He shrugged. 'Just a feeling I've got.' But then, as if to substantiate what he had said: 'When I first stuck my head out, all I could see was smoke, but I could hear him running off down King Street.'

'You're sure it was him?'

'Pretty sure.'

'He was apprehended, you know.'

'What's that mean? Ap . . . '

'Apprehended. It means 'caught.''

'Well, I'd like to get a look at him — or not see him exactly, just hear his voice.'

'You think you could identify him by his voice alone?'

'I've got a good ear for voices, and a good memory, too.'

'All right,' said I, 'then come to Bow Street Court about ten-thirty or eleven. As for now, we're going to bring you to a lodging house in the Strand — you and all you can carry. We'll help.'

And that, reader, was just what we did, each of us with our arms fully loaded with clothes, knickknacks, odds and ends. It was not a great distance to the Globe and Anchor, and Hannah's innocent prattle made it seem even shorter. She must have mouthed every cheering proverb and aphorism ever conceived to lift the spirits of those in dire straits. It seemed she had thought of every one from 'Tomorrow is another day' to 'It always seems darkest before dawn.' But no, Clarissa contributed another and then another, as did I. Even Deekin remembered one: 'Happiness lies just round the corner.' And then it was Hannah's turn once more. Thus we played it as a game — laughing all the way.

When we arrived in this manner at the Globe and Anchor, we must have looked a bit like a drunken party of revelers. In any case, that is what I read in the face of him who came to the door. Only reluctantly did he open it, and that just wide enough to get a look at us. It was plain to me that he did not like what he saw.

'Yes? What is it you wish?'

'A room for these good people,' said I.

'All of you?'

'No, good sir, we wish your hospitality only

246

for this charming couple. They have been burned out of their domicile, and they bring with them all the belongings which they were able to save from the fire. Sir John Fielding, magistrate of this City of Westminster, guarantees payment for their room.'

The name of Sir John Fielding did, of course, change things a great deal. The night clerk forced a smile and threw the door open wide. It took but a minute or two, no more, to get them assigned a room.

'Ordinarily,' said I to Mr. Deekin at our parting, 'I would advise you to try to get some sleep.'

'No, I'm too uneasy for that, I fear.'

'Well, since that be the case, I would ask you to spend your time calculating the extent of the damage done by the fire and the amount of money it would take to make all right again.'

'Aw, now wait,' said he, 'I know magistrates get paid a proper large amount, but he can't — '

I interrupted him: 'Now, Mr. Deekin, I have known Sir John a number of years, and I have found that it is best to make no assumptions or guesses as to his intended course of action. Just do as he asks, and add up the damages.'

'All right,' said he, 'I will.'

★ ★ ★

Ever since the Great Fire of the last century, which destroyed four hundred acres of the City of London, arson has been the most certainly punishable of all offenses; 'a sure ticket to Tyburn' is how it was once put to me. Word had gotten out round Covent Garden that Sir John would try an arsonist at his noonday session. Therefore a full house was present at the Bow Street Court when it came time to beat with the gavel upon the table and call all to order. Actually, it was near a quarter of an hour later than was scheduled. I had held things up searching for a witness, one of the bucket brigade from Tom King's Coffeehouse. When at last I found my man, it was near to midday, and it was all I could do to find my place beside Sir John as the session began.

Just getting my bearings, I checked the number of prisoners in Mr. Fuller's charge and found there were but three. The first was a man of middling years who was brought in by Constable Sheedy for public drunkenness. (Sir John fined him ten shillings and sent him on his way.) The second, Matthew Treacher, was the hapless fellow whom Mr. Brede had encountered carrying a near-empty bucket of lamp oil, running down King Street, away from the fire he had set. I had the opportunity to interview him following Sir John's interrogation; he was still in tears and unable at first to make much sense, but eventually I got from him an acceptable minimum of personal information and passed it on to Sir John. And immediately thereafter was I sent out on my search for one of Tom King's men. And thus did I miss the apprehension of one who had grown quite familiar to me without managing to win my respect — *Doctor Hippocrates Grenfell*. On Sir John's orders, Mr. Fuller had brought him in, and his interrogation had taken place in the magistrate's chambers. Dr. Grenfell's usual manner — gruff and overbearing — seemed to have left him altogether. In its place was naught but uneasiness and a fear that he tried his best to hide.

I glanced round me and managed to locate a number who might serve as witnesses. I noted Mr. Brede's presence and saw also Mr. Deekin and Hannah. Indeed I happened to catch Mr. Deekin's eye, and he winked at me. I returned a frown, for such expressions of familiarity were out of place in the courtroom — any courtroom.

Following the swift disposal of the case of the man brought in by Constable Sheedy on the charge of public drunkenness, Sir John had me call out the next, which we referred to by then simply as 'Arson, et cetera.' As agreed upon, I invited Constable Brede and Matthew Treacher to take their places before Sir John, which they did without much ado. They were sworn in, as were all who followed. Sir John began with his constable.

'Mr. Brede,' said he, 'can you tell us of your first meeting with Mr. Treacher?'

'I can, and I will, sir. I was walking northwards on Bedford Street, and I heard footsteps round the corner on King Street. Naturally I was suspicious.'

'Why was that natural, Mr. Brede?' Sir John asked.

'Oh, yes, sir, I forgot to say. It was just four o'clock in the morning — and pitch-dark it was. That time of night you have to be suspicious of anybody who comes along on a dark street, specially when they're running.'

'Ah, running steps, was it? I would say your principle is fairly sound, Mr. Brede, and your suspicion was justified, so by all means continue your story.'

'Well, I had a pretty good idea from all the noise he was making just where he'd come out, so I took up a place on Bedford just shy of the corner, and just as he was coming, I took a step out and stops him right there. Right off, I noticed he was carrying a bucket that was just about empty. He dropped the bucket, y'see, and it rolled right to my feet. I says to him, 'What's in that bucket?' 'Oil,' he says. 'What are you doing with it?' 'I just started a fire,' says he. 'Let's go see that fire,' says I.'

'He was as frank with the truth as all that, was he?'

'He was, sir. We walked back together, and there wasn't any trouble finding that fire he set. I'd say it was just about at its peak then. But they'd organized a bucket brigade, and it looked to me like they had everything under control. Truth to tell, the fire wasn't very well set — or so it appeared to me. So since that's how it was, and he'd confessed everything and all, I charged him with arson and marched him off to Bow Street.'

'In your judgment, then,' said Sir John, 'there was no danger to the surrounding buildings?'

'None, sir.'

'And no need to notify the Lord Mayor?'

'No to that, too, Sir John.'

'All right then, Mr. Brede, you may leave the court with my thanks.'

Which is what he did, tracking down the long aisle and out the door to Bow Street.

As he did, Sir John turned to me and whispered that he wished my fellow from the bucket brigade to take Mr. Brede's place before him.

And so I summoned him by name. 'Will Joshua Tilley take a place before Sir John, please?'

I should perhaps say a word now about how Matthew Treacher was taking all of this. Now that the inquiry had actually begun, he seemed much more in control of himself than before — and certainly more than when I had followed Sir John to the strong room and found the poor fellow in tears. Yet on that visit I secured all the necessary information regarding his person which Sir John now used to begin his questioning.

'Your name, sir?'

'Matthew Treacher.'

'And where do you reside?'

'In Pater Noster Row, next the hatter's.'

'You heard Mr. Brede's account of your apprehension, did you not?'

'I did, yes.'

'And did you find it complete and accurate?'

'Well, it was accurate, so far as it went, but there was some things could be added.'

'Then add them, by all means.'

'There was this matter of how good the fire I set proved to be. I knew it wasn't well set. That's as I intended.' Clearly, Mr. Treacher had regained a bit of confidence.

'Hold please, sir,' said Sir John. 'I wish to hear your additions, as you name them, nevertheless I wish at this point to talk to Joshua Tilley. You are here?'

'Right in front of you, sir.'

'Good. That is where I wish you to be. Your name is Joshua Tilley?'

'It is.'

'And where do you reside, Mr. Tilley?'

'In King Street, sir. It ain't much of a room, and it ain't much of a street — but it suits me.'

'How so, then?'

'Well, it's near my work, so it is.'

'And what work have you?'

'I'm a greengrocer in Covent Garden. I do right well there. I run a good-sized stall, and I employ three people — a helper and two barrow women. It takes up most of a day — starts early, goes late.'

'You say it starts early? That explains your presence there in Tom King's Coffeehouse.'

'Yessir. Start the day there — half a loaf of sweetbread and coffee with a flash of lightning.'

'When did you hear of the fire round the corner?'

'A minute or two after it was started. We all heard the alarum raised, and we run for the door, each of us grabbin' a bucket on the way out.'

'The buckets are stored there?'

'It's a natural place to keep them, because King's never closes.'

'Yes, well, go on with your tale, Mr. Tilley.'

'Right you are, sir. Well, I got them organized into a bucket brigade, stretched from the pump outside of here, around the corner to where the wagon was burnin'.'

'But why you? Why did it fall to you to organize the bucket brigade?'

'Not to brag, but around the Garden I'm considered sort of an expert on fire. I set the bonfire every Guy Fawkes Day.'

'Ah,' said Sir John, 'just what I was getting to. What do you, as an expert on fires, think of the one set by our Mr. Treacher?'

'In all truth, sir, I didn't think much of it.'

'And why did you not?'

'Well, rock oil — or lamp oil, whatever you wish to call it — just isn't much good for starting fires. Just doesn't have enough push to it. I knew right away that's what'd been used, 'cause you could smell it. Now, whether it'd been used on purpose, or out of ignorance, I couldn't say. It burns for hours and hours. That's why they use it in lamps — but it burns slow. That much I do know. Why, there wouldn't been any fire at all if this fellow next to me, or whoever did it, hadn't lit the cloth of the tent in the back of the wagon. That caught right quick. Cloth always does.'

'All right then, Mr. Tilley. We needed an expert opinion, and you provided one. You may return to your seat, or leave the courtroom, as you see fit. You are, to put it to you direct, dismissed.'

I noted, reader, that Joshua Tilley returned to his seat.

'Now,' said Sir John, 'please continue, if you will, Mr. Treacher. And let us hasten along, for we still have much to hear from you.'

'Yes sir,' said Mr. Treacher. 'There is also the matter of the warning which I gave to those sleeping in the wagon.'

'Ah yes, tell us of that.'

'Well, I had thought at first simply to beat upon the wagon in order to wake them, but when I lit the wagon's cloth cover, it burned so quickly I was fearful that they might be caught inside.'

'And what then did you do?'

'I both beat upon the wheels of the wagon and yelled a warning to those inside.'

'And what was the warning you shouted?'

'Oh, sir, I forget the exact words, for I was most excited.'

'Perhaps one of the occupants of the wagon

will confirm your efforts to wake them and remember the words of your warning.' At that, Sir John paused, took a moment, and then called out: 'Is Joseph Deekin in the courtroom?'

'Here I be, sir.' Deekin sang it out loud and clear, though he was but a few feet away.

'Very well, Mr. Deekin. If you will but keep your place and stand, that should be sufficient.' But his nudge reminded me that it was up to me to bring the Bible to Deekin that he might take his solemn oath. And to the courtroom crowd, Sir John said: 'Let it be known that this person is Joseph Deekin by name, and he is the victim of this intended arson. I see no need to identify him further.' He turned in Deekin's direction. 'Sir, I have but two or three questions for you. First I must ask if you heard the voice warning you that your wagon was afire.'

To that, he responded quickly and directly. 'Yes, sir, I did,' said he. 'I was just beginning to wake when I heard the voice.'

'And what were the words of warning?'

'Well, it was something like this: 'Hello, inside the wagon. You're on fire, so you'd better get out right now!' Oh, I remember real well, sir. We got out the back — about the only way we could.'

'Did you see him?'

'No, but I heard him.'

'You mean . . . you heard what was said?'

'No, I mean I heard the voice, the sound of it. Matter of fact, I've been hearing it for a good half hour now.'

'You mean . . . ?'

'That's right, Sir John, this man here — this Mr. Treacher — he's the man shouted into the wagon just like I said — warning us and telling us to get out and save ourselves.'

'You're sure of that?'

'Oh, I'm sure, all right. I've a good memory for voices.'

'So have I, Mr. Deekin,' said Sir John, 'and so I accept your identification of Matthew Treacher as positive.'

'He's the man who roused us. You might say he's the man who saved our lives.'

At that, the magistrate's courtroom quite exploded into whispers, mutters, and mumbles; there was even a bit of discreet applause. No cheers, no loud stamping upon the floor (they would not have dared), but still and all, it was an interruption, and Sir John would have none of it. He accompanied his calls for order with blows of his gavel. And when at last the place had been quietened, he dismissed Joseph Deekin with thanks and turned his attention back to Matthew Treacher.

'Now, Mr. Treacher, it seems to be established that either by ignorance or by your own intention you set the sort of fire that would have smoldered long before it burned. Not only that, sir, but when the cloth cover of the wagon, referred to by some as the tent, caught fire and burned with a threatening intensity, you took it upon yourself to warn those sleeping within of the danger to them — danger which you yourself had put them in. Frankly, I'm confused. You are either the least able arsonist who has passed my way, or the most reluctant. Tell me, which is it?'

Faced with such a question, and bowing under such responsibility, Mr. Treacher was of a sudden quite stunned to silence. So long did he stand dumb, Sir John felt obliged to prompt him.

'Mr. Treacher?'

'It is now that I speak in my own defense?'

'This is the time.'

'Thank you, sir. I will. I, well, I think of myself as the most reluctant of arsonists. Truth to tell, I hardly think of myself as an arsonist at all. Where to begin?' Another pause. 'Let it be here: My wife fell ill a little over a year ago — or perhaps a little longer. To say a year ago does no more than mark the time I put her in the care of Dr. Grenfell.

258

He came highly recommended, and he told me that he could help her. I loved my wife, and I wanted only to help her, and so that was enough for me. I should have kept a closer eye upon the expense for it mounted in a way that was most frightening.'

'And what nature of illness had your wife?' asked Sir John.

'That of the female sort,' he answered.

Sir John seemed about to ask him to be more specific, but he said nothing and let the moment pass as Mr. Treacher resumed.

' 'Twas only after my wife had died that Dr. Grenfell presented me with his bill which came to no less than two hundred pounds. By far the largest single item on it was the doctor's own elixir which he claimed would cure any and all illnesses. Well, it did not cure her. When I confronted him with this and other facts, he simply said that I had brought her to him too late. The disease was too far along — so he said. Finally, I went to a chemist and asked him to analyze the contents of this so-called elixir. It was one of a dozen or so left over when she died. He said it had a bit of honey for taste, a good measure of opium, and the rest was alcohol. No wonder my good wife — God rest her soul — fell into such a deep sleep whenever she took her dram!'

'Opium is sometimes prescribed for pain, you know,' said Sir John.

(That I did know well, for I remembered, as he did, that Mr. Donnelly had done so for the first Lady Fielding to ease her last days.)

'Oh, indeed I do know, sir — but a hundred and twenty pounds worth of it? Let it go, though, and let me speak of his methods of collection.' He sighed. 'Now, Dr. Grenfell's bill was just a bit more than I make in a year.'

'What is your work, sir? I should have asked you earlier.'

'I'm naught but a clerk — or I was.'

'Explain yourself, please.'

'I tried to arrange to pay him a bit at a time, but he demanded larger payments than I could possibly manage. We argued back and forth on the matter. A week ago he sent a letter to my employer citing the debt and demanding that my wages be garnished at the rate of a pound a month — again, more than I could pay. My employer wanted nothing to do with arrangements of that sort, and so he told me that I need not report for work until I had satisfied Dr. Grenfell.'

'And who is — or was — your employer?' asked Sir John.

'The East India Company, shipping division.'

'Make a note of that, Jeremy,' Sir John whispered to me.

'I despaired of my future, seeing only debtors' prison ahead. But then, quite by surprise, Dr. Grenfell sent for me. He told me in such a way as he might if telling a secret that he had a deed he wished done and for which he would forgive my debt. 'I wish you to engage in a bit of arson for me,' said he. 'Arson is against the law,' said I. 'And so is running up debts you cannot pay.' Thus I was forced to agree to his terms. Yet when I discovered that what he wished burned was the wagon in the street below, I asked if there would be people inside, and he told me that was a matter that need not concern me greatly. 'Just be careful you do your arson on a night with no wind,' said he to me. 'I'll not have you burning me or my neighbors out.''

'You've quoted him exact?' Sir John asked.

'I have, sir.'

'Dr. Grenfell, come forward,' said Sir John. The medico complied.

To me, the magistrate whispered, 'Go to him. Have him put his hand upon the Bible.'

I did as he said and had the opportunity to look deep into Grenfell's eyes. He was troubled, no doubt of it. Nay, more. He was greatly worried. Yet in his response to Sir John, it soon became evident that he had made up his mind to deny all — and he remained doggedly true to his decision.

'Doctor, you have heard the testimony of Mr. Treacher in his own behalf. Tell me, what think you of it?'

'Why, I think nothing of it.'

'How is that, sir?'

'From first to last, it is naught but a well-woven tissue of lies. *None* of it is true.'

'Oh, come now.' Sir John said it indulgently, as one might when talking to a child. 'Surely there are some parts of it which ring true.'

'None.'

'None, is it? Well, it so happens that during my interview with him, Mr. Treacher passed on to me certain papers which I tucked away, giving no thought to them. He said that they were important, but not having my clerk about to read them to me, I simply forgot I had them. How foolish of me, eh?'

So saying, he proceeded to make a great show of going through all the pockets of his coat, muttering, 'No, not there' and 'This is most embarrassing,' and finally, 'Ah yes, *here* they are.' He had them tucked in his hat. I strongly suspicioned that he knew all the time where they were. They were neither stained with the sweat of his brow, nor were they even slightly damp with it. I glanced over them as

Sir John settled himself to listen.

'Just read them as they come up,' said he. 'I'm sure that we can fit them in correctly.'

The first was the bill from Dr. Grenfell. It was dated but two weeks past. I began to read the itemized account aloud — visits, personal consultations, et cetera, and a figure posted for each one. I stumbled over some words in Latin. At that moment Sir John chose to interrupt: 'That will do nicely, Jeremy,' said he. 'But for now, just read us the figure at the bottom of the column — the total.'

I glanced down and read the figure aloud: 'One hundred ninety-four pounds, eight shillings, and ten pence.'

'*There!*' shouted Grenfell. 'You see? He lied right there. He said I billed him two hundred pounds, and I did nothing of the kind. You must admit that!' Sir John did not respond.

Next was a letter from Dr. Grenfell declining Mr. Treacher's offer to return a dozen bottles of Grenfell's Elixir for credit on his bill.

'Why did you refuse?' asked the magistrate.

'They might have been opened. They lose their strength then.'

'Ah!' said Sir John — and only that.

There were other items of interest among the papers. One of them was a letter from a chemist containing his analysis of the elixir. The proportions were the same as Mr. Treacher had given, but they were written in a chemist's code of which I knew naught. I explained my difficulty to Sir John, and he urged me on. Grenfell claimed it as a victory.

There was a letter from an assistant director of the East India Company who governed the shipping division. Though I do not recall its wording exact, it announced to Mr. Treacher that until he settled this matter with his physician, he could no longer consider himself an employee of the East India Company.

In these documents and a few others Matthew Treacher's story, given in testimony, was given confirmation. They had obviously been carefully arranged to tell the story, and the final document told its sad ending. It had been drawn up in such a way that it might appear as a legal document. But it had no validity as such, for it was couched in the most vague and unspecific terms possible: 'The two parties signed below agree that the debt owed will be forgiven upon the successful completion of certain labors, as agreed upon' — that sort of thing. Below all this were their signatures. I noted, by the bye, that Mr. Treacher's was the more practiced hand; he indeed had written out the body of the text.

Dr. Grenfell had no immediate comment.

Sir John, on the other hand, treated the document with a certain respect, as if all were revealed by it. In truth, naught was revealed — except that the doctor had actually signed it. That he admitted after viewing the two names at the bottom of the page.

Finally, commenting upon this in the course of his summing-up, the magistrate allowed that taken as it was, it had little value. 'Nevertheless, when taken in the context of what we have heard in testimony and been given in documentary evidence, we can suppose what that harmless-seeming phrase would mean — ' . . . upon the successful completion of certain labors, as agreed upon.' Oh, indeed we can.'

He considered the two who stood before him. 'What am I do to with you?' He put the question to them rhetorically, I think, for I was fairly certain that by the time he had taken us thus far, he knew well just what he would do. 'Both of you know, I hope, that if I were to pass you on to the Criminal Court, you would be condemned and hanged in a week's time. There is more than enough to convict you. There is one charge, arson, against you both — yet how different your stories, how unlike your motives.

'Mr. Treacher, you, it strikes me, are one of the victims of this lamentable affair. Yet looked at in another way, you are the most fortunate of all. If either of the occupants of the wagon had died in the fire, or even been injured, I should certainly have to send you on to Old Bailey. But after setting your fire, you did all you could to waken those inside, thus saving them from a death by fire or smoke. Yet you are nevertheless a victim — a victim of Dr. Grenfell's greed. You did not know Joseph Deekin. You had no grudge against him. You had no reason to burn his wagon and endanger his life. It is certain that you, Mr. Treacher, should have kept closer watch on your bills, but it is just as certain that you are not a murderer. I sentence you to three months, which is the maximum penalty which I can give under law. It is to be served in the Fleet Prison, which you know is a debtors' prison. That seems appropriate.' He brought down his gavel.

It was evident that Mr. Treacher was more than satisfied with the sentence. He felt that he had been dealt with generously. It was writ upon his face.

'But now, Dr. Grenfell, you present a much different set of problems. Essentially, *you* set the fire in King Street, because in forgiving the amount that was owed you, nearly — though not quite — two hundred pounds, you were paying Mr. Treacher that amount for doing the job for you. There was considerable damage to Mr. Deekin's property. All this has been set forth and itemized by Mr. Deekin here.' Sir John produced a paper for all to see. 'The amount in total is twenty-eight pounds. It is a figure I am sure you can pay. I order you to do so.'

'Have I any choice in this matter?' asked Dr. Grenfell.

'None at all,' said the magistrate. 'You may pay by cash or by cheque, as suits you best.'

Having heard that, the doctor stepped forward and pulled forth his cheque book. I offered him my quill, which he took. Then did he use the table at which Sir John and I sat to steady his hand and wrote out a cheque. 'There,' said he when he had done.

'Present it to my clerk,' said Sir John — and then to me: 'Is everything in order, Jeremy?'

'Of course it is,' said Grenfell quite indignantly. 'It is a draft upon the Bank of England for the exact amount.'

I ignored him. 'It seems to be,' said I, tucking away the cheque.

'Now, Dr. Grenfell, we come to the more difficult part of your sentencing. In spite of your callous remarks to Mr. Treacher as to what should happen to Joseph Deekin and his companion, I do not believe that you wished them dead. In any case, they did not die, and that is your good fortune. You are in every way more culpable in this than Matthew Treacher. Nevertheless, having sentenced him to three months, I cannot give you a longer sentence without finding you fit for trial and sending you on to Old Bailey. That would mean an almost certain death sentence. And somehow I cannot bring myself to believe that even you deserve that — thus my dilemma. But if you and Mr. Treacher must serve an equal length of time for the same crime, you need not serve it in the same prison. That then was my reasoning, and why I now sentence you to three months, which is to be served in Newgate Gaol.' He hammered once again upon the table and instructed Mr. Fuller to take them away.

Dr. Grenfell looked wildly about him, as if reckoning his chances of escape. He must have reckoned they were by no means good, for he took to calling countersuggestions to the magistrate as he was led out.

'What about a fine? Oh, make it a large fine! One hundred pounds perhaps? Two hundred?'

'That will be quite enough, sir. You will

need all your money for favors in Newgate.'

For some odd reason the courtroom crowd thought that exchange quite comical. They laughed and laughed whilst Grenfell commenced to blubber quite without restraint.

Toward the end of the afternoon Sir John was paid an expected visit by the Lord Chief Justice. There was no way that Lord Mansfield could have avoided the meeting, for had he not put forth the formula — or 'rules of engagement' — by which Lady Lammermoor might be questioned? In effect, the agreement between the two men was that if she should refuse to talk to Sir John, then she *must* answer Lord Mansfield's inquiries. Otherwise would she be guilty of an insult to the King's entire judiciary. Not even such a one as she would dare that.

And so there came the usual prelude: The door slammed open; there were the usual rapid steps down the long hall. Sir John listened and nodded knowingly. He grasped my arm, indicating he wanted me to remain. We both managed to regard Lord Mansfield with a look of surprise as he came through the door to the magistrate's chambers.

'Sir John,' said he, 'I've come to give you a report on my interview with Lady Lammermoor.'

'Ah! Lord Mansfield, is it?' said he, rising.

'Do come in and sit down, won't you?'

'Much as I'd like to, I cannot. Too much to do, far too much. I'll just give you the gist of it, then hurry on to the Lord Mayor's office to discuss a matter of which I have only a vague understanding.'

'Well then, do tell me how the interview with Lady Lammermoor went.'

He shrugged. 'It went well enough, I suppose. She's quite a charming woman, actually.' Then did he hesitate. 'Now, what was it you wished to know from her? I've not got your letter in front of me, nor did I when I spoke with her, but I'm sure we must have covered all.'

Sir John let escape a slight sigh of disappointment. 'All right,' said he, 'I was eager to have her account for her time on the night her husband died — the *entire* evening.'

'What do you mean by that — 'the *entire* evening'?'

'Well, her son has given it that she was with him at their residence right up to midnight when he himself went to bed.'

'Then you have it,' said Lord Mansfield. 'She's not likely to have stayed up much past midnight.'

'But I would like to hear it from others, as well — her servants.'

'Ah, servants, is it? That can be a rather

sticky business, you know.'

'And why is that?' asked Sir John, all innocent ignorance.

'Servants tend to hold grudges; they think the house belongs to them, and you're just getting in the way. That sort of thing. Not a good idea to talk to servants — that's my personal view. *But*, lucky for you, Lady Lammermoor takes a more liberal view. The place should be the Lammermoor residence, which seems only sensible to me. As for the time, that should be arranged in advance, so that she may be absent. There! You couldn't ask for more, could you? Not only does she throw open her home to you, she even declines to sit in on your interviews with the servants so that they may feel free to talk.'

'Yes, those seem to me like satisfactory arrangements. But what about Dr. Goldsworthy?'

Lord Mansfield's face took on a rather vague expression, as if he couldn't quite remember who that might be. 'I . . . don't . . . believe . . . I . . . No, I don't recall asking her about any such . . . Was that in your letter?'

'It was, yes. You'll perhaps remember that I asked you to find out if she had spoken to Goldsworthy whilst in Liverpool.'

'No, sorry, I don't recall . . . but that name,

Goldsworthy. It's an unusual one, isn't it? I've seen it recently.'

'Oh?'

'Yes, it was . . . ' He searched his memory until — 'Now I have it. I get a monthly report on crime from every magistrate in Britain. It has some use, I suppose, though I know not what it might be. That name appeared in the latest such compilation. I was turning through it just today, and there it was — Goldsworthy.'

'What sort of crime?' Sir John asked. 'Where was it?'

'Indeed, where was it? In Lancashire, as I recall, somewhere outside Liverpool. Homicide it was. He took a ball right through the heart from some highwayman, I suppose. He was brought in dead by the driver and footman. Seems he had resisted the highwayman's demand for money.'

Sir John gave no response.

'Well then,' said the Lord Chief Justice. 'Sorry I couldn't have been of more help to you. But you've got the servants to question. That should keep you busy awhile, eh?'

Having said that, he waved, then turned away, and then turned back again: 'Did Lady Lammermoor give you her theory of the crime?'

'You mean the murder of Dr. Goldsworthy?'

'No, I mean the murder of my dear friend,

Lord Lammermoor.'

'The one involving whom?'

'The one involving that actress from the Drury Lane Theatre.'

'Oh, that. Yes, indeed she did.'

'Then perhaps you ought to interview her.'

'Interview her? I have already — twice.'

'Well, then, do it a third time. After all, she used to be your cook, did she not?'

'Yes, she did.' All that Sir John would not allow himself to say was audible in those three words — all that he might have said.

'Yes indeed, Lady L. made that point, and that being the case, I think it important that you give special attention to this Annie . . . Annie whatever-her-name. I'm not saying you should pass her on to me at Old Bailey — just give her some attention, will you? I'll not have my magistrates compromised.'

Sir John said not a word in reply. Indeed, as I recall, he said not a word the rest of the day, so great was his anger.

9

*In which a day is
lost in interrogation
then found again*

After an exchange of notes in which I participated, it was settled that Sir John and I would visit the Lammermoor residence next day, just as soon as his court session was done. Though sullen and brooding through most of the morning, Sir John was sufficiently recovered from Lord Mansfield's insulting behavior to discuss the case with me as we walked to keep our appointment in Blooms-bury Square. The discussion had been occasioned by one of my usual obtuse questions — the sort I seemed to ask far too often at that stage of my legal education.

'Sir,' I had said; 'I cannot understand how it is that you say that the death of Dr. Goldsworthy is in some sense a good thing for us.'

'Well, not an entirely bad thing in any case.'

'Still, I don't understand. His death

deprives you of the chance to question him. I don't doubt you could've gotten much from him had you done so.'

'There you are, looking on the dark side. You often do that. You seem to prefer it. Note I said it was not an *entirely* bad thing.'

'Meaning, of course, that there is some good in it.'

'Yes.'

'What is the good in it?'

'It tells us, for one thing, that my theory on the manner in which Lord Lammermoor was murdered is not at all wild speculation, as even I feared it to be.'

'We know now how he was murdered?'

'We know how he could have been murdered.'

'Then you put no store whatever in what Lord Mansfield seems to believe — that he was the victim of a highwayman.'

'None at all. As long as there is an obvious explanation, Lord Mansfield will never look beyond it. He is the great champion of the obvious.'

So convincing had he earlier been that I had accepted without question what he now admitted may have sounded quite like 'wild speculation.' My first impulse was to argue with him. Yet knowing what little good that would do, I decided (wisely) it might be better simply to ask questions — and so that is what I did.

'How is it, sir, that the death of Dr. Goldsworthy out on the highway proves — or better said, suggests — the validity of your speculation?'

'Well, from the little we were told, we know that the doctor did not walk a distance near to Liverpool in order to present himself as a target to a highwayman.'

'That's certain,' said I. 'He had to have a conveyance of some sort take him there. If he was found by the side of the road, how did he get there?'

'Precisely — and so we must write to the magistrate of Liverpool when we return, and find out if an investigation was held and what — if anything — that investigation had revealed.'

'Well, if I may, Sir John, I can suggest something that may be pertinent.'

'Then out with it, Jeremy, my lad, out with it.'

'Yes, sir. I recall from his own lips that Mr. Donnelly called upon Dr. Goldsworthy the day after the demonstration to put a few questions to him. And he called upon him at the Lammermoor residence, for he had found out that it was there that the doctor had stayed for a few days before the demonstration.'

'But you never told me this.'

'It seemed of little importance at the time. But to continue, sir — '

'Yes, by all means.'

'Since he departed for Liverpool from the Lammermoor residence, it only stands to reason that one of those in the house must have engaged the coach and team for him.'

'So it does,' said he, 'so it does.'

By that time we were close upon Bloomsbury Square, and I noted from a distance what had previously escaped me: In that cluster of buildings, large and grand, the Lammermoor residence was the largest and grandest of them all. What wealth, what power was concentrated therein I could only guess. Of all cities, London must surely be the richest, I thought.

'We must be nearing Bloomsbury,' said Sir John.

'Why yes,' said I. 'How could you tell?'

'Please, Jeremy, I may be blind, but I still have a nose.'

What an odd response, thought I. 'I don't quite follow.'

'The lilacs, of course. They're all over here, are they not? This time of the year their lovely odor pervades all. You smell them, don't you?'

'Now that you mention it, sir.'

It seemed to me that if I had managed to

raise Sir John out of his earlier state of mind and interest him in the smell of lilacs once again, then I had done a great deal. Earlier, he would have ignored them. I had, by that time, seen Sir John Fielding in every mood, yet in all truth I do not believe I had ever seen him in a state so low for so long — and all was due to the rudeness of the Lord Chief Justice.

* * *

The afternoon, which we spent interviewing the staff of servants was, all in all, a rather trying ordeal. There were so many of them that we could scarce avoid a feeling of repetition. Or could that have been because the servants were so well-drilled in their responses? One after another they came before us and said essentially the same thing. Only a few stand out from the rest; there were thirty in all, brought in by the butler.

Though she was not the first to be brought to us, she was, in any case, among the first few. A pretty girl, she was, introduced as a chambermaid. Her name was Abigail, and she came to us by way of Sussex — a farm girl who rose (if that is quite the word) from pitching hay to emptying chamber pots. We had begun, even that early in our questioning, to perceive a pattern in the responses of the servants to Sir John's simple questions. Therefore we were certainly not surprised when we began to hear a few of the same words and phrases repeated from one to the next. After the butler had brought her in and introduced her as 'Abigail, a chambermaid,' he left us to stand outside the door: 'In order,' he had said, 'that I may be certain you are not disturbed by any of the staff.' This was quite considerate of him, of course, yet I could not help but notice his station just beyond the closed door made it easy to hear what was said inside the room.

'Come forward, child,' said Sir John to her, 'and tell us your full name.'

'Abigail Hardy,' said she, giving to us a pretty curtsey. 'I am not long in London, though I am happy to be here and specially fortunate in my position in this noble household.'

(I was certain we had heard that last from one of the girls who had preceded her.)

'As chambermaid?' Sir John sounded quite dubious.

'Oh, indeed, sir. The master and missus have been great entertainers. I doubles as a serving maid, and there are vails aplenty from the guests at every dinner. 'Course not now 'cause of the master's death, but . . . '

Was it my imagination, or was Abigail inching forward from the place she had taken when first she entered the room in the company of the butler? I studied her face, and not her feet, and I found that the girl — she could not have been more than fourteen — was attempting to signal something with her eyes — widening them, rolling them. What odd behavior! What was she trying to signal?

'I understand what you say,' said he, 'but can you tell me, Abigail, how did Lord and Lady Lammermoor get on?'

'How do you mean that, sir?'

She made a dash on tiptoe for the desk — my side of it — and threw down a piece of many-folded notepaper and pointed into her pocket, indicating that she wished me to put it in my own. I nodded and tucked it away into my waistcoat as she retired to her former place.

All this preceded as Sir John hemmed and hawed over his response to her question in this manner: 'How *do* I mean that? Well, I suppose as anyone might. When one meets a married couple, it is perfectly normal to wonder how they get on. Are there frequent fights? Or perhaps long silences at the dinner table? Is all right between them? And so on. You see what I mean, of course.'

It was quite unlike him to circle about in such a vague manner. Something was up, and Sir John knew it. He usually did speak direct and to the point.

'Oh, of course I see,' said she, by then safely settled. 'And I would say, sir, that there was never a couple happier than them. They laughed and joked together and called each other lovey names, like a pair just been married.'

'So much in love, were they?'

'Oh yes, sir.'

'There really remains only one more question, Miss — er, what was your name again?'

'Hardy, sir, Abigail Hardy.'

'You have that, Jeremy?'

'I do, sir.'

'Good, now that question has to do with the hour of Lady Lammermoor's retirement on the night her husband fell to his death from Westminster Bridge. Would that be something you would know?'

'Oh yes, sir,' said she. 'Around the midnight hour, or just before it, Lady Lammermoor rang and asked me to help her into her nightgown and turn down her bed. She wished to retire.'

'Would that have been an early hour or late for her to retire?'

'Oh, late,' said she. 'Except when she entertains, she usually goes to bed at least an hour earlier. As it seems to me, she was reading something that quite held her. A book it was.'

'And was young Mr. Talley reading in the same room as his mother?'

'As near as I can remember, yes, he was. He went up at about the same hour.'

'And what was this room in which both passed the evening whilst reading?'

'The library, sir.'

'Hmmm. Seems quite appropriate, doesn't it?' said he. 'You may go now, Mistress Hardy.'

With a quick curtsey and a final thank-you-sir, she whirled about and rushed for the door. Nevertheless, before she arrived, the butler had the door open to bring in the next girl before she slipped out. Obviously, he had been listening.

We then examined a goodly number of women and girls, boys and men until, as we talked to the last five or ten of the servants, a row broke out just beyond the door. There were shouting, cries, and threats until Sir John was forced to break off his interrogation of one of the kitchen slaveys and send me out into the hall to investigate the cause of the interruption. I ran out into the hall and found the butler locked in a struggle with two men, holding tightly to the arm of one and to the coattail of the other. I could tell by their dress that both were coachmen. One yelled at the top of his voice that they were leaving, whether the butler liked it or not.

'Well, surely you can stay long enough to have the magistrate examine you two,' the butler insisted.

'That's just what we can't do. She wanted us at her dressmaker's by five, and I don't know where she'll want us after that.'

'Well, she told me no one was to go till she gave permission.'

'Oh, that's the rest of them. We got to leave.'

The butler was a strapping, forceful fellow, yet there were two for him to hold on to, and they soon proved altogether too much for him. No fists were thrown. No kicks were delivered. There was nothing as crude as all that. The two simply wrenched free and stalked off for the door to the outside. The butler, for his part, seemed to feel that they were not worth further trouble and simply let them go. Only then did he notice me out in the hall, staring at him. It was evident that he was embarrassed.

'Begging your pardon for the interruption,' said he. 'All is now in order. And if you would pass my apologies on to Sir John?'

'Certainly,' said I.

We hurried through the remainder of the staff, asking the same questions over and over again, getting the same answers. Thus we passed the remainder of the afternoon. Though it was well after five when we came to the last of them, we did so without the intrusion of Lady Lammermoor. No doubt she had other stops to make. But let me amend that as follows:

When the butler opened the door allowing the last of the kitchen slaveys to depart, he remained long enough to inform us that there were no more to be interviewed.

'By my count,' said Sir John, 'there are three more to talk to.'

'Oh? Well, of course you have not talked to the two coachmen. I doubt that they will have much to tell, but perhaps at a later date it could be arranged. But who else had you in mind?'

'Why, you, sir. Had you thought I would neglect you?'

The man was, of a sudden, visibly abashed. He smiled uncertainly as his face slowly began to redden.

'Why, certainly, Sir John, if you feel that I can be of any help to you, I should be glad to answer any questions you might have.'

'Why not sit down? I've no doubt you've been on your feet all day. You must indeed be tired.'

'Thank you, sir,' said the butler as he settled into a nicely padded chair. ' 'Tired' just ain't the word for it.' He sighed deeply.

'I was wondering,' said the magistrate, 'if you could — or would — tell me a bit about that altercation in the hall.'

'Ah, well, I'm not a bit surprised to hear you wonder at that. I myself cannot say from one day to the next just what goes on, nor who's in charge.'

'Not you? In every grand home I've entered, 'twas the butler in charge of the staff.'

'That's how it was here, as well — until a few months back.'

'What was it happened then?'

'Oh, all kinds of things. First, Lord Lammermoor became quite sudden uninterested in the house and all that went on here. I don't know what it was, exactly. Maybe it was the war in America took all his attention or maybe it was him getting interested in some woman. There were rumors about him and some actress at the Drury Lane. But as he let the reins slip, so to speak, he didn't hand them over to me, which would have been the only proper thing to do; he just let them drop right out of his hands — and Lady L. picked them up.'

'Is that how it came about that those two villains came to work here?'

'Isn't it? Oh, isn't it indeed? Lady Lammermoor just took it into her head to sack our coachmen. She said they were impertinent. Not likely. Those boys worked here near five years without a murmur. Lord Lammermoor gave them both a good character when they left. But the real damage was done. The two of them — the *new* coachmen — started to work the next day. Now, you can just make a bet that she had the new ones hired even before the old ones was fired.'

'And now?'

'Now everything is just topsy-turvy. They take their orders from her — and only from her. The horses ain't given proper attention. The master gets killed in a way could only be suicide. He had no reason to kill himself! And then Lady L. sends them off to Liverpool to start this doctor on his tour.'

At that, Sir John sat up sharply in his chair. '*They* took him to Liverpool?'

'Oh, indeed they did. Took a long time coming back, too. And in the meantime, they had all of us running up to High Holbourn to get hackney coaches for this one and that one.'

'What are their names, those two?'

'Hyde and Howell is what they told me. Hyde is the little one. They sound like a firm of undertakers, don't they?'

'Just one more question,' said Sir John. 'You were listening at the door, were you not?'

'Yes, I was following Lady L.'s orders. I tried to make it just as plain and open as I could, so you wouldn't take me for a spy in truth. I'd never been told to do such things before.'

'Well, you now have a clear conscience.'

'Her Ladyship wanted to be sure that all told the same story — and 'course that's what they did. You must have counted it a day wasted.'

'Oh no, not entirely.'

Soon as ever we were out of sight and earshot of the great house in Bloomsbury Square, I told Sir John of the note that was passed to me by the chambermaid. He said he was not surprised. We fell to cackling and rubbing our hands in anticipation.

'Shall I out with it and read it now?' I asked Sir John.

'No, just keep a firm hand upon it till we get back to Bow Street,' said Sir John. 'Better to get good news at home.'

(He quoted that last as if it were an ancient saw, a proverb known to all, yet I had never heard such words of wisdom before he uttered them, nor have I heard such since. Quite frankly, I see no sense to it.)

★　★　★

As we entered Number 4 Bow Street, the place was in the usual state of turmoil you would find it in at that particular hour. Crime — and in particular, burglary and theft of all kinds — is most commonly conducted at night. Therefore do the Bow Street Runners go forth at nightfall to challenge the miscreants on their home turf. They hold the line.

A round of hellos greeted Sir John as we arrived. About halfway down the long hall, the night jailer and armorer, Mr. Baker, stopped us with a call from behind the strong room where he maintained his little office.

'Hi! Sir John, I've something for you here.'

The magistrate turned his head in Baker's direction as the latter came forward, waving a letter.

'Ah, Mr. Baker, what have you?'

'Something brought over by one you know

at the Post Coach House, someone name of Evers.'

'Ah yes, he's been helpful before. A letter, is it?'

'Indeed it is. This Evers fellow said he's never seen one to match it for being marked up the way this one is.'

'Marked up in what way?'

'Well, prob'ly Jeremy can do a better job of describing it than I can, but it's got more than just your name on it. Here in one corner it says 'Rush!' — with one of those exclamation marks. And here it says, 'Court Business.' And on the back of it, in big letters, it says, 'Do not delay.' And each one of these *special* messages is in a different-colored ink.'

'Sounds colorful indeed. I wish I could see it properly.' Sir John accepted the letter. He took it and crammed it carelessly into his pocket. Then, thanking him, he gave a nod to me, and we set out once again for his chambers.

The moment he had eased into the chair behind his massive desk, he turned in my direction and ordered me as follows: 'Jeremy, lad, I would like you, first, to close the door that we may have some semblance of privacy. Then will you read to me the billet-doux given you by our Mistress Hardy — was that not her name?'

'So it was, Sir John,' said I, as I began the work of unfolding the notepaper. It was more difficult than you might suppose, reader, for it had been folded so tight and so often that I feared it might come apart in my hand. At last, however, I had it open, and though slightly stained with perspiration, it was quite legible. It had been written out carefully in block letters: MEET ME IN BACK PEW — ST. PAUL'S COVENT GARDEN, NOON MASS, SUNDAY. MUCH TO TELL.

I read the message aloud to Sir John. Frown lines appeared upon his forehead, just above the black silk band which covered his blind eyes.

'What do you make of it?' I asked him.

'Well, it all seems quite straightforward,' said he to me. 'We must wait until Sunday to find out what, if anything, she knows.'

'Probably nothing, eh?'

'Not necessarily. It is not so much in the future, after all — just the day after tomorrow.'

'Ah, so it is,' said I. 'I'd quite forgotten. Perhaps we could both go. You could ask the questions, and I could take down her answers. I could bring her here. That would make it easier for you.'

'No, I believe I have better ways to spend my time. I do, however, have a suggestion on whom you might take with you on Sunday's risky undertaking.'

Risky undertaking? His little joke, surely. 'I should be happy to take your advice in that particular matter, sir. Which of the constables had you in mind?'

'None of them,' said he. 'Our purpose would be best served if you were to bring with you your wife-to-be, Mistress Clarissa Roundtree.'

I'd feared something of this sort. And so, even though I was well aware of how little was my chance of winning, I set out to argue the matter with Sir John: 'But, sir, what could she possibly contribute to this investigation? She has no notion of interrogation techniques. She — '

'Jeremy,' he interrupted, 'I should think it would be obvious to you. First of all, her mere presence with you there in church will be of aid to you.'

'How do you mean that, Sir John?'

'Why, in church, a man without a wife upon his arm would appear half dressed.'

'I have no wife,' said I.

'Oh, Jeremy, please don't quibble. If you have no wife now, you will have in a week or two, and she will be Clarissa.'

'Twelve days,' I muttered.

'There! You see? In any case, there is

another far better reason.'

'And what is that?'

'Women talk more easily to other women — or did you not know that? Had you not noticed?'

'Well, yes,' I admitted. 'I suppose I had.'

'There are likely to be matters that she would broach in the presence of Clarissa of which she would never speak to you.'

'But,' said I, raising one last obstacle, 'what of the hour appointed by Mistress Hardy? Noon Mass? That, after all, is when you hold your court — is it not? I cannot then discharge my duties as clerk, nor can Clarissa take my place if she is, as you describe, there in church upon my arm.'

'Oh, Jeremy, leave off, won't you? You're thinking now as a lawyer in exactly the wrong way! In all my days I've not heard such pettifogging. If neither of my clerks is available, then I believe I shall have to alter the usual time to an earlier one. I am, after all, more flexible than you seem to realize.'

With each sentence, my head drooped a bit lower. I know I should have been glad at the result, for by moving the time both of us got what we said we wanted. But perhaps what I wanted most was to keep Clarissa at arm's distance from Sir John's investigations. If she were allowed close, she would be sure to start giving advice — to me, Sir John, to any who would listen. Nevertheless, there was little doubt that he was right on this matter of females talking more readily to others of their kind. Still, right or wrong, I was embarrassed and somewhat undone by our conversation and wished to beat an orderly retreat as quickly as possible. I said something about my need to organize my notes from the court session. He then dismissed me with a curt nod and sent me on my way.

I got no further than the door to his chambers when, quite unexpected, I was struck by a thought. I turned about to face him and fair shouted my reminder: 'Sir, the letter!'

'Letter? What letter?'

'Why, that one given you by Mr. Baker as we entered.'

'Ah yes, I'd quite forgotten it. Now, where was it I put that?'

'Try your coat pocket,' said I, 'the one on the left.'

He then delved where I had suggested and came up with the parti-colored missive, described in detail by the night jailer; there was no mistaking it. He held it out to me. 'Jeremy,' said he, 'if you would, please? It may be something important.'

And it was. I gave it a quick examination

before opening it and noted its sender. 'It's from the office of the Liverpool magistrate.'

'Why, read it, lad, read it!'

That I did, whilst Sir John, seated at his desk, gave to me his rapt attention.

My dear esteemed and justly famed colleague:

Allow me, first of all, to express my admiration for all that I have heard about you and your brave band of constables who are known, as I understand, as the Bow Street Runners. Indeed, sir, I have heard so much that you have become a sort of model to me in the discharge of my duties here in this far outpost of the West. In this manner, have I often asked myself, What would Sir John Fielding do in this situation or that? And thus guided, have I managed to maintain a remarkable degree of order in this port city. For this I offer you the sincere thanks which is due unto you.

I have ever sought an occasion to write you and give you my thanks in this manner, and now it has come to me. Though the matter of it may be trifling, there is a principle of some importance involved. Allow me to describe the circumstances to you, and I'm sure you will agree.

On an evening but four days past, I was

called away from home by one of my constables and two coachmen in livery. It seemed, or so the coachmen said, that they had been waylaid by a pair of highwaymen outside the city. Their passenger, a Doctor Goldsworthy, quite foolishly pulled from his pockets two pistols, with which he attempted to do battle with the robbers. They shot him down without hesitation, picked over his body for money and valuables, and robbed the coachmen, as well. When we arrived at the site of the affray I discovered a number of things which did make me wonder.

First of all was the body, which was in the roadway, over to one side. When I asked the two of them why one hadn't stayed with the body whilst the other came to fetch me, neither could give an answer which satisfied me.

Secondly, though in telling their tale to me, they had said they had been set upon by two highwaymen, and that this Dr. Goldsworthy had drawn *two* pistols with which to do battle, there was but one to be found at the scene.

Thirdly, though the doctor's body had fallen in such a way as to indicate that the robbers were before him, the entry wound at the back of the doctor's head suggested otherwise. And furthermore, there were powder burns round the wound so as to indicate that he had been shot at very close range.

Finally, when I asked the coachmen to demonstrate just how all this had taken place — who stood where, et cetera, it was soon evident that, given the sequence of events, it would have been very difficult, if not impossible, for things to have happened as they said they had.

With all these doubts in my mind, I could in all conscience do naught but hold them longer in order to question them further. Then, too, it would be necessary to notify their mistress, Lady Lammermoor (*Lord* Lammermoor, it seemed, had just died under unusual circumstances), and ask her to verify their presence here in Liverpool. I explained this to the coachmen and said that I would have to hold them till I heard from Lady Lammermoor. The charge would be leaving a body unattended. Though this sat ill with them, they agreed to come along and wait for her response as long as necessary. Their cooperation lasted only as long as I could keep up the pretense that I was satisfied with the story they had told me. When I began to question them in earnest, they became sullen, withdrawn, and uncooperative.

Whilst out with my constables on a call which lasted well into the night, the prisoners managed to escape. Their names, by the bye, are Thomas Hyde and Henry Howell. They managed to hoodwink the proprietor of the stable into releasing the coach and horses — and off they went! No doubt they are back in London as I write this — or soon will be.

Could you apprehend these two so that they may be returned to Liverpool? It may well be that they are telling the truth, after their fashion, for inconsistent though they may be, they are not contradictory. And it is certainly true that there are highwaymen working the roads in the vicinity of Liverpool. As it now stands, I did not feel that I have sufficient evidence against them at this time so that I might send them forward for trial by the Criminal Court. Indeed, I must admit, too, that they used no violent means in escaping our little jail; they simply tricked the jailer.

Though I have but two constables at my disposal, I should be happy to send one of them along. As I said when I began this long letter, it is the principle of the matter. Don't you agree, sir?

I remain your loyal, admiring, and obedient servant, Daniel Ball, Magistrate, City of Liverpool. P.S.: Just today, following the escape, a letter from Lady Lammermoor arrived. It praised the coachmen in glowing terms and demanded their release.

'Well, Jeremy, what think you of that?'

'What should I say? He offers lavish praise to you, and you deserve it all. I would say, too, that he writes a good, direct English sentence. Do you know this Daniel Ball?'

'Indeed, I've never met the man.'

'Perhaps you should.'

'How do you mean that?' He leaned forward, obviously intrigued.

'You two obviously have hold of two ends of the same horse,' said I. 'Why not invite him here? Then, rather than allow the interrogation to go on by letter ad infinitum, you two magistrates would be able to offer questions together, compare notes, discuss strategy. You often say that it would be a great blessing if magistrates could work together upon cases which call for that sort of treatment. This case does. You'll never have a better opportunity to try your theory than this one.'

★ ★ ★

And so it was settled. We sat down together as of old and composed a letter to Daniel Ball. Though short and direct, it was none the worse for it. In Sir John's name I thanked him for the exceedingly generous praise he had offered. Then did I congratulate him on his analysis of the crime from the scene (all this came direct from the magistrate). The questions and doubts that plagued Mr. Ball were precisely those which would have bothered Sir John. 'As it happens,' I wrote in his stead — 'Hyde and Howell are involved in another homicide here in London, though their part in it has yet to be established. Would it be possible that you might come here so that we might work on the two, compare notes, et cetera. Frankly, I believe you could be a great help to me in every aspect of this strange and most complicated case. I do understand, however, that you are but one man and have only two constables to do your bidding. Thus it may not be possible for you to get away in the manner I have proposed. If this be the case, rest assured that you will have Hyde and Howell delivered safely to you in chains by a pair of my men.'

Sir John heaved a great sigh once he had appended his signature scrawl to this document. 'Now,' said he to me, 'if you hasten upon your way, I believe you may still find the Post Coach House open. Why not do that?'

I was greatly pleased that he had so welcomed my suggestion; so much so that had he asked me to run the letter direct to Liverpool, I believe I should have done so. 'Certainly I will, sir,' said I. 'Now, if you will but pass me your signet ring?'

I was gone in a minute's time.

10

*In which Annie Oakum
survives an attempt
upon her life*

'Twas upon that selfsame Westminster Bridge
from which Lord Lammermoor leaped to his
death that the attack upon Annie took place.
As it happened, Lady Lammermoor had
casually promised to lift the threat she had
made against Annie. (She assured Sir John
that it was naught but a joke made to frighten
the girl, in any case.) Nevertheless, he must
have put little faith in her assurances, for in
spite of them, he kept Constable Will Patley
on the job accompanying Annie each night
from the Drury Lane Theatre to her rooms
just over the bridge in Southwark.

What happened was this: Mr. Patley had
come by for her at the appointed hour and
was waiting for her when she stepped out the
stage door. Annie declared her preference for
a walk that night, and the constable was glad
to oblige. He had enjoyed their nightly

meetings, and even though they had not led where he hoped that they might, he was just pleased to make her acquaintance and enjoyed talking with her as he had not before with any other member of her sex. He found her witty, charming, and quite without pretension. In short, he liked her.

He chose for them a more respectable route — along the Strand, et cetera. It being early Saturday morning, the streets were crowded and as safe as any London streets would ever be of a warm spring night. Both felt justifiably safe; Mr. Patley felt doubly so, because of the two pistols he carried, one in each coat pocket. There were shorter routes than the one they had taken, yet it suited their lighthearted mood that night. Yet when they turned off Parliament Street and onto the bridge Mr. Patley experienced an almost physical change, a shiver, a premonitory chill which put him on the alert quicker than any shout could have done. Of a sudden did he fall silent and watchful.

Annie could not help but notice. 'What is it then, Will?'

'Aw, nothin' much,' said he. 'It's just that I got a peculiar feeling just now.'

'Peculiar? What sort?'

'Oh, like maybe I'd best walk on ahead of you a bit — till we get cross the bridge, anyways. And maybe if us two kept over to the left side of the bridge, so the coaches and wagons are coming towards us.'

'But . . . but why?' she asked. 'Wouldn't it be better if we —'

'Just do it the way I say so for once, won't you?' said he, turning, interrupting, shouting his annoyance at her.

The thought shot then through Mr. Patley's mind that she was reacting awfully strongly to his harsh words: wide-eyed she was, with a look of terror upon her face. But then he saw that she pointed to something ahead of them. He whirled round and saw that a coach-and-four had left its lane and was bearing down direct upon them, gathering speed as it came. He grabbed Annie by the wrist and began running fast as he could, pulling her along.

Annie, on the other hand, was thinking: 'The man has gone completely mad, for he is taking us *toward* that runaway coach and not away from it. What chance have we?'

What Constable Patley had earlier noticed and Annie had not was that atop each of the stanchions supporting the bridge was a shelter of sorts built into the stone. The one to which he led them lay just their side of the coach-and-four that was now hurtling down upon them. They reached the shelter just in time for the constable to throw Annie inside and take up a position protecting her. He had a pistol in his hand. There was barely time enough to shout out a warning before he cocked it and pulled the trigger.

It was an old piece of military ordnance, scraped and nicked, and probably twenty or thirty years old. Nevertheless, it still did well what it was designed to do. When given the option to bear arms, this was the pistol he would choose, invariably and without hesitation.

There was no telling if he had hit his mark or not. Nevertheless, he felt he had. Though the shot was rushed, Mr. Patley knew he had a good eye and a steady arm. It would have hit somewhere in the area of the driver's middle. There were two men sitting up there on the driver's box; he had shot the one on the right. He had also gotten a momentary glimpse of the man inside the coach. He might not have seen him as clear as he did, except the mysterious passenger had his face pressed against the glass of the coach window so that he might miss nothing. Nevertheless, Constable Patley did not recognize him. Annie, however, thought that she did.

This story came to me, for the most part, from Mr. Patley and was given in bits and pieces over the next few days. Annie, I'm sure, must have contributed, too. Still, Mr. Patley and I were sent off by Sir John on the sort of errand that should, I thought, prove interesting.

It was after eleven when Patley and Annie returned from their adventure on the bridge. There was much to tell, and I listened for a short while, but then Sir John suggested that the constable and I hie ourselves off to Mr. Donnelly's surgery on the chance that the man shot by Patley might be there if he were still alive. He treated this matter with some gravity, for he had a strong notion of just who was behind it.

I admit, however, that I was a bit puzzled by his unwillingness to say more.

'Well, who *is* behind it?' I wanted to know.

'I'd rather you found that out by yourself. Then perhaps you'll tell me.' His little joke.

In any case, we two — Mr. Patley and I — were off on a late evening visit to Gabriel Donnelly's surgery. We made just one intermediate stop. At Patley's urging, we stopped off at Mr. Baker's for a pistol that I might take along. Whilst we attended to that, Patley reloaded his pistol. Then, out into the night we went, uneasy at what might lie ahead.

We were not long upon our way when Mr. Patley turned to me and said: 'I hope he don't die.'

I had no need to ask just who it was he meant. He could but have reference to the man he had shot.

'Well . . . yes,' said I. 'It certainly wouldn't be a good thing to have on your conscience.'

'Oh, I ain't worried about that too much. It's just that coach that tried to run us down must've belonged to somebody pretty important. They ain't goin' to like it if I killed their driver.'

'Did you shout a warning?'

'Oh, I did. But with all the noise the horses were making, I doubt they could hear me. Still, they wouldn't have stopped.'

'Why do you say that? How could you tell?'

'Because they were laughin'.'

'Laughing?'

'Oh yes. They were havin' a merry old time up there, so they were — just watching us run for cover.'

'Are you certain?'

''Course I am.'

'Well, be sure to tell Sir John about that.'

'Oh, I will. Don't you worry none.'

For the moment, that was the end of our discussion. Nevertheless, though he told me not to worry, I could tell that he himself was as weighted with worry as I had ever seen him.

As for me, I was quite taken up by the

question of whether the man at whom Constable Patley had shot was Hyde or Howell. They sound like a firm of undertakers — now, who was it had said that? Why, it was none other than the butler at the Lammermoor residence in Bloomsbury. I recalled that he had added that Hyde was the smaller of the two. That suggested to me that Mr. Patley's victim was Howell, a large man by description, the sort who could handle a team of four horses.

Yet it was the smaller rat-faced Hyde who lay upon the narrow bed in Mr. Donnelly's examination room. I had seen him, if only briefly, in the hall of the Lammermoor residence during the coachmen's set-to with the butler. He slept deeply, quite undisturbed when the three of us came trooping into his room. Nevertheless, Mr. Donnelly beckoned us out when Constable Patley commenced speaking in a normal tone.

'Sorry,' said he, once out into the waiting room. 'He was sleeping so well I didn't suppose I'd wake him up.'

'Oh, you probably wouldn't,' said Mr. Donnelly. 'There was no ball in his shoulder. It must have gone straight through. Still, I gave him a stiff draught of laudanum. That should keep him quiet till morning. I take it he's your man?'

'That must be,' said Patley.

'I've even seen him once myself,' said I. 'He certainly looks like the man. What name did he give?'

'Harris, I believe. I've got it written down.'

'Hyde might be closer to the mark,' said I. 'Who brought him in?'

'Oh, a rather tall fellow. Strong he was, with a shifty look. Actually, I'd seen them both before. They brought in Lord Lammermoor.'

'Of course!' said I.

Constable Patley cleared his throat in a plea for attention. Donnelly caught it and turned to him.

'Yes, Constable,' said he. 'What was it you wanted?'

'Beggin' your pardon, Mr. Donnelly, but you said the wound was in his shoulder?'

'That's correct — the lower right shoulder, just above the chest. It was a lucky shot — lucky, that is, for this fellow Harris, or Hyde, or whatever his name. An inch or less lower, and it would have nicked one of his critical arteries.'

'Well, I usually hit what I aim at, and I aimed lower than that.'

Remembering Mr. Patley's unease of a few minutes ago regarding Hyde's wound and whether or not it might prove fatal, I could not help but laugh at the sudden change in him.

'Forgive me, Mr. Patley,' said I to him, 'but you sang quite a different song on the way here, did you not?'

'Oh, I did. It's true. Like most, if you take one worry away from me, I'll find something else to trouble me in no time at all.'

'All right, you two, I know not how you intend to settle this, but I intend to go back to bed whilst there is still a bit of the night left to sleep in. I take it you intend to make a prisoner of that fellow in the next room?'

I nodded.

'Well then, you have a couple of choices: You may either attempt to wake him up, though with all the laudanum he has in him now, you may not have much success at that. Nor would he likely be able to make the march to Number Four Bow Street if indeed you managed to get him to his feet.'

'You spoke of a couple of choices,' said I.

'So I did. The more practical thing to do might be simply to wait until the man wakes. You could sleep upon chairs, or stretch out upon the floor, if you've a mind. But please don't tell me that you'll return for your prisoner in the morning, for now that I know of what he is capable, I'm convinced the only way to handle him is roughly and with a pistol in hand. And if you believe that cowardly of me, I urge you to remember that I have a wife sleeping in the room down the hall from my examination room, and I want no violence round her. You understand, I'm sure.'

There was obviously but one choice, reader, and we chose it — Mr. Patley curled up in a chair, and I stretched out upon the floor.

I must confess that I believe I slept well, but I came awake abruptly to the sound of voices. From the position and weakness of the sunlight from the windows, I had a sense that it was still quite early, though I had not yet opened my eyes. I was reluctant to do so, for hearing as much as I had in the first minute or two, I realized that Mr. Patley and I, as well as the Donnellys in the back room, were all in great danger.

The voice of him who threatened us all was as deep and rasping as any I'd ever heard. It belonged not to Gabriel Donnelly, nor to Constable Patley, nor even to the opium-thralled Hyde who was probably still asleep; and so, of course, it had to belong to none but his accomplice, the enraged Howell who had burst into Mr. Donnelly's surgery, only to learn that his friend was now prisoner. As I opened my eyes I saw that Mr. Patley had his hands outstretched, being relieved of his pistol. Then taking leave of caution, I came quietly to my feet, spying my pistol on the table but a short distance from Howell's reach.

My next move proved near fatal; here then is what occurred:

In my deepest voice, I called out to the intruder: 'I must warn you that you are interfering with constables who are under the direct command and protection of Sir John Fielding, Magistrate of Westminster and the City of London!'

'Bugger, you fool!' he shouted. He swung his pistol toward me as I dove for his legs. (I failed to prevent him from clubbing me on the head, which did cost me my senses for a moment, as well the chance to retrieve my weapon.)

After a moment my head cleared as I spied my pistol clutched in his other hand. My thoughts raced. Was I never to see Clarissa again?

'Ya make a move on me again, chum,' said he, 'and yer as good as dead.'

I said nothing, merely stayed down, trying to think how I might detain him.

'Ever seen anyone with his brains blown out his head?' he taunted. 'Ya get a gush of blood so sudden that ya never know what hit ya.'

'I believe you'd do it, right enough,' said I to him. 'You need not convince me. Only one as stupid as you would do such a thing.'

'I ain't stupid,' he snarled. 'I kilt the only witness against me.'

'And now you'll have more witnesses if you kill us.'

'What'cha mean by sayin' that?'

'There's voices in the hall and footsteps . . . You'll have a lot of killing to do, and that won't be easy.'

At that, Howell, quite nonplussed by my remark, made his move on Mr. Patley, whipping his pistol cross the constable's face and saying: 'Fetch me friend and carry him outside. Put him in the carriage before I finish the lotta you!'

Here then is what followed: Mr. Patley lifted Hyde off the table, carrying him to the door as Howell simultaneous opened it. The two stood in the doorway now. I saw that Hyde was near awake. I rose slowly to my feet, noting that Howell moved with a limp and had a cloth tied round his middle.

Of a sudden a shot was fired, and Constable Patley dove back into the room, hitting the floor just as the hackney raced off. The shot summoned the Donnellys. There was no time to explain, however.

'Hurry, Jeremy,' said Mr. Patley . . . 'I ain't waitin'!'

Ever pressed to see a man run faster, Constable Patley was out in front motioning at a wagon coming in our direction:

'In the name of Sir John Fielding, magistrate of London, surrender your wagon,' ordered the constable.

The driver would have none of his demands, but Constable Patley pulled the reins from the teamster who then leapt down to confront his foe, insisting that his wagon was in no wise for hire, pointing to a coffin that lay in the wagon bed. Paying no heed to the driver, we climbed unto the wagon box and drove off, leaving the angry fellow at the steps of the Donnelly surgery.

Mr. Patley whipped the reins something fierce. The leathers snapped in the air as I spied our quarry in the distance, diminishing along Hart Street. Our horses responded at a gallop just as I noticed the blur of a wheel nearing cans of milk set at curbstone. Then, of a sudden, I felt the wagon shudder and heard a crash. I turned quickly round and glanced the wheel hitting the cans like tenpins. But Patley's eyes were fixed on his prey (truth be told, his gaze was focused as if entranced or possessed by the spirit of the jockey Deuteronomy Plummer).

Hyde and Howell skidded left onto Peter Street, which would lead them across the High Holbourn, direct into Covent Garden.

'Faster — faster!' shouted Will Patley, mad with chase.

We were nearing the turn where they'd made to the south. Mr. Patley jerked the reins to redirect the horses into the lane ahead. The wagon shook, and the strap holding the coffin split with the force of the turn — skating it into the railing. I held to the wagon box as tight as I could to prevent myself from slipping, which I knew would impact upon Constable Patley so sudden as to throw him from the wagon unto the ground beneath our wheels. I held my breath briefly and when I recovered I saw that we now were closing upon the forward hackney.

Then, reader, what now occurred was this: Crisscrossing our path, bearing trays of bread, came two lads, their eyes gone wide as they sprang out of the wagon's path, dashing their loads against the sides of our conveyance. And 'twas in this stretch of a moment, for a reason then unknown to me, that I was overcome with a terrible sensation — I could not bring myself to demand that Mr. Patley pull back the reins to stop this pursuit most immediate. Fear overcame my reasoning. And there upon the wagon box I sat, like a lump, chilled by this physical change. Mr. Patley noticed not my condition, though I was glad to hear his voice cheer as the lane did open up where it would cross the larger artery of the High Holbourn.

Ahead, not far apace was Howell, whipping his horse into the great artery as riders and horses reared, their hooves flailing the air; passersby scattered and a coach-and-four near slammed into a building to avoid colliding with the hackney. Then I spied that the hackney had now disappeared down a dark lane, on the far side of the highway.

As we approached the great avenue most rapid, my senses revived enough so that I could not imagine how we might escape colliding with the traffic ahead. I pointed to the nearest side lane as Mr. Patley snapped the reins hard. And then of a sudden a thought did finally reach my brain: Cupping my hands over my mouth I yelled in the strongest voice, 'Fire! . . . Fire! . . . Fire! . . . '

A pedestrian scrambled out of the way of our vehicle, brandishing his umbrella as if to break our necks with it. Then Mr. Patley did at last jerk the reins, slowing, just as a dray wagon loaded with kegs of beer came full into our direction. And though Mr. Patley did all he could to swerve, we caught the rear of the dray, flipping it over and hurtling its cargo unto the road where the teamsters lay dazed.

We'd crossed the broad road unto Drury Lane. Whatever we'd gained on the hackney was gone. Yet Constable Patley's rage had not abated, and he pressed on.

'Gardyloo!' a voice warned. Mr. Patley did manage to avoid that indignity and said: 'Trust me, lad, we are gaining.'

Following the hackney onto Russell Street, we did seem to be gaining. Covent Garden was ahead . . . streaming with humanity. When we entered the market square, there was naught but chaos awaiting . . . stalls ripped asunder, women and children wide-eyed with terror. I grabbed the reins from Constable Patley and reined to a halt. Then in the distance, the hackney disappeared into Floral Street.

I sighed, admitting to myself how weary I was. I was all in turmoil, wanting nothing better than to go to my own bed. Yet that, I feared, would be sometime in the future. It appeared that we were in for a long day of it.

★　★　★

Thus went we to Bloomsbury Square to return what we'd taken from the teamster we now did hope to find. Therefore, with naught but trepidation, we approached the Donnelly

316

surgery. However, we knew with confidence that Gabriel and Molly were unharmed and that they would greet us with warmth, since our failures had come after our sudden exit from the surgery and not from before.

I gave three stout thumps upon the door, and in a moment it opened. I then did look with pleasure upon the face of Gabriel Donnelly. 'Twas the face of a friend whom I would soon greatly miss when he and Molly would depart London for their new life together in Dublin.

'Come in, lads,' said Mr. Donnelly with a look of concern writ upon his brow.

'We've naught but a moment or two,' said I with a most serious mien.

'I believe I know already what you've come searching for . . . or rather whom it is you wish to find. Am I correct in my assumption?'

'Why . . . yes, sir . . . your intuition is as good as your skill as a medico.'

'Alas, praise shall get you where you'd like to be,' said he smiling . . . 'which may be into my Molly's kitchen . . . Again, am I correct?'

'Sadly, I must decline your invitation. That's the truth of it,' said I abruptly, knowing full well that Sir John would need to be apprised of Hyde and Howell's escape and other matters . . . 'Nevertheless, can you tell me if you've seen the man whose wagon Mr.

Patley and I . . . borrowed?' said I haltingly.

'Do you mean my fellow countryman?'

'Well . . . yes. I did not know that he was an Irishman, but I'm much pleased if you've already spoken with him.'

'Well, perhaps I can help you there, lad,' said the medico, rather pleased with himself.

And thus Mr. Patley, who stood sullenly throughout our brief discussion, did follow behind me as Mr. Donnelly led the way to the couple's kitchen next their quarters off the side of the surgery.

'Twas Irish-blooded luck that did prevail in our favor! For there at Molly's good table sat the teamster, now devouring a plate of her famous scones. And with the sight of that, I breathed a sigh of gratitude and a gasp of hope that he, at the least, would hear our apology; and that with his increase of appetite, so might there be in reverse a slackening of the man's temper.

★ ★ ★

And so it was that Mick Spiker (as was his name) did happily agree to accept whatever compensation might be granted to pay for damages to his wagon and costs for delaying the deliverance of his solemn cargo. Both Mr. Patley and myself were satisfied (though our stomachs were not) that we had begun our atonement in the proper manner. And so we bade good-bye to the Donnellys and Mr. Spiker and set out on our walk homewards.

★ ★ ★

We entered Number 4 Bow Street to the strong aroma of breakfast. I knew that after telling the tale we had to tell, we would not be asked to join the feast that Clarissa had prepared for Sir John and Lady Fielding.

This is what occurred:

Mr. Patley began in earnest to give his report.

At first, Sir John cut him off in midsentence, so infuriated was he by what he heard. But he let him continue until Sir John's jaw could drop no further and he said to his wife, 'Kate, I do believe that at this moment I will need help to stand.'

'Jack, you cannot be serious?'

Clarissa covered her face with her hands.

Then followed this:

'Jeremy,' said Sir John in an exasperated tone, 'I take it you were aboard the wagon that Mr. Patley seized?'

'Yes, sir. As was also the coffin in the wagon bed.'

'The coffin?' shouted he.

I gave no response. Only a look of chagrin.

'Sir, there was no time to remove it.'

'This is your defense? . . . '

'Is that all you have to say, Jeremy?'

'No, sir. Certainly not.'

It was then that Constable Patley did speak up on my behalf, taking blame upon himself for pursuing the villains in such a way.

'Sir John,' said I, 'I have more to tell.'

'Yes, then out with it!'

'There are the damages to report as well — some we know of, some we do not yet know of,' I stammered.

(Reader, I had never before known Sir John to gnash his teeth. He was at boiling point.)

'Mr. Patley, your job should now be to find the owner of the wagon and obtain from him an accounting of the damages to his property and for his time as well.'

'Sir John, that has been done, sir.'

'Well, then fine,' grunted he.

Then having had his say, he clapped together his hands, signaling an end to it, and rose from the table.

Lady Fielding had no need to assist him. She did glare at me most displeased. 'I think it best for you and Jack to settle this matter alone in his study. Please help him up the stairs and so forth,' said Lady Fielding emphatically.

'I do not wish help, Kate. But I do want Jeremy to come with me.' Sir John took leave, moving with a slight limp, which was his wont from the time he had sustained an injury to his left hip on route to Great Mongeham.

Then, as Mr. Patley and I exited the kitchen, I noted that Lady Fielding's face bore an expression of concern that I'd never seen before, and Clarissa did shake her head from side to side. Though she did not look into my eyes, I knew she was disappointed in me. Would I not ever meet her expectations? thought I.

And so Sir John and I repaired to his study, where we sat a moment or two in silence and darkness until he asked me to light a few candles: ''Twould be better that you observe me as we have our talk,' said he.

'Jeremy. Listen — and listen well. There will also be damages to vehicles yet to be assessed. Write down what you and Constable Patley have reported and what you have not, and we will petition the Lord Chief Justice for a grant — perhaps my dear Kate can call upon a contact of hers to defray the costs of your and Mr. Patley's misadventure. We will see what can be done . . . ' He then sighed heavily and said:

'Now I will put this to you as best as can — you must take control of your wits. Good judgment is the essence of what you will make of yourself and 'tis your judgment that seems to have been impaired in some way or other. You seem to be ever so frenetic these past days.' Here he paused, clasping his hands, shaking them stiffly at me as he said: 'Tell me — have you also the wish to burn yourself alive? No!' he bellowed, 'do not even answer that.' I sat in disbelief at what I'd just heard. (Reader, 'twas not Clarissa who broke my request for secrecy upon the matter. And still to this day, I do not know how he learned of my escapade — but to say this: The Blind Beak had his sources.)

'Now tell me this: Why did you not demand Will Patley bring that chase to an end when surely you realized the danger — not only to those in your path but to yourselves.'

'Well, I . . . I.'

'Speak!' he then did thunder. 'You sound as if something has you by the tail. What is the matter with you, lad?'

'Sir, it is fear,' admitted I.

'Fear? Of what? There's no logic in that. If it was fear you had, you should have then stopped.'

'Yes, of course. I know that, sir.'

'Then what could you fear more than accelerating towards your death as that calamity near caused. Surely you do not take pleasure in such?' What an odd question, thought I. Though I had not the wherewithal to cobble together a proper response to it.

Thus Sir John eased off and said in his even-tempered fashion, 'Yes, that's it. I believe that is the reason.'

'What, sir? What is the reason?'

'Be patient a moment and I will tell you,' said Sir John, his lips poised, moving silently. And then: 'You have heard it told before how it happened that I lost my sight. Have you not?'

'Yes, Sir John. 'Twas the siege of Cartagena, in the war with the French and Spanish.'

'Just so. I was a young midshipman charged with duty to country and to my mates. And it was from one such mate, a dead marine, that I took his fallen musket and fired with it at the fort. The great flash from that overloaded musket was what did blind me. And though I had some sight in my left eye through the battle, I lost the rest of it to the maggots during the voyage back to England. Are you following me, lad? You seem not at all with me.'

'Sir, I am listening. But truth be told, I was caught in a memory of something else.'

'And what, pray tell, was that memory?

Give it me precisely!'

"'Twas, sir, of my father's sorry end . . . when last I did see him alive. And I do admit to frequent lapses of this kind, at times most recent, whilst I'm overcome with thoughts of my past. Oddly, these memories appear like ghosts . . . 'tis as if I'm standing in their midst elsewhere altogether — I suppose, not exactly 'together' — so it seems, does it not, sir?' said I, puzzling at what I'd described.

'Jeremy, lad, do you recall when this curious effect beset you?'

'No . . . sir . . . not exactly — I am certain, however, that I did discover a degree of fear that I'd not ever afore experienced when Dr. Goldsworthy ordered Clarissa to shoot to kill me.'

'So then, perhaps it is I who is to blame for these changes that have come over you — though surely not directly. Nonetheless, 'twas I who sent you to 'restrain' Clarissa, and after all I did naught to prevent him from carrying on with his damnable experiment, or demonstration, as he would call it . . . and now I wonder — could it have produced an aftereffect upon your brain, so subtle that you were and are not even now conscious of it?'

And so there we sat both thinking upon Sir John's theory. Then he said this to himself:

'To unblind the hoodwinkt world.' And at hearing this I looked at him in bewilderment.

'Sir. Beg pardon. But what do you mean by that?'

''Twas a quotation from Mr. John Milton.'

'Oh,' said I, still perplexed.

And then he explained: 'You've been hoodwinked, lad. 'Twould be far more difficult to hoodwink a blind man than to do it to one who can see.' Sir John then paused briefly.

'Tell me this, Can you remember any signal from Dr. Goldsworthy that could be construed to confuse you?'

'No, sir, I cannot. I do not recall even a word that you did not also hear from where you sat. Though . . . Then these thoughts did flash through my brain . . . '

'What is it, Jeremy? Tell me, please!' said Sir John with urgency.

'My eyes were squinted so that I could keep watch over Clarissa. And though I did not perceive Dr. Goldsworthy's lips to move, there came a muttering of sorts — nondescript — from what I now believe was his throat. I thought at the time 'twas naught but nonsense. That it was not I who was entranced, 'twas Clarissa, though a gnawing of sickness did pass to my stomach, which I dismissed as nothing at all. But the truth is, sir, I have the queasies even now.'

'I see,' said Sir John. 'I wish I could interrogate Dr. Goldsworthy. That man who called himself a medico and a man of science. Pish-posh! How many men of science do you suppose have broken their oath — if such an oath there be. Remember, lad, they are men of science — not much better and no worse than men in most other fields. I believe that you, as well as Mr. Docker, were invited onto the stage to play the fool. And if Goldsworthy did with malice — as I assume — influence your mind in some way, we must be clever to discover what this was about and why he did it. No doubt it has to do with Lady Lammermoor as well. And I must add that it is the tragic incident on Westminster Bridge that's getting us both 'down at the mouth,' figuratively speaking, don't you think?'

'Yes, sir. I do see your point.'

'Now then . . . Hmmm,' Sir John murmured. 'Let's see — where was I? I seem to be taking one of those digressive excursions not unlike Clarissa's wont.' I smiled, and Sir John made a chuckling laugh.

He then continued: 'For now, I can only help you in practical ways to undo what was done to you. We do not know if it was 'animal magnetism' used upon you. Nevertheless, if a condition persists 'twould be wise to seek advice from Mr. Robert Levet, who is Dr. Johnson's good friend and adviser on matters of health. He is not a medico; however, he has experience with 'nervous conditions' — such as they are called. And I am told that he's a fine fellow.'

'Very well, sir. I shall remember that. Thank you.'

'Nothing at all, nothing at all,' said he. Then raising his brow a bit and rubbing his chin with a slight grin on his lips, Sir John put this comment forward: 'I am reminded by my own words of a moment ago of something that Dr. Johnson once said at table to Clarissa whilst offering her advice on improving her skills as a writer. Do you remember what it was?'

'Frankly, I do not, sir. I do recall an argument — of sorts — that she had with Dr. Johnson at his home quite aways back, but nothing on the order of what you've suggested.'

'No matter. Perhaps you were helping Annie in the kitchen whence he delivered it. Never mind, lad. There's no contest in this — 'Twas simply this: He said that 'gloom and silence produce composure of mind and concentration of ideas.' And I believe this to be true. It is a worthwhile pursuit for one who must use his head in his life's work. Just as you will soon need to do, more and more. You've not forgotten, have you, that your examinations for the law will take place soon after your wedding?'

'Of course I have not forgotten, sir.'

'Then we will need to get back to our work and prepare. You have a bright future that awaits you, Jeremy . . . ' (and he did pound his fist once upon the table so hard it shook) — 'and I will see to it that I give you all I have to give to make it so.'

(Reader, and when he had finished these words, I did spy from where I sat more than one tear wash down his face from beneath the black band that did cover the spaces that were once his eyes.)

'Now again a question: Do you fear death?'

I waited naught to give my response: 'Yes, sir. I do.'

'And that is proper for a man of your years. Jeremy, your own fear reminds me of my own, which did not leave me 'til darkness took the place of my sight. 'Tis the unknown that causes the fear within us. Do you agree?'

'Yes. That does make sense, though I do not readily accept it.'

'You are correct. It is more complicated than that. It may take you far longer to learn than the years I have to live. But you will learn to accept it, and when you do, it will not weaken you but will make you stronger for it.' We sighed together at what he'd just spoken in that room. And though he could not see it, he heard that I did hold back sobs, which I would not allow myself to release.

He waited for my composure to return.

'As you know, I practice no religion, though I believe the Almighty exists. I have no use for clergymen, though there is one I consider to be wise. Do you remember Rabbi Gershon of the Hasidim?'

'Yes I do, Sir John. He called me by my Jewish name, from the prophet Jeremiah. And he did once say a blessing to help me to take good care of you — for he said that you were a good man — a good man in a bad time, as all good men have been in all past times.'

'I'm not surprised, though flattered I am. I hope I can continue to live up to his words. But it is you, Jeremy, who has lived up to his wish and blessing — for you have taken good care of me, lad — better than you realize. You have acted bravely on my behalf and continue to watch my every step. But now — you must look after yourself more than ever before. Do you understand?'

(Reader, I did not need reply, for he had said this with as deep and solemn a tone as ever I'd heard.)

'Allow me to go on a bit further and then

leave this matter,' said he as he continued without interruption. 'When the rabbi spoke with us in his house of worship, I did not then full comprehend his storytelling. Now I do; he wished to give comfort as I do now to you:

'All men die — though that in itself,
is no cause for mourning.
For him who dies it may be a cause for
   rejoicing.
Who can tell?''

Thus I left Sir John alone in his study whilst I retreated towards the kitchen, passing Clarissa along the way, carrying cloth that was soon to be cut into the dress that she would wear on our wedding day. I received no greeting or question of concern from her; instead, there was naught but suspicion in her eyes as she jerked back her head in a gesture of disapproval. I wondered what had caused this hostility in her manner? Perhaps Lady Fielding's anger had given rise to her own. I had too much to think about to worry over such gossip. So I put it out of my mind for the moment, knowing that Sir John would speak with his wife on my behalf and harmony would prevail in our little household.

And to my surprise and delight, there upon

the kitchen table Clarissa had set out for me a plate of bread and drippings. I poured myself a cup of tea and there as I sat and chewed, I spied a manuscript, quite thick, tidily arranged at a corner of the table. I knew that it could only be Clarissa's 'book' that I'd so eagerly awaited to read — though perhaps, in truth, my eagerness was but to see how I'd been portrayed. But on this morning, all but my own worries were of importance. Still — my attention was drawn to the pages which lay before me. I scrutinized the title page, boldly faced in Clarissa's elegant hand: *The Orphan's Quest*. I liked that. She had a way with words (and still does!). Though she'd not taken Dr. Johnson's advice in taking a masculine pen name . . . There it was: By Clarissa Roundtree. Plucky as ever. Yet I had to agree with Sir John that she was proof incarnate that women are, in ways uncounted, equal, if not superior to men.

I began to read: 'In that corner of our kingdom known as the West Midlands, there is a village in Staffordshire named Lichfield, where there lived an honest yet poor family. Their name was Turnwood . . . ' I lifted several more pages but found that by page fifty-seven, 'Mary Frances Turnwood' was yet an infant! And knowing that I had no time to spend 'questing' for my entrance into the tale,

I placed the manuscript into its proper shape and finished my bread.

Just then Clarissa ran toward me, hugging me from behind with all her might, kissing my aching head. 'Oh, Jeremy, you have endured such a terrible morning. I am so sorry for your trouble!'

'Thank you for that,' said I, relieved that perhaps Sir John had already calmed the waters for me.

'Jeremy. Did you see? Look! Look!' referring to her manuscript.

'Yes indeed I have, 'Mistress Mary Turnwood.''

She then gave me a smile, pleased that I'd noted coincidence in her heroine's name.

'It's quite right to alter a name as I have when the story approaches near to truth.' It was clear by the tone in her voice that she wished reassurance from me that she'd nonetheless been clever to disguise the name.

'But who could mistake it? Round-tree and Turn-wood?'

'Ooohhh . . . You're making fun of me, aren't you, Jeremy? I think my novel is very good and strong, full of true feelings and sentiments. It's sad, then very romantic — just as life should be.'

'I'd like to skip the sad part for now, if I may.'

'But it brings such joy when obstacles are overcome! Does it not?' She was irrepressible, almost dancing; I was letting her down, no doubt. But I simply could not keep up with her energy.

'I shall read it soon, Clarissa. I promise you.'

She must have sensed my lack of enthusiasm, for then she said: 'After today you'll have to beg me to see it.'

She then gathered the manuscript together and prepared to march off with it. Nevertheless I did not allow her to fume at me for naught.

'Clarissa, please do not be offended. I've had a most unsettling talk with Sir John. And I must not fail him in his investigation. He needs me now more than ever, though he says otherwise. In fact, tomorrow he has asked you to accompany me to St. Paul's where we are to interrogate Mistress Hardy, a chambermaid at the Lammermoor residence. Though Sir John did already question her, she passed me a note which indicates that she has something of great importance to tell. And Sir John believes, wholeheartedly, that women talk more freely when another is present. I insist you help us in this way. Do you not remember how important your role was in the capture of the gang of smugglers in Deal?

Surely you remember the ghost of Great Mongeham?' And with that she did break into a full-throated laugh. Smiling at me with all her charm, she did make my morning brighten somewhat.

The rest of the afternoon did pass in the routine of chores of the magistrate's office, those judged incomplete and needing disposal in the relative calm of the weekend. I took down several letters for Sir John, drafted and filed his writs, and counted out sums of foreign banknotes found by a jailer (abandoned by a pickpocket in one of the holding cells). Therefore the day had not entirely been a disaster so that my mood upped from doom to mere gloom. I decided then to spend the remaining hours of daylight reviewing some of the more interesting cases that had been brought before Sir John in the time previous to my appearance in his courtroom at age thirteen.

I was immersed in a file which dealt with the 'Begging-letter imposters' — a fascination of mine still in these years after I read law with Sir John Fielding. London is proverbial the world over for the number and ingenuity of the tricks which are daily practiced in it; but perhaps there is no department of roguery in which a greater amount of ingenuity is displayed than in that of begging.

One case which drew my interest at that moment involved a man who claimed to be both blind and lame in one letter and in the next an orphan seeking asylum in a noble family. He had been quite ingenious in his capacity to fake his afflictions; however, he wrote one too many begging letters to a nobleman who decided to investigate the fellow who had an entire retinue of clerks in his service as well as a number of imposters who had entered with him into a sort of partnership. Sir John's file revealed the success with which he could change his personal appearance. In the course of one day he could assume and sustain, with admirable effect, seven or eight different characters; so that those who saw him, and were conversing with him, at ten o'clock in the morning might have been in his company at twelve, and never had the slightest suspicion of the fact. It was Sir John who put an end to his career when blind William did fail to perform in a manner befitting a blind man.

All things considered, I was pleased that the investigations I had participated in had, in so many ways, been far the better and more stimulating than those I'd just read through. And though the Lammermoor case was perhaps the most mysterious yet, I was confident that it would be solved.

As I was returning the file, I heard a racket in the entrance to Sir John's chambers. I made haste to the spot and witnessed this: Constable Baker was in heated discussion with a man I recognized as the secretary to Bishop John Talley. And next to this fellow stood a woman dressed in the oddest fashion. In truth she looked like one of those characters from the file that I'd been reading not but a minute past.

She was portly as a man, with youthful face, though whiskered; she wore a kilt with man's blouse, was sporting a wig the color of straw, and held to a staff that was gilt to a degree I'd never seen before. Just as I began to think her face familiar, she ripped off the wig to reveal Bishop John Talley: 'I require a change of clothing most immediate,' demanded he. 'I must see Sir John Fielding at once!' I did spy several constables engaged in merrymaking (one did a little Scottish gigue to a tune that Constable Sheedy whistled). Bishop Talley's wish was nevertheless granted, and I escorted him upstairs to Sir John's study. I knocked on the door and was asked to enter alone. This did not please the Bishop, whose brow was now speckled with sweat. I entered and did apprise Sir John of the situation, lit a few candles for the Bishop, and bade him to enter.

Bishop Talley heaved a sigh as he sat down and commenced his tale of an attack upon his person by two armed culprits, whilst a third waited in a nearby coach.

'As you know, I sometimes feel the need to get out and stretch my legs a bit, especial after long, contentious meetings. And so it was that I was strolling about Lambeth gardens round two when a coach did begin a rapid approach, gaining momentum in my direction. Faster and faster it came, until 'twas but for the grace of God that I was able to step — jump — into a hedge to protect myself from those madmen!'

'Your Grace,' said Sir John, 'was this a coach-and-four or a smaller conveyance?'

''Twas a coach-and-four, sir. May I go on?'

'By all means, do.'

'I fear that I know not how to convey what happened to me without it sounding a mockery!'

'Let me be the judge of that, Your Grace. Please relate the facts,' said Sir John, a bit snappish.

''Twas then that the coach halted and the driver climbed down. Another exited the coach door. Then both scoundrels made for me, aiming pistols and giving shout at me.

They were perhaps attempting to fright me into tripping. But I kept afoot, I did, and retreated as quick as I could behind the tree nearest me just as I heard a shot fired in my direction. I looked back, and what I saw was quite preposterous. Though they were attempting to give chase upon me, both of these would-be assassins appeared to be lame as they hobbled and staggered forward a few paces, requiring each the other for support. Once more they fired and then reloaded their weapons, but made no progress in my direction.'

'Bishop Talley. Have you been invested with your title?' asked Sir John.

'No, sir. That is for Monday a week. There will be a celebration afterward.'

'Then it is possible this attempt on your life was to prevent your becoming the next Lord Lammermoor.'

'Or 'twas an attack by the bloody Papists, in order to disrupt our conference and its plans.'

'Can you give me a description of your assailants in greater detail?' asked Sir John.

'Ah . . . 'twere like Punchello and Puncherino.'

'Do you follow me, Bishop?' said Sir John, his patience wearing, 'Give it me, man! Plain and direct.'

'Well, then . . . I suppose the driver of the

coach was rather tall and thin. His voice was churlish. The other villain was quite short and had the look of a rodent.'

'Twas then I interrupted: 'Sir John, may I question the Bishop?'

'Why, yes, Jeremy,' said Sir John.

'Your Grace,' said I confidently. 'Could you describe where on their bodies your assailants were wounded?'

Bishop Talley then turned toward me: 'Well, perhaps the taller of the two was wounded in the belly. He did have a light-colored cloth wrapped round his middle.'

The Bishop paused a moment just as I noticed a look of surprise appear on Sir John's face. Then continuing: 'And the shorter man had been wounded in his upper part. I know this since his shoulder bore a proper bandage.'

'Sir John. I have a theory. May I summon Constable Patley?'

'Please do, lad.' And I did just that, returning in no more than a minute. We entered the study together, and Sir John spoke immediate.

'Constable Patley, you will oblige Jeremy by answering his questions.'

'Yes, sir,' said Mr. Patley as he turned to face me.

'Mr. Patley,' said I, 'in the course of the

attack upon Annie Oakum and yourself, how many shots did you fire?'

'One. I had no time to reload or draw another pistol.'

'And where was your shot aimed?'

'At the man's middle.'

'Which man's middle?'

''Twas the taller one. He was the man with the reins, driving down upon us all a-fury.'

'And do you always hit your mark, Mr. Patley?'

'Without fail. It's perplexin' indeed, since the man in Mr. Donnelly's surgery was wounded in the shoulder.'

'Let's leave that point for the moment. Yours is a military issue, and is it not powerful?'

''Tis indeed, Jeremy . . . Mr. Proctor. Others may be more so today, some less.'

The Bishop interrupted: 'I say, here, if you don't mind, I should like to put a move on things so that I can proceed on my way. I've a pressing engagement this evening, and I do not wish to be late!'

Sir John (making a dismissive motion): 'Bishop Talley,' said he, 'assuming that you did not imagine this attempt upon your life, I must ask you to remain until we have finished with our meeting here. There may well be some intrinsic importance to these details which we seek.'

Bishop Talley was henceforth silent.

I resumed my questioning of Mr. Patley: 'How close were the two men atop the coach?'

'They were leaning each into the other. The coach was moving most rapid.'

'Now, as exact as you can remember, can you describe where the coach was when you fired off your shot?'

'In truth, I remember its position well. I believe that near the railing of Westminster Bridge there is a row of kerbstones which marks a small raised footway for those crossing the bridge afoot. The coach wheels hit unto the kerbstones just as I fired my pistol.'

Thus I said to Sir John: 'Sir, I have a theory of the wounding of the culprits, who do appear to be the same men who attacked Bishop Talley. May I continue?'

'Let us hear it.'

'According to Mr. Donnelly, no ball was to be found in Thomas Hyde's shoulder. I believe Constable Patley fired at the coach just as it jumped abruptly, hitting the kerbstones. It was then that Hyde was briefly thrown in front of Howell so that the shot passed through his shoulder and struck or did graze Howell in his middle, where it was aimed. Therefore, the difference in their heights accounts for the position of their wounds. I believe that no other explanation will suffice.'

'Ahhh . . . it is good to hear your powers of reason at work. In that spirit, have you heard tell of 'Occam's razor'?'

'No I have not, sir, though I've heard this expression before.'

'It is a principle of logic dating from William of Occam. It requires that in scientific reasoning, the least number of assumptions should be made, entities or conceptions should not be multiplied unnecessarily, and that, usually, simplicity should be the guiding principle. It has been claimed, as a basis for this principle, that the same simplicity operates in the natural world . . . that Nature achieves its end by the simplest effective means. Mr. Patley, if you could perfect this technique you've developed you might again employ it when necessary,' said Sir John with a hint of a smile. 'Never mind, 'twas but a bad joke. Bishop Talley, if there is nothing further for you to tell, you may leave. I will continue my investigation into this matter. However, use caution in your goings and comings, since we do not know the whereabouts of these men; though whoever was sitting in the coach knows exactly where they are hiding.'

'Thank you, Sir John . . . There is but one other thing.'

'And what is that?'

"Tis the matter of my appearance,' said the Bishop.

'If you mean your clothing, it matters not to me what you are dressed in,' said Sir John in a curt manner. 'Surely the Runners will see to the matter.'

'I charge you, Mr. Patley, with escorting the Bishop and his assistant to Lambeth Palace.'

'Yes, Sir John.'

I remained with Sir John awhile as we continued to discuss matters pertaining to the Lammermoor case.

"Tis tomorrow that you meet with Mistress Hardy?'

'Yes, Sir John.'

'And Clarissa will accompany you?'

'Yes. That has been arranged.'

'Jeremy, I am puzzled by the twists and turns of this case. There is no doubt that the threat upon Bishop Talley is to be taken seriously. Who else but his stepmother and brother would wish him dead? Surely it had to be one or the other waiting in the coach. We are running out of time, and I fear that Lady Lammermoor will soon again pounce if we do not succeed in catching her in the act.

If only I could lay a trap for her. What else can we do?' He sighed and lapsed once more into silence for a moment. 'There is little chance today. Let us leave it rest for the day.'

There was one more matter, quite unrelated: 'I wonder, Jeremy, if you could go to the apothecary shop before dinner and get from him some preparation to bind my bowels. I've been troubled all day ever since breakfast.'

11

*In which we come
face-to-face
with an evil woman*

Next morning — the Sunday that Clarissa
and I were to meet with Abigail Hardy
— began early. I was awakened by a loud
rapping upon the door of Number 4 Bow
Street. That night I had lain awake, it seemed,
for many hours, pondering the change that
had beset me; a result from the demonstration of animal magnetism. I was in no wise of
the mood to arise at such an hour and tried
to ignore the pounding at the door; until it
came a second time, bringing me thankfully
to my senses. Startled, I bolted from bed with
this thought in my brain: Could there be a
mob of our victims, come to find me and Will
Patley to exact their revenge?

And, knowing that Mr. Patley had the night
watch, I dressed quickly, preparing, if need
be, to help defend Sir John and the Bow
Street Court. Fearing the worst, I bounded

down the stairs; and letting my grip on the balustrade slip, I slammed into Mr. Patley's back at the foot of the stairs below. Swiftly as I could, I pushed myself up, encountering a tallish man shuffling forward to assist us. From the candlelight I perceived that he had a clubfoot.

Mr. Patley recovered his composure first and introduced me to Daniel Ball, magistrate of the City of Liverpool. Mr. Ball then explained that he had journeyed through the night, taking to heart Sir John's proposal that he could be of assistance in the magistrate's investigation. I then offered to make him some tea whilst he waited.

'If you would oblige me, young sir, and ask your stable boy to see to my mount,' said he motioning at the entrance to Number 4 Bow Street. Through the door, which was slightly ajar, I spied a well-blooded mount showing the sweating of a hard night's ride.

'Sir, consider it done,' announced Mr. Patley.

I showed Mr. Ball to the kitchen, where I set things right in the fireplace; striking flint against metal, blowing on the sparks.

'A cup of tea will suit me well. For I feel a chill in my leg,' said he.

Mr. Ball settled at table with a sigh. And as the kettle began to boil, I introduced myself to the visitor, explaining that I was a student of the law and Sir John's 'man Friday.' He seemed impressed. Then did I realize, recalling Mr. Ball's letter to Sir John, that we had both come near to apprehending Hyde and Howell though we'd also suffered their escape. Therefore I brought him up-to-date on the Lammermoor investigation.

And so there I was, describing Hyde and Howell's escape from Mr. Donnelly's office, when the door opened and Clarissa entered with a look of surprise on her face:

'What have we here, gentlemen?'

I introduced her to Mr. Ball, explaining that like myself, she was Sir John's ward and had been taken into his household; also that with Lady Fielding's urgings she had been helped to blossom. Looking at her with a smile, I noticed that she was not pleased by this. Then with a reproving tone she said: 'I do not feel much like a 'blossom' at this hour.'

'Why not, Mistress Roundtree?

'From the fields the flowers and plants allure,
Where nature was most plain and pure.''

'Oh my . . . 'Tis Andrew Marvell, is it not, sir?'

'Yes, indeed. My wife and I read his poetry to each other of an evening,' said he.

'If there's time, perhaps you can recite more, sir. But now, I must set to the matter of breakfast. Jeremy, do continue with your tale.'

Just as I concluded, Sir John emerged from his bedroom in breeches and shirt, asked Clarissa for a dish of tea, and me he asked to shave him. She quickly heated water for the shaving pan, poured the tea, and bade me wait a moment for some sugar. Then with a hand she brushed my check and said: 'Mr. Ball, this gentleman and I are to be wed. Do you not think he shall make a fine husband?' I felt a flush on my face as I broke into a grin.

'Knowing what I do of Sir John Fielding, I am certain that you are meant each for the other,' said he with authority and a wink. There was naught he could have said that would have pleased us more.

Sir John called again: 'Jeremy! Where are you?'

'Pardon me, Mr. Ball. I must help Sir John.'

'Of course, Mr. Proctor. I'll occupy myself in conversation with Mistress Roundtree.'

As I mounted the stairs, I heard Clarissa begin to tell about her book. I knew that would take a while so that time remained for me to talk with Sir John whilst I shaved him. I knocked on the door and entered simultaneous since Sir John was in a hurry.

'There you are, lad. Shave me close,' said he to me. 'It might be well to do the job twice.'

I did as he wished, taking care, drawing no blood; after I had finished, he tested his cheeks with his fingertips and nodded approval. His manner that morning was most direct. I took this not as a sign of his displeasure, for as yet I had done naught to displease him, but rather that he was preoccupied by his consideration of matters that lay ahead.

'What's Daniel Ball like?'

'He seems quite learned in poetry and is a gentleman; dignified, though he walks with some difficulty due to a clubfoot.'

'Hmmm . . . Interesting. And he came by mount from Liverpool,' said Sir John in a thoughtful manner. 'So far, I like what I hear.'

I helped Sir John with the remainder of his clothing and, as we readied to join the others, I brought up the subject of the Lammermoor investigation.

'Sir, in the night, while tossing and turning, I remembered things perhaps pertinent to my condition which I seem now to be aware of.'

'Indeed,' said Sir John. 'I'm afraid that now is not the time. However, you should go into them as soon as possible,' said he.

'Quite right, sir,' said I.

'Why not wait until I get a feel for the magistrate.'

'Certainly,' I agreed.

'I assume you've already given Mr. Ball a rundown of the investigation?'

'Yes, sir. Leaving out my own difficulties,' said I.

'Understandable. This is what we do: Once we settle in, I'll give him the facts. Then you'll have the chance to relate your findings.'

★ ★ ★

'Let's proceed.'

Thus we made our way to the kitchen, where Sir John made a grand entrance, reaching out with his great hand to shake the magistrate's.

''Tis indeed an honor, Sir John. I've waited a long while for this moment.'

'The honor, sir, is all mine,' said Sir John. 'You've made a considerable journey, and you must be exhausted.'

'In truth, I am, sir.'

'Then Clarissa's culinary talents will revive you,' announced Sir John as Clarissa began to fill the table with food: rashers of bacon, delicious scones, bread and dripping with a dish of beans and mutton, served piping hot.

Just then Lady Fielding made her entrance, and introductions were now complete. Across from Mr. Ball sat Sir John with Lady Fielding at his side. Next to Daniel Ball sat I whilst Clarissa hovered over us making sure that we were satisfied.

Conversation flowed as we breakfasted. I was glad that I had urged Sir John to invite Daniel Ball to London. It seemed now that our family had grown. I observed Mr. Ball aware that Sir John was sizing him up discreetly, as he folded his arms over his capacious belly, leaned back in his chair, and listened. I could tell he liked the man. So did I.

As usual, Lady Fielding hurried through her meal saying little but to give her regrets at having to leave so quickly: 'Mr. Ball, I am sorry to rush away like this,' said she as she rose. 'Please excuse me, sir. I must meet with Mr. Joseph Hanway, who has now joined the board of the Magdalene Home for Penitent Prostitutes, a charitable enterprise which with Sir John's assistance was brought into being. Mr. Hanway is a man of wealth who also may be of assistance in other matters,' said Lady Fielding, looking positively through me. 'I trust that my husband will offer his hospitality in my absence.'

'Lady Fielding, 'tis ever gracious of you to have shared with me this memorable meal,' said he, rising from the table. Then, reaching for her hand, he leaned forward to kiss it as a Frenchman might. I noted that she blushed yet returned a generous smile. Then she kissed Sir John and was off.

Thanking Clarissa for the meal, it was hence to Sir John's study that we three went. Clarissa offered to come for me before noon so that we'd not be late for our meeting with Abigail Hardy at St. Paul's.

I lit a few candles for our guest, and we sat waiting for Sir John to speak.

'Mr. Ball, had you heard of 'animal magnetism' prior to this investigation?'

'Yes, Sir John, but only recent. And Mr. Proctor has given me the idea that its use may be involved in Lord Lammermoor's death,' said Mr. Ball. 'I should like to know more about it from you, however.'

Then Sir John gave a full summary of the Lammermoor case, including each demonstration of animal magnetism given by Dr. Goldsworthy, including assessment of Mr. Deekin's technique. After taking a moment or two to allow Mr. Ball to digest the contents of his account, Sir John brought himself upright in his chair, planted his elbows on the desk, and leaned toward us.

'All my years I've been opposed to quacks of all types. However, I've noted this: I believe my own blindness has allowed me to develop such concentration that may even sometimes enter into a trance state. From time to time, whilst engaging in thought, my focus upon the matter is so intense that my other senses simply fade. It is similar to the occult communications from the realm of dreams; surely you have witnessed the phenomenon in which a person speaks whilst he sleeps. This does appear to resemble Dr. Goldsworthy's demonstrations as well as Mr. Deekin's. Does it not, Jeremy?'

'Yes, sir,' said I. 'Though there is something else that flashed into my brain. I believe it is of importance to your investigation.'

'Let's hear it.'

''Tis a combination of things I've witnessed, both in Dr. Goldsworthy's demonstrations and in Lady Lammermoor's behavior. A puzzle emerges that I cannot fit together.'

'Start at the beginning, lad, and we will do what we can to make sense of it all,' said Sir John.

'Do you recall you asked Archibald Talley why he had taken the medical report prepared by Mr. Donnelly for the coroner's inquest?'

'Yes — go on,' said Sir John.

'At first I thought this incident but a perfectly timed illusion. But now I believe it was nothing of the sort: Just as young Mr. Talley was opening his mouth to respond to your question, Lady Lammermoor spoke up, saying, 'Oh, I can answer that Sir John' ... and so did she; although it was as if her words were issuing from the lips of her son, not from her own. I was of a sudden taken aback. And so I laughed. Mr. Talley gave me an odd look, and his mother fixed me with one of scorn. And you, Sir John, lacking sight, could only frown.'

'Hmmm.' Sir John put his hands to his chin and then to his brow, pinching his flesh together over the black silk that covered his eyes. Then he said: 'My lack of sight is proving a disadvantage for us in this investigation. And it is likely that if Dr. Goldsworthy and Lady Lammermoor conspired to kill Lord Lammermoor using occult means, they would seek to prevent one such as you from gaining information that could help resolve this investigation.'

'Mr. Proctor, what else can you tell us?'

'It seemed, as I've said before, that Dr. Goldsworthy muttered from his throat and also whispered. I recall that in the treatment of Mr. Ginder, he made sounds that not even his patient could discern. But what comes next to mind, sir, is this: When I was describing it all, softly, to you how Dr. Goldsworthy was preparing his treatment for his patient, it surprised you so that you burst into laughter.'

'Oh, yes. I did indeed have the giggles — and enjoyed them very much,' said hc.

'However, sir, you could not see that as you laughed Lady Lammermoor gave you the sort of glare that could turn men to stone. Is it not odd that she would fix her eyes in such a manner upon a blind man?'

'It is in no wise a good sign! What more do you remember?' (All the while Sir John and I spoke, Mr. Ball sat at full attention to every detail of our exchange.)

'Nor did your laughter escape the notice of Dr. Goldsworthy. He turned a fierce eye to us both, giving a hint of the power that Mr. Donnelly had said was in that gaze.'

Then I paused a moment and said: 'Sir, I'm almost to the end of my revelations.'

'Don't stop.'

'Dr. Goldsworthy was using his hands in a circling motion, moving them this way and that, keeping Mr. Ginder in his gaze at all times. And as his hands moved, so did his lips. He was saying something, perhaps whispering, that could not be heard, not even by Ginder. But now I wonder was it whispering at all and from whence were the sounds emitted? It mattered not if Dr. Goldsworthy was heard or no. Those eyes of the doctor's were at once sympathetic and fierce. And they could have held Mr. Ginder in any case. And in my case, the doctor also stared in such a way, penetrating far more deeply than I did then realize. But it was that trick with the voice; those mutterings and whisperings — with or without the movement of his lips — with glaring as Lady Lammermoor has done which are so very different from the treatments described by Mr. Donnelly that are credited to Anton Mesmer.'

'Jeremy, is that all?'

'Yes.'

I felt quite tired — truly exhausted.

Silence reigned for a good long stretch of time. Then:

'I believe what you've described, in bits and pieces, is the act of ventriloquy. And if this be so, what in heaven's name has ventriloquy got to do with animal magnetism?'

Then did I see Sir John in full fury as he began to boil over:

'Damn — damnation! They have confounded me with this infernal matter of

356

glaring and staring and mutterings. 'Tis I who is being made the fool! I dare say the late Dr. Goldsworthy and Lady Lammermoor were involved in the murder of her husband: I have no doubt. Oh, such a case — a nightmare, it is. How can I arrest this woman because of what I now suspect to be the workings of an even more evil plot than I earlier surmised?' Just then a knock came upon the door.

'Go, Jeremy. Get what you can from Abigail Hardy. Off with you, lad! Mr. Ball and I will consult upon the matter whilst you and Clarissa are at St. Paul's. My head requires some good London air. Mr. Ball, let us make our way together. My left hip is giving me trouble these days and though I have my stick, a sturdy arm will help to boost my confidence.'

'Sir John, 'twould be a great pleasure to accompany you.'

★　★　★

Clarissa and I stepped out of Bow Street and made our way to St. Paul's, a short distance by any measure. Russell and Great Hart streets were thronging with people making for the garden. In truth it was loud, chaotic, and disordered, and yet usually I quite liked it.

But today I wished not to retrace the route that Mr. Patley and I had taken on our chase, so that I took pains to guide us through the alleyways that serpentined through the great city.

'Jeremy, why are we going round this way? St. Paul's is just over there,' said she, pointing.

Without a reply I continued my way.

'You are becoming as stubborn as I,' said she with a tilt of her head and a chuckle.

Still I held my response from her, and she let the matter rest. I knew that her thoughts were elsewhere. On her dress perhaps, which was to have a fitting the day next. And then Clarissa said: 'I must choose my best maid. Should it be Molly or Annie?'

'Annie, I suppose, since a 'best maid' must be unwed.'

'Then Annie it is,' she replied with a serious mien, and then said this: 'Have you sorted out your clothing for our trip afterwards?'

'After when?' said I, my thoughts slipping into a knot. 'I've not the time, Clarissa, even to read your book. Now there's a thought.'

'What kind of thought?' she asked.

'We could take your novel on our trip,' said I with a twinkle.

She then put her arms round me ever so

tight and kissed me sweetly. Perhaps I had now redeemed myself in her eyes, thought I.

We entered St. Paul's to the muted sound of an organ. And there in the very last pew, sat Mistress Hardy, looking quite pretty. She looked at me, motioning with her hand for me to sit beside her. Since Abigail Hardy knew not that Clarissa and I were together, she frowned as I led Clarissa behind me to where she sat. And though I introduced Clarissa, I failed to make clear our relationship.

'Jeremy,' said she, 'I must speak softly.' She did seem rather forward with my name. This did not escape Clarissa's notice; nor did she overlook that Abigail rested her hand on my shoulder whilst she whispered in my ear, 'There's spies even here.'

'That will do, young lady,' said Clarissa boldly, as she stood and came along the pew, knocking against my knees in the space between myself and the kneeling rail. She then sat herself betwixt Abigail and me and said, 'You may whisper in my ear. I am Jeremy's betrothed, and we keep no secrets.'

But Abigail did not appear surprised nor hindered by this interruption and began to speak in a normal manner, all fear of spies forgot:

'When we spoke at the Lammermoor

House, I told to your Sir John that Her Ladyship had that night been in the library reading with her son. Afterwards she ask'd for help with her bedtime preparations. That was round midnight. 'Twas the truth but not all of it. That's the reason I gave you the note to meet me here.'

'We thank you. Now please continue.'

'Well, ya see, I had trouble sleepin' that night 'cause the floor were so cold.'

'What? You don't even have a pallet to sleep upon?' asked Clarissa with naught but sympathy in her tone.

'Do please go on with your tale,' said I.

''Twas 'bout half pass'd midnight when I heard noises below in the coachway. So I poked my head through the dormer to have a look-see. And that's when I saw the coach-and-four pull up. There she was. Her Ladyship, all cloaked and hatted, steppin' out from some hidin' place in the garden. Y'see, there's a great many secret places in that palace of a house. Somehow they all connect to the bedchamber of the master and missus.'

Right then, all of a sudden, an official of the church came up behind me and pounded his staff down upon my shoulder.

'Ouch!' I blurted out.

'Hush, you three!' demanded he. At this, Clarissa and Abigail began to giggle in such a way that I did suggest that we quickly take our leave. And so I escorted my companions outside into the churchyard, where we found a suitable place to sit: upon a ledge amongst the tufts of hawkweed and snapdragon scattered round the church wall. (The sunlight there seemed strangely brilliant after the darkness inside the church. The transient glittering of some seagulls remote in the blue was as if I could glimpse, now and then, fleeting hints of what is immaculate in heaven.)

There in our little refuge we did proceed, as Abigail Hardy went on with what she'd seen on the night in question.

'I didn't see Her Ladyship's face that night. Yet I know that walk of hers: *Strut, strut. strut.* Straight as a board she holds herself when she walks — like a man — she puts one foot down and then the other.'

'Abigail, I get the sense that you are not fond of Her Ladyship,' said Clarissa.

'No, I ain't. She's a taskmaster, and she ain't got a heart, I tell ya. She's cold as ice. That's what she's.'

'Sir John was told that she and Lord Lammermoor called each other 'lovey' names.'

Then Abigail did tighten her lips as she waited a moment before saying this: 'Well

. . . that's all lies. Those two wasn't like a man and wife, if ya know what I mean. They didn't make the noise that lovers do. 'Twas spoken downstairs that each had a lover — p'rhaps many,' said she, looking straight into Clarissa's face and not at mine.

''Twas just after I was new at the house,' continued Abigail, 'right as I was passin' by their bedchamber when I smelled something burning in the room. A sweet odor. So I stopped what I were doing and listened right there. And what I heard gave me the chills.'

'What exactly did you hear?' said I.

'I admit to you both — and I hope you don't think bad of me — that curiosity was my only reason for standin' there behind their door. For what I'd heard about them did make me wonder what they was doin' in there. 'Twas terrible strange, indeed,' said she.

'What was strange?' I asked.

'The lady — I think it was her — was makin' these mumbly noises. Then all a sudden, the voice would change — go all deep and hollow like . . . ' She stopped a moment to think. 'Like the death rattle. 'Twas like someone was dyin' in there or like a ghost was talkin' outa the ground.'

'Good God,' Clarissa said while I did wonder what next the girl would reveal.

'Is there anything more you want to tell us? You're being most helpful. I am quite sure that Sir John will help you to find employment elsewhere if you so wish to leave the Lammermoor household.'

'Oh, I do. Sure as I'm sittin' here. I wish I could get outta there right aways. They got acquaintances that'er just as awful — even one who calls himself a medico. Imagine that. They come in the middle of the night — even before His Lordship was dead — and I heard tell that somedays Her Ladyship don't eat. Not even a bite of food. Instead she has cook give her especial some bones from a cow or sheep. And nobody knows what Lady Lammermoor even does with 'em. Truth be tellin', that last's what I heard she did the day before Lord Lammermoor took his dive. I swears that's all I know.'

As Abigail finished her tale, my stomach once more began to churn. And my head began to pain. The girls, quite unaware of my discomfort, talked as friends. Of a sudden, I realized that I'd not heard a word of what they'd spoken to each other. Then Clarissa said urgently to me:

'Jeremy, go direct to Sir John and inform him of what we've learned. I'll go as quick as I can with Abigail whilst she collects her belongings. Then we will hurry to Bow Street.' This, reader, is what followed: Fearing for the girls' safety, as near to Lady Lammermoor they would come, I was much against their plan. I argued and made demand that they not proceed with it, though I failed to convince Clarissa of the danger. Abigail assured us that Lady Lammermoor had gone out for the day and would not return until much later. So at last, Clarissa convinced me there could be no danger in midday since they were two, not one alone, and if need be, far more quick to trick rather than be duped by 'that old bat,' as they'd dubbed her. Reluctantly, against all good judgment, I gave assent. Nevertheless, they agreed to travel by hackney to and fro, which might bring them to Bow Street not much after myself. They happily agreed to accept the shillings I provided from my pockets.

After hailing them transport, I started back to Bow Street; but then did hazard that Sir John and Daniel Ball might still be engaged in their walk so that I need not make haste homeward. (Reader, on more than one occasion, I've recalled to mind this error so grievous, and I confess that I failed in my duty to protect Clarissa and Abigail Hardy.) Although 'twould require a detour, I saw opportunity to purchase a gift for my bride.

The idea had nagged since morning when Mr. Ball had charmed Clarissa with his quoting of Andrew Marvell. Truth be told, I longed for relief from the turmoil I again felt upon hearing the goings-on between Lady and Lord Lammermoor. This had sent me into more confusion. Would it ever leave me? What was it about that expression 'the death rattle' that had so unnerved me and reminded of Dr. Goldsworthy's mutterings as if he were speaking from his armpits? I could not even remember if I'd told Sir John this, though he'd asked time and time again for details of great import. Heaviness and disappointment overcame me. I had failed in my duty to Sir John; although in truth, I was not to blame for the nature of my condition.

What I now resolved was this: I would seek quietude and briefly stop at my favorite bookshop. And what better place could there be to focus my mind but amongst the bookstalls that were to be found just east of Grub Street. Thus I set out at a jog-trot for quite some stretch, but as my feet trampled the ground, of a sudden unexpected thoughts once again came into my mind. These were of my first love: a poor Italian girl named Mariah, how I had first glimpsed her as an acrobat when first she came to London; how, when her family returned to Italy, she had been seduced in to staying and then sold into prostitution. Alas, she was the final victim of the Raker. Just as I recalled this so did I remember words of Mr. Donnelly, who helped me to bury her with dignity: 'Life is not just, Jeremy. It is simply a space of time that is given to us. We do with it what we can.'

I pressed on at a slowed but even pace, until I arrived at Duntun's Bookshop, the sight of which did lift my spirits. There on wooden tables spreading along the kerbstones were books of all types, in a disorderly jumble; more often by size than subject.

'You've returned, lad,' said David Duntun, smiling.

'Your bookshop, sir, has become a favorite of mine,' said I.

''Tis ever a pleasure to promote the education of a lad so bright as yourself,' said he as he was called away by a gentlemen, giving me the opportunity to pounce upon the books that caught my eye. And then, I espied, as if put right upon that table, the *Miscellaneous Poems of Andrew Marvell*. I scanned its pages, turning each with care; and finding no scribblings in the margins nor corners bent or torn, I decided this the perfect gift for my bride. As I held the book, I resolved to write a poem of my own creation for Clarissa, to copy it tidily and nestle it beside Marvell's 'To His Coy Mistress.' I had in my mind the image of Clarissa making her discovery of it and of her coming at a run with arms open to embrace me. Therefore satisfied and feeling somewhat purged of the brooding in my brain, I searched for another that might help expedite my recovery.

Putting trust in my former luck, I rummaged quickly and made my second find. Though my surprise in discovering what lay open on the table did cause me to gasp aloud.

'Are you all right, lad?' said Mr. Duntun

'I suppose I am, sir.'

'What disturbed you?'

'This pamphlet; the illustrations in it,' said I.

'Oh, yes, that one. The cover, I daresay, was ripped away whilst my back was turned. Though I'd be able to get you another, since the publisher down the road distributes this 'type' of literature,' said David Duntun in a low tone. 'We must keep an open mind. After all, a free press is the sign of a free nation.'

'I agree,' said I, staring at the pamphlet. 'What's its title, since I do not know the French language.'

'*C'est très exotique, n'est-ce pas?* Translated it reads: *The Practise of the Occult Art of Necromancy.* You'll notice that these diagrams and illustrations have explanations as well in that tongue,' said he. 'Beg pardon, lad — but you don't look the sort to have interests of this kind.'

'Truly I have not. However, I am involved in an inquiry under the supervision of Sir John Fielding, magistrate of the Bow Street Court where I am clerk as well. I regret I cannot divulge the nature of the investigation. Nevertheless, this pamphlet reveals certain practices which may shed light upon events that need further illumination.'

'Say no more . . . Take it with you. 'Tis a gift from David Duntun to Sir John Fielding. May it be of great benefit in his investigation! *Oh, là, là!*' said Mr. Duntun, displaying affection for the French tongue he seemed to have mastered. 'This is all rather stimulating!'

'Thank you much. May I pay you for the book of poetry?'

'No, you may not. A man so young as yourself has needs for his future. And you look as if you will have a fine one,' said he pointing his finger upward. 'Remember these words of D.W. Duntun . . . 'Every shilling counts toward the next.' '

And with that said, he smiled as we shook hands heartily.

I tucked the books under my arm and made a dash for home, choosing the shortest route to take me quickly to Bow Street.

Running as fast as my legs would carry me, heart pounding in my chest, I finally reached James Street, where I spied Sir John and Daniel Ball ahead of me on Great Hart Street just as they turned right unto Bow Street.

'Sir John! Sir John!' I shouted, near breathless. 'Wait! I'll catch you up. There's something I must show you and Mr. Ball.'

In a few moments I stood there on the steps of Bow Street, where they waited. I could hear myself sputtering as I told them about what I'd found in the bookshop.

'Calm yourself, Jeremy. If you've something of such great import to show us, we must first go inside.' And so we did. I expected to see Clarissa inside awaiting us.

'Where're Clarissa and Abigail Hardy?' said I in a panic.

'Jeremy! What's happened? Are you having one of those blasted spells? Surely you remember that you left with Clarissa for St. Paul's. Where is she, indeed? Tell me,' said Sir John furiously — erupting in anger.

We sat at table, Sir John across from me and Mr. Ball to my right. I explained what Abigail had told and placed the pamphlet open for Mr. Ball to see as I described to Sir John its portentous contents: drawings of the positions assumed whilst engaging in necromancy. Positions that resembled Dr.

Goldsworthy's. Mr. Ball spoke French and translated writings marked on the pages within circles, indicating what the necromancer should mutter or whisper at his subject. The necromancer was a woman: dressed as Lady Lammermoor was the night Lord Lammermoor leaped to his death. The puzzle came together, with the feeling that something was terribly wrong. Nay, it was more than a feeling, but rather an awful, frightening certitude.

'What have I done?' said I, covering my face with my hands. It was this that changed my fate.

'Jeremy, look at me!' Sir John bellowed. And then he placed both his hands flat down on the tabletop, pushing up as he leaned his body forward as if looking into my face. And in one swoop of the hand did strike my cheek with such force that I near fell to the floor. Stunned yet relieved, I was in that instant brought to my senses.

'There. I've put an end to it,' said Sir John.

'An end to what, sir?' said I rubbing my face, which still bore the imprint of his great hand.

'An end to your grumblings and fears. You've erred on one hand, but by chance, you've made headway. Hear me out,' he said sharply.

'We can now be certain that Lady Lammermoor was involved in the murder of Lord Lammermoor; whether by entrancing him under the guise of animal magnetism or by a combination of the occult practices in which they all took part. What their exact roles were, we may never know. Dead or alive, Lady Lammermoor will not tell; nor will that reprobate son of hers. I must arrest her. And the disappearance of Clarissa and Abigail indicates that the rules of engagement have changed. Still, there is the matter of trespass. We will proceed direct to Lord Mansfield for a warrant to search the premises and to arrest her and her son.'

'Sir, I would deem it an honor to accompany you,' said Daniel Ball.

'I'm sure you will provide a great deal of help, and I shall need all I can get.'

'Jeremy, inform Mr. Bailey to sound the alarum. All Runners must assemble. And have Mr. Ball's mount brought round. We'll need much transport. And tell him this: The Bow Street Runners shall go forth to challenge the miscreants on their own turf!'

Sir John rose to his feet and began searching the surface of the table for his tricorn and stick as I went to speak with Benjamin Bailey. Mr. Bailey, who was with the prisoners, shot to his feet and responded in sharp, soldierly manner. Knowing that Sir John would wish it so, I left word with the jailer remaining, to apprise Lady Fielding of our whereabouts.

When we emerged from Number 4 Bow Street, I was armed and ready. Sir John gave the order for Constable Patley to take the lead with Mr. Ball at the reins of his horse. Mr. Patley looked uncertain as he took a leg up, his sword on one shoulder and his rifled musket (held with a strap which ran from the bottom of the stick to the barrel) simply slung over the other, thus both hands free to hold onto the waist of Mr. Ball. On Sir John's behalf, Constable Brede commandeered a coach and two hackneys to carry the dozen or so constables as well as Sir John and myself. All were in a state of pulsating excitement as the Runners mounted conveyances.

Positioned to leave, Sir John gave the order, plain and simple.

'*Away!*' Our hackney carriage thundered through the streets of Westminster, with determination as fierce as ever I've seen.

Sir John was silent and deep in thought. I watched him, knowing full well that a plan of action was being devised as we moved closer and closer to our appointment with the villains.

Led by Mr. Benjamin Bailey, the main

body of Runners pulled up in the coachway of the Lammermoor residence while Sir John bade Constable Sheedy halt in front of Lord Mansfield's residence.

The magistrate jumped down, as he usually did, but I was on hand to steady him and made sure he did not fall. We then made our way up the walkway.

'Well, my lad. If you just position me, I shall give this door as threatening a knock as ever it has had.'

With that, Sir John let loose a flurry of blows upon the door, which immediately silenced the voices and the music inside the house. There was a significant pause, footsteps beyond, and then through the door:

'Who is there who dares interrupt this social evening,' said my nemesis.

'I will see the Lord Chief Justice, immediately!' said Sir John.

That familiar cadaverous face appeared, distant and unamused.

'Do you have an appointment, sir?' said the butler.

'My business is of utmost urgency,' said Sir John.

The butler was unmoved and said: 'The Lord Chief Justice will not be disturbed.'

Then with a great phlegmy rumble, Sir John cleared his throat and said: 'I am Sir

John Fielding, magistrate of the City of London and the City of Westminster. I will have you before the bench for obstruction of justice, if you so wish it.'

'Please wait, Sir John.'

'The man is detestable!' said Sir John, before the butler passed from earshot.

Then, shortly thereafter, the door swung wide. Lord Mansfield appeared, seething with annoyance. Sir John wasted nary a moment in describing the reason for our visit.

'Sir John, you cannot expect me to disrupt my amusements to hear such outrageous accusations for which you have no absolute proof.' (I had come to know the Lord Chief Justice fairly well during his flying visits to Sir John, and him I judged to be proud — often excessively so — and one who bore the traits of many proud men: a choleric disposition and an overweening certainty of the rightness of his own causes and opinions.)

'Proof you want, sir? Is it not enough that your good friend Lord Lammermoor leaped off a bridge as if he could fly? Lady Lammermoor is our primary suspect. She was seen by her own maid leaving her house shortly after midnight, though denying it when I questioned her. She is a liar, and she will escape if we do not act quickly.

Furthermore, her practices of animal magnetism are but a cloak for her evil purposes, which now may be putting the lives of two young ladies at ultimate risk.'

Lord Mansfield hesitated, thinking upon Sir John's tirade.

Sir John, emboldened by this pause, took the advantage and bellowed forth: 'Lord Mansfield. You commit a grave misjudgment if you do not grant me immediate access to the Lammermoor residence.'

And with that pronouncement Lord Mansfield did clench his fists, raising stiffened arms in anger, shouting, 'So be it! So be it! I shall accompany you. And we will just see where this leads us. I warn you, Sir John, Her Ladyship is second cousin to our King. She must not be mistreated!'

He heaved a sigh, blustering away, and banged the door shut behind him; but not before I spied his guests in the doorway, wide-eyed.

Sir John and I then followed him cross the square, where Sir John commanded the Runners to surround the residence, securing all exits; and then finally to 'Batter down the door!'

Lord Mansfield's spirits did then collapse as he himself halted with jaw agape, looking upon Mr. Benjamin Bailey (all six and a half feet of him) as he swung his ax. Three blows were sufficient to crush the lock. And with a great rush the Runners swooped into the hallway, with Daniel Ball following their lead.

I led Sir John into the house with my hand on his shoulder as he barked orders to all: 'Spread out. Leave no room unsearched. Clarissa and Abigail are within these walls. Keep your weapons at the ready. Hyde and Howell are hereabouts.'

Off somewhere in search, Daniel Ball called out: 'I've found the butler; but I need a hand. Here beneath the stairs. I need help to carry him up.'

Constable Patley descended the stairs at a run, and it was he alone who carried the butler over his shoulder to the hallway. He laid the man on the floor as Mr. Ball approached, carrying a huge old fowling piece.

'Sir,' said Mr. Ball. 'I found this instrument lying next the butler.'

I described it to Sir John.

'Is he alive?'

Mr. Ball bent over him. 'He breathes, sir, in irregular fashion.'

'Take him to the library and someone get cloth, wet it, and place it over the poor man's head. I regret we cannot stop our search further to tend to him,' said Sir John.

Lord Mansfield stood in silence, a curious look on his face.

'Sir John, I'll fetch my butler; they're on friendly terms. I'll have him brought to my house, and the doctor will be sent for.'

'Good of you, M'Lord,' said Sir John.

Just then Constable Brede hollered from the floor above.

'I've got me a prisoner, Sir John. Found 'im in the water closet, wouldya believe?' And down they came, Mr. Brede pushing and pulling Archibald Talley.

'You can wriggle all ya like, you ain't escapin' me.'

'Here he is, Sir John. A squamy fellar he is. Just look at his face, Jeremy.'

Young Mr. Talley was covered from head to hands in a rash of scales and pustules. He squirmed and babbled in his high fluting voice that he'd been afflicted with a nervous condition brought on by his mother; though she'd attempted to effect a cure upon him with salves and powders.

'Stop your groveling this moment, Mr. Talley. If you wish any manner of indulgence, you will tell me this instant where Clarissa Roundtree and Abigail Hardy have been taken; and where Lady Lammermoor is.'

Choking back his sobs, Talley said naught. Sir John would have none of his denials and gave a nod to Constable Brede, who then took the prisoner by the nape of the neck and gave him a good shaking.

'They're below. Below the house. Somewhere off one of the passageways. I've refused to ever go there with my mother and her friends. 'Tis the only thing I've not let her bully me into.'

'Sir John,' said I, 'he's telling the truth. Abigail's story confirms it.'

'Then, Mr. Talley, lead the way. *Now!*'

We followed our host along the great hallway to where he placed a chair beneath a sconce. Then with a circular motion, he cranked the apparatus as it slowly opened a wide panel of the wall.

'Ah-hah! There it is, Jeremy. Lead me in,' said Sir John, as he signaled the Runners to go swiftly hither, Daniel Ball following us.

'Describe what surrounds us.'

'We're in a narrow chasm lit from above by skylights and mirrors.'

Archibald Talley of a sudden spoke up.

'Sir John, these passageways lead into secret rooms within the house; it was designed for my great-grandfather — of the Catholic faith. There is even a chapel, which was once visited by his many guests. Priests and such.'

'Enough with your family history, Talley.

Runners! Find the girls, and beware — the villains are yet to be reckoned with. They are armed to kill.'

The Runners began their search, roaming the cavernous halls, leading this way and that into cell after cell, opening door after door, much like a monastery. One stood guard as the other would enter. And though faint noises were heard, the girls were nowhere to be found.

'Mr. Talley, are there any other passages you've not revealed?'

'My mother has keys she keeps with her at all times. I believe, sir, that other corridors run beside the one we now stand in, and below us as well.'

'How do we enter them? Speak up, man. Two lives are in the balance — as well as your own.'

'I know naught the way, sir.'

At that very moment, Daniel Ball let out a call:

'Here! I detect noises beyond.' He then pointed to a place in a panel. We rushed forward to examine it but could find no entrance nor protrusion to be manipulated. Mr. Ball did not relent. He rapped his fist hard until a hollow sound was detected.

'Mr. Bailey. I believe 'tis time for the ax.'

'Consider it done, Sir John.' It took but one

sharp blow; then several more to clear the way for us to pass through.

Mr. Bailey crawled first. A gunshot was fired, and he backed out in haste.

''Twas him. The man described as Howell.'

'He's come behind us and gone this way,' said Mr. Patley, pointing to his right.

As the Runners surged in that direction, Sir John grasped onto my shirt and that of Mr. Ball's. 'Don't move,' said he, sensing something we did not.

'Tell me about this opening we've come through.'

I bent down but could see naught but darkness through and through; it was a crawl space with an odor of molding earth.

'It's a tunnel; scarce the girth of a human and dark as a grave.'

Archibald Talley, still standing by in a foolish pose, did scratch at his arms.

'Sir John, perhaps this connects to another corridor used by workmen during construction. Or it might have provided a route of escape for the priests.'

'No matter what it is, I shall need to go in and investigate where it leads,' said Sir John.

'In that case, I shan't accompany you farther,' Mr. Talley did whine.

'Then I order you to remain at this opening. Inform the constables of our location.'

'Awright, Sir John. I shall. Surely you must believe me.'

'I believe naught of you. But I'll have your hide if you disobey me.'

Then Sir John asked me to position him.

'Sir, I must now intervene.'

'You will do no such thing, Jeremy. You will assist me as you've done in the past. And remember, no one is more suited to explore darkness than I. And if I'm correct, this will take us to the girls. But we must have two candles; you will carry one and Mr. Ball the other.'

'There might be candles in one of the rooms. If you allow me, sir, I'll see to it,' said Archibald Talley.

'Do it.'

In but a few minutes, Mr. Talley returned with candles in hand, which he passed to me. (Along with a pocket knife, I also carried implements with which I could set the flame, so I handed the candles to Mr. Ball and did just that.)

'Well done, Jeremy,' said Sir John as he sniffed his approval. 'Time is growing short, and I fear for those girls. Let us proceed. I'm going in ahead of you.'

As Sir John followed his nose into the chasm, I crawled behind, using a hand to hold onto the candle. Sir John felt his way with his hands touching the sides of the burrow, which was but packed earth that was, thankfully, damp. Sir John was making progress, remarkably; thrusting himself forward, then pulling along, digging his hands through the cavern.

'Are you all right?'

Of a sudden I heard his breathing, taken in gasps, and then he said, 'Something ahead . . . '

His feet kicked, driving him forward. Reaching in close as could, I saw that he could move no further. His body was crammed tight against the impacted earth. I apprised Mr. Ball of the situation.

'We'll pull you out, if we must!' I shouted. I then heard him pummel the earth round him, reminding me of his fists on the table at Bow Street. Then, at last, I did hear him call, 'Push . . . Push me! Now!' (Sir John was braver than ever I'd seen him.)

And so I pushed with all my might, until at last a thump did resound and a wisp of air even more stale and warmed did pass over us. I scurried onward, following muffled cries until my head banged down on Sir John's boot.

'I believe the girls are near,' said he. 'There's an odor. 'Tis incense.'

I continued in his path, Mr. Ball faithfully

behind. Until of a sudden the trail ended as we did enter a room about the size of Sir John's study. Sir John lay exhausted on his back, panting through his mouth. And there I beheld Clarissa and Abigail. Alive.

'Clarissa!' Straightening my legs, I held onto the candle, which I placed on a table. My only thoughts were to release the girls from the chairs they were bound to. Mr. Ball was now resting next to Sir John.

'Jeremy, I presume the girls are all right?'

'Yes, indeed they are.'

Hurriedly I removed the mantles from their heads; and next the rags round their mouths. They both gasped . . . then the ropes of braided leather that held Clarissa's arms. When free, she reached for me in such a way as never before. It was necessary to pull back from her grasp as gentle as I could. Just as I untied Abigail, the poor girl fainted. I caught her before she slipped and carried her to lie against the wall next Sir John and Mr. Ball. She then did awaken as I set her head against Clarissa's shoulder. And just then a door slammed behind hind me; Mr. Ball quickly stood, staring at a trapdoor that had snapped tightly shut: the same (no doubt) through which we could have made our exit.

'Jeremy, I'm assuming that this room is tantamount to the chamber of a necromancer. But describe what you see.'

Herewith, reader, is what I saw in this mysterious place: The table where my candle flickered was draped with a black cloth emblazoned with odd-shaped symbols. There in the center was a human skull surrounded by small bones and silver dishes of incense. Direct across the room, on the wall opposite, was an altar of sorts; graven images made of silver sat on both sides of a silver chalice; and beneath all that were branches of dried oleander. (All of which were indicated in the booklet I'd discovered earlier that day.) But there was something else that was not in the pamphlet: wrist irons nailed to the wall.

'I see,' said Sir John, as he fell into a protracted silence, musing with bowed head there in the near-vanished light. Then he said:

'Clarissa, give me the details of your imprisonment.'

She then told how Lady Lammermoor had tried to make the girls drink from the chalice, threatening to put them both in wrist irons if they did not. But Clarissa surmised that the liquid was poison, and did bite the hand of Lady Lammermoor in a struggle with her.

Sir John then took charge. He would abide

no delay in our search for an exit from this tomb.

'Clarissa, you did well. But tell me, how did Lady Lammermoor make her exit?'

'Sir John, we could not see. Our faces were shrouded before she left. Her accomplice, a man, dragged us in here and then tied us to the chairs.' She then began to sob.

But there was no time to waste. The air in the chamber was thin.

'Sir John . . . truly I cannot take a breath without a pain in my throat,' said Mr. Ball.

'Jeremy, extinguish a candle. We must save what little air there is. And make as little movement as possible.' We did as bade.

'Sir John, I can hear footsteps striding across the floor above.'

'So do I . . . Go, sir, immediately, to that spot yonder and pound rhythmically on it. Take a chair if you must,' said Sir John in a whisper.

Mr. Ball began to knock his fist against the ceiling, to no avail.

'Surely one as pernicious as she would not come into this dungeon without having an exit,' said Sir John.

The chamber, now illumined by a single candle, pulsed with undulating shadows, casting a most macabre hue upon our predicament. I strained cross the space between Clarissa and myself to hold her in my arms whilst she held Abigail.

'Does anyone see the merest seam in these walls — anything that could be manipulated to spring us free?' said Sir John.

And then Abigail did speak. 'I remember only this, sir. Lady Lammermoor did walk away from us . . . in that direction,' she said, pointing a finger. 'So if we were there, in those chairs, then she went near the corner of the chamber. Right there!'

'Mistress Hardy, your senses have heeded the urgings of reason whilst reaching conclusions from information provided by them. It is thus that I experience all things and events. You've a good head on you, lass!'

(And that, Reader, was the brightest of compliments that Abigail Hardy had no doubt ever known.)

'This is what we must do. Mr. Ball, Jeremy. Have you still your pistols?'

'Yes,' we replied simultaneously.

'Then go to the spot that Abigail has indicated. Examine it further. And if I'm not mistaken, you'll discover there to be a different color or texture thereabouts.'

We found exactly that.

'Back away, far enough to make aim. Jeremy, use your knife to make a mark on the wall so you both will have a target.'

'Sir, 'tis done.'

'Positions. I will give the command to fire.'

'Pistols at the ready.' (Reader, I did get the notion from Sir John's tone, bold as it was, that he did relish once again being in the midst of the sally of battle.)

'Girls, help me to my feet.'

'Yes, Sir John,' they piped.

Mr. Ball and I marched forward and threw back our shoulders, all but saluting.

'To whom does the night belong?' said Sir John Fielding. Then: 'Fire!!!'

Our single volley reached its mark. The breach was made.

★ ★ ★

'That was close, Lieutenant!' said the voice of a man, faint but near enough to hear through the rupture we'd made.

'Hold positions!' issued from another.

'I believe that is the voice of Corporal Otis Sperling of the Grenadier Guards,' said Sir John jubilantly. Just then the wall burst inward, followed by a small troop of red-coated soldiers. I, too, recognized the one who had testified in Sir John's court four or five years before.

'Lieutenant Sperling, sir, at your service.

And you are Sir John Fielding, magistrate of renown!'

'Yes. That I am. Lieutenant Sperling: How can we thank you enough for coming to our rescue?'

'No need for that, sir. 'Twas the Lord Chief Justice who did send for us.'

'Indeed.'

Lord Mansfield peered in at us, making a grimace at the sight he beheld.

'Oh, dear! What is the purpose of such a room . . . or chamber of . . . Whatever is it?'

'M'Lord, if my guess is correct, it is the den of a necromancer, perhaps even used for other purposes — ' said Sir John.

'I see. I daresay, 'tis most distasteful. Sir John, let us say no more about it.

'I am glad to find you and the others alive and well. I did think the worst, so I summoned help. But you managed to reach the girls in time to save them. Well done!'

'No need to congratulate. Our mission is not completed. I assume that Lady Lammermoor has not been found?'

'Correct.'

'Then we must move swiftly,' said Sir John.

'But, sir, the doors are well guarded.'

'Hmmm . . . ' Sir John cleared his throat. 'That, sir, is not enough to hold such a creature as Lady Lammermoor. As you see from this odd cavity I'm standing in, there are hiding places and perhaps exits that we've not discovered. Therefore I must proceed with my plan.'

'Well enough. Do as you must,' said Lord Mansfield, tightening his lips.

'But, Sir John, there's another matter to be addressed.'

'What is that?'

'Archibald Talley. Poor chap. He's sitting in the library rather glum.'

'He has good reason, since I'll be soon placing him under arrest.'

'But what on earth for? It's my understanding he has been forthcoming in this investigation.'

'Lord Mansfield, with all due respect, he has not. He's deceived us at every opportunity. He feigns helplessness and is not what he appears to be. I grant that his mother is a 'demanding' lady. However, 'twas he who chose to lie to me throughout our investigation, and for that he shall answer.

'Are you aware, M'Lord, that my constables found him hiding in the water closet?'

'No.'

'He knew full well that my ward, Clarissa Roundtree, and Mistress Hardy, a chambermaid in his household, had been abducted by his mother and were in gravest danger; he thought it graver still that he himself suffers a rash. Furthermore he's surely witness to the bludgeoning of his butler, and I've good reason to hazard that he knows exactly why his father leaped from Westminster Bridge and why Dr. Goldsworthy was murdered. And lastly, where Lady Lammermoor is as we speak. He shall not be spared. I will arrest him — on this I insist. Now, sir, I must get out of this chamber and breathe proper air. Jeremy, if you will.'

'Yes, sir. Just step with me,' said I as Lord Mansfield stood back.

Sir John asked Lieutenant Sperling to escort Clarissa and Abigail to Bow Street whilst Mr. Ball and I reloaded our pistols.

As I waved my good-bye to Clarissa (and blew her a kiss, which she returned), Mr. Benjamin Bailey informed Sir John that a woman's voice was heard below, though no stairway could be found.

'And I hear horses outside,' said Sir John. Mr. Ball flew into action and ran for all he was worth. Sure enough, I also heard the wheels of a conveyance moving along gravel upon the coachway back of the house. I rushed to follow as he quickly managed to find a way out. Several Runners spotted us and joined.

In a flash we were past the Grenadier

Guards and through French doors at the rear of the grand salon. There was no moon to light the way; however, windows shed enough brightness to see the carriage looming. But more important, Daniel Ball had fixed his attention upon something else. I followed his eyes to what he spied and saw this: the iron cover of a coal chute began to open, ever so slowly. And there into the night stepped Lady Lammermoor, quietly moving through the ivy, seeking darkness at the south side of her property. She did blend well but for the valise she carried.

'Halt!' called Daniel Ball. 'You are under arrest!'

'You trespass here!' she did announce.

'I charge you to remain. Do not move another step!' he warned.

'I do say this is most absurd. I am merely taking a brief holiday to visit a cousin.'

'Surely you do not exit your house by the coal chute, Lady Lammermoor,' said Mr. Ball.

She then began to walk stealthily toward us, shifting her head this way and that, with her mouth in a mocking smile, until she said most calm: 'Oh the curious portals and mazes of this grand old house.' She turned to face Daniel Ball, putting forth her hand in a greeting manner (as if to assure him of her good intentions). 'Our cellar now serves well to store luggage and the like,' said she, flipping her hand. 'Please do stand aside, sir.'

'Tell me, Lady Lammermoor, why is your hand wrapped in such a way, and how did two young ladies come to be imprisoned in your house?'

She gave this explanation: 'My hand? 'Tis but a rash — some contagion my son Archie spread to me. As to the girls, they had permission from me to reclaim some belongings and it is obvious, is it not, that whilst they were skulking about they simply lost their way. Perhaps a gust of wind blew the door shut. It is most regrettable. However they are all right, are they not?'

Just then several Runners, followed by the Lord Chief Justice, led Sir John outside where he stood for a moment as he listened.

'She's here. Is she not?'

'Indeed she is,' said Daniel Ball.

'Seize her!' roared Sir John.

With that, Lady Lammermoor faced Sir John, her eyes ablaze with fury. (All those present retreated a pace as if driven back by what might be described as an evil eye.)

Of a sudden, Sir John did shout: 'Be alert! There are others!'

At that moment a shot was fired from the carriage. The horses reared and set off.

Daniel Ball was closest and took off after the coach to prevent its escape, just as Mr. Patley and I hastened to take Lady Lammermoor into custody. She glowered at me. Hate was writ upon her face.

Yet another shot.

'Jeremy, find Daniel Ball!' Sir John shouted.

I drew my pistols, leaving the prisoner with Mr. Patley, and dashed down the path to where the shot had been fired. Two constables trailed me as I sped toward a shape crouching low and aiming at the coach. He fired. The flash showed the face of Daniel Ball. There was a flurry of shots in ragged succession — *pop* — *pop* — *pop* — so that it took near half a minute as we volleyed at the coach. I struggled to reload, as did the Runners.

But then the coach clattered away just as I spied the trunk of a man lying on the ground. I knew that instant who it was.

I rushed to him and stooped to see if he was alive. I felt a wisp of air against my face, as I placed my cheek against his. But blood oozed from the corner of his shoulder. I pressed my hand cross the wound as Constable Brede and Mr. Bailey stood over me and lifted the man off the ground.

Sir John awaited us as we walked to the house carrying Mr. Ball. And as they took him away, I remained with Sir John to answer any questions he might have. And then in a grave voice he said, 'It is worse than I thought and as bad as ever I feared. Ah, Jeremy.'

'No, sir. Mr. Ball is alive. I cannot say how serious is his injury. He bleeds from the shoulder and is not conscious.'

'I see.'

He said nothing for a long moment.

Then, in the deepest and darkest of tones: 'The evil of our immoral age, in which human life is given so little respect and taken with so little regard. Was it always so?' he said then, answering himself. 'Yes, alas, it was always so.'

12

*In which there
is cause
for celebration*

"Twas to be an eventful week, for both the
Bow Street Runners and our household,
commencing with our return to Number 4
Bow Street after the raid upon Lammermoor
House, with Lady Lammermoor herself and
Archibald Talley under arrest, and Clarissa
and Abigail restored to safety.

Without protest the prisoners were
escorted to a cell; Mr. Benjamin Bailey
pushing Archibald Talley forward with no
difficulty, and Mr. Patley followed close
behind, gripping Lady Lammermoor by the
collar. It was remarkable how swiftly the two
culprits had taken on the appearance of
common street criminals now that they were
in the hands of the law: Mr. Talley was
whining and squealing as loudly as any
seven-year-old might; Lady Lammermoor
(keeping to her sly and sinister manner) had

torn her cloak in the coach, and her hat was askew.

Soon after, word arrived that Daniel Ball was safe under Mr. Donnelly's care and would most probably recover use of his wounded arm, though he was feverish yet and we would be advised to find him a bed where he might be tended to; Mr. Donnelly's small surgery would not function as a hospital. I volunteered my own quarters, whereupon Sir John dictated a letter to be sent posthaste to the wife of Daniel Ball. (Just as later we learned that the Lammermoor' butler had narrowly survived his wounds.)

Upon my return from the post dispatch, much of the turmoil at Number 4 Bow Street had subsided, as Sir John prepared to interrogate Archibald Talley in his study, where I sat myself in a corner to take notes.

'Well, Mr. Talley, what do you have to tell us about your role in the death of your father?'

'Well . . . um . . . what could I know of that, Sir John?'

'Let me remind you that you are speaking to a magistrate of the Crown, and in this investigation I have the consent of the Crown's direct representative to arrest and indict even royal blood should it become necessary.'

At Sir John's pronouncement, the man was clearly taken aback.

'Archibald Talley,' said Sir John, leaning forward, 'all is discovered. Do believe it. You may face the gallows, except if you co-operate with the Crown, beginning now. This is your last chance to escape dire punishment.'

'But, I — I had nothing — ' Again sniveling, it took him but a few moments more, between gasps and clearing his nose in a handkerchief, to admit to Sir John that our suspicions were correct — that Lady Lammermoor had coveted control of her husband's property ever since she had become Lord Lammermoor's second wife, which she had long plotted. To further her plans, and seeing her husband's infatuation with Mesmerism, she traveled to Vienna to make the acquaintance of Dr. Goldsworthy, British master of animal magnetism. Together, they hatched a plot: Using the techniques of animal magnetism and the occult arts of necromancy, they convinced Lord Lammermoor that he could 'fly through the air' to visit with his father in the afterlife and yet return to the present. Dr. Goldsworthy had induced the trance whilst Lady Lammermoor uttered the signals which did propel her husband to his death. Then when the deed was done, a falling-out occurred. Threats were made; Dr. Goldsworthy refused to participate (as in the previous manner) in the murder of Bishop Talley (but fearing loss of her sponsorship, he did finally assent); they traveled to Liverpool, where Lady Lammermoor ended the game. Dr. Goldsworthy was killed, and Henry Howell did the deed. Archibald Talley had been witness to it all; though he maintained it was his mother who rode in the coach attempting to trample Annie Oakum and his stepbrother, Bishop John Talley.

Mr. Talley fell silent for a moment. Then he said, 'How would you feel having a mother like that? I wished naught more of life than my fancies for women and gambling.'

A teasing smile twitched at the corners of Sir John's mouth. 'It strikes me that with such noble ambitions it would be a shame to foil your plans.'

Thus ended our interrogation.

Just as I was taking Archibald Talley to his cell, I passed Mr. Bailey on his way up to Sir John.

'Jeremy, there's a Mr. Joseph Hanway to see Sir John. I'll take the prisoner whilst you escort Mr. Hanway to Sir John's study. He says he's here on business to do with damages at Covent Garden.'

He took the prisoner, and as we descended I spied a top hat in the entry and then an umbrella clutched in a well-manicured hand.

As we reached the ground floor the man greeted me as if we'd met. I greeted him back in a friendly manner (trusting that Lady Fielding had prevailed upon his generosity). And then as he raised his umbrella in a kind salute, a vision popped into my head. It struck me indeed that this man was the very same that had brandished his umbrella at us in outrage; nay, the man we near trampled.

I then escorted him to Sir John's study and knocked upon the door.

'Come,' said Sir John.

''Tis Mr. Joseph Hanway, sir.'

'Good. Please show him in, light a candle, and be on your way, lad — you've a busy week ahead.'

As I passed beyond the door which separated the Bow Street residence from the cells, I found Mr. Patley with his back to the entryway. His eyes were wide. ''Tis him — it is,' stammered he. 'The man we near trampled!'

'Yes, I know. Don't worry. He's with Sir John, and I believe that our woes will be resolved.' This seemed to satisfy him.

I repaired to my eyrie to make ready to receive the wounded Mr. Ball. Yet within minutes Clarissa had found me. Apparently I had calmed Mr. Patley sufficient for him to help Annie rehearse her lines for her performance tomorrow. Clarissa wished me to witness their preparations, for which they had repaired to the coach yard.

'You know, he is besotted with her?' said Clarissa.

'I know nothing of the sort,' said I.

Standing at the window, this is what we witnessed.

Mr. Patley stood facing Annie, holding a sheaf of papers near his face to read shortsightedly. ''Laertes. Punctuation. This nothing's . . . more than . . . matter,'' read he in a halting style. 'Annie, I don't understand the sense of this line.'

'Hush, Willie. It is but to prompt me.'

Clarissa and I met eyes: How familiar Annie had become!

''There's Rosemary, that's for remembrance. Pray you, love, remember. And there is pansies, that's for thoughts.''

It was a remarkable change in her — of a sudden she had become a different girl, an airy girl from a prosperous family, a girl near mad. She did pluck imaginary flowers, one hand from the other, and her voice did tremble with care. I did not know the play *Hamlet*, though I had heard high opinion of it, but with these few words Annie was making me eager to attend.

''Laertes,'' said Mr. Patley. ''Punctuation.

A document in madness . . . thoughts and remembrance . . . fitted.''

''There's fennel for you, and columbines. There's rue for you, and here's some for me. We may call it herb of grace o' Sundays. O, you must wear your rue with a difference. There's a daisy. I would give you some violets, but they withered all when my father died. They say he made a good end.'' Then began Annie to sing, in a voice carrying much pain: ''For bonnie sweet Robin is all my joy.''

Whereupon I retreated from the window, wishing no more to eavesdrop. 'Let us go down and greet them in the open,' said I.

'I think my point is well taken, do you not agree?' said Clarissa. 'They are much in love.'

'As usual, you race to conclusions. If they are, let them say it direct, not glimpsed in secret.'

So we hurried down to the coach yard, arriving just as they paused to rest. After we exchanged greetings, Annie did kiss Will Patley on the cheek. 'Isn't he a sweet man, to help me practice my lines so? Well, Jeremy, am I singing them yet, do you think?'

'I'm not sure I would know,' said I. How I would have liked to compliment her acting, reader, but to do so I would have had to admit our little conspiracy at the window.

'Did you not oversee us these last

minutes?' asked Annie, pointing upward with a finger. A smile appeared on her face.

Clarissa burst into laughter.

'You were most wonderful,' admitted I to Annie.

'I did adore what I heard!' said Clarissa. 'Is this the scene in the play in which you go mad for love of Hamlet? I hear it is a splendid play, full of ghosts and sword fights and very fine speeches.'

'Indeed,' said Annie. 'I sing a full song next and then I get to die of love. Unfortunately, my last breath is offstage.'

That all seemed rather strong to me, this dying-of-love business. 'Do you poison yourself, or how are you meant to die?' asked I.

'I just die of love, Jeremy,' insisted Annie. 'I have such a passion for my Hamlet that I cannot bear to live when he rejects me, and my heart breaks in two.'

'Hmmm, well, I don't believe people die of love,' said I. 'They may kill themselves from despair, but do they simply die?'

'Hold on, Jeremy,' said Mr. Patley. He looked most grave. 'I believe love is very strong and may take us unawares. Love can be a fire burning in your heart. When a person falls in love, he can't eat, nor sleep. He can't even think of his duties, for he thinks only of his beloved each minute of the day. To feel like that and then to be rejected — I can certainly believe one might fall into death.'

Could this be the Will Patley I knew? Perhaps Clarissa was right about the constable — that he had fallen in love with Annie. He did seem to be speaking from his heart. I was saved from further argument with them by a summons from Mr. Bailey to return to Sir John's quarters.

This was the result of the meeting that had just taken place: Joseph Hanway had come to Sir John, not to chastise Mr. Patley and myself, nor demand recompense, but at Lady Fielding's urgings, to offer his purse for our cause. He proposed to settle claims arising from our misadventure in Covent Garden! And so it came to be that Joseph Hanway (patron of Lady Fielding) became our benefactor as well.

★   ★   ★

The Drury Lane Theatre lay under a hush. Hamlet, the great Prince of Denmark, played by David Garrick, lay dead upon the boards, having been struck by the poisoned blade, and also lying dead were the King, and Gertrude, Hamlet's mother, Ophelia's brother Laertes — and much earlier, Ophelia herself (our

Annie). I had no idea that the final scene was to be such a massacre. And I gave such attention to the action that I was no longer aware of Sir John and Lady Fielding to my right, nor Clarissa to my left.

Then came the tread of military boots, striding amongst the bodies onstage, the tall Fortinbras who gave me a thrill with his rasp of German tone.

'Let four captains,
Bear Hamlet like a soldier from the stage.'

(I learned that David Garrick did direct the actor to use foreign sounds to give sinister quality to the scene in which all die and a foreign soldier becomes inheritor of a land emptied of its heroes.)

Fortinbras stamped a foot again and raised his musket high.

'For he was likely, had he been put on,
To have proved most royal; and for his
    passage
The soldiers' music and the rites of war
Speak loudly for him.
Take up the bodies. Such a sight as this
Becomes the field, but here shows much
    amiss.
Go, bid the soldiers shoot.'

The play ended thus: The motionless Hamlet was borne off-stage by soldiers, with David Garrick first back onto the boards for his bows; and then he did reach behind to bring forth Ophelia.

'Oh, John, our Annie comes for her bow,' said Lady Fielding proudly, and Sir John led us all in rising to our feet to cheer and bang our hands together. Will Patley did hurl roses to Annie as she blew him a kiss, still the Ophelia of delicate wounded spirit. Clarissa and I had seen her perform in other roles, but never so touchingly. Tonight she did become a star! The cheering and huzzahing went on for some time as the rest of the cast came forward to bow low, also with fervent whistles and catcalls for Fortinbras and the evil king.

Clarissa and I led the way afterward through the lower depths of Mr. Garrick's theater to the dressing rooms. And there was Annie with a host of admirers, including David Garrick. I heard Fortinbras — or whatever was his true name — speak kindly to her and was much surprised to hear a London voice. 'You was grite tonight, gal.' Clarissa then broke from me and pressed through the crowd to embrace Annie.

David Garrick, elegant as the Prince of Denmark, greeted Sir John: 'You have seen

Hamlet many times, Sir John. What did you think?'

'What do I think? Hmmm, well . . . ' Sir John paused. 'Truly, 'twas your finest moment. And I congratulate you on your company.'

And Sir John having said that, Garrick bowed most graciously. 'I value your opinion, sir. Have you heard of the splendid renovations soon to take place here at the Drury Lane?'

'Yes, I have indeed been apprised of your plans, David.'

With that he gave a polite little bow to the magistrate and a wave to me. He whispered good-bye and left for his own dressing room.

And as Sir John and Lady Fielding made their way toward Annie, I spied Will Patley standing beside her, with his arm shyly upon her shoulder. Just then Clarissa took my arm in great excitement to tell me that they had declared their troth.

★   ★   ★

Over the next week, Clarissa and Lady Fielding made their plans for our wedding. Daniel Ball was brought from Mr. Donnelly's surgery to my garret room to recover, and Mistress Hardy became his nurse for the time that it took for his wife to arrive to transport him back to Liverpool. At this same time, against Sir John's wishes, Bow Street was forced to release Lady Lammermoor to Lord Mansfield's custody. We were informed that her solicitors and the King's counsel were going to attempt a plea of madness and diminished reasoning. I knew this did worry Sir John.

To make matters worse, Lord Mansfield allowed Lady Lammermoor to be visited by Prince William, third son of George III, who was rumored to have been her lover . . . (setting the stage for what followed). Lady Lammermoor slipped the bonds of custody and vanished.

The Runners did their best to find her. They learned that a tall lady had taken ship at Glasgow, but the shipper swore by post dispatch that the passenger was not Lady Lammermoor but his cousin, and a report arrived that a mysterious lady in a cloak had taken refuge in a papish cloister; but the lady who came to the barred gate to show her face to the Runner was certainly not Lady L. We turned up fleeing women of every description — a Negro scullery maid running from her cruel mistress, a prostitute escaping her lecher from Seven Dials, and girls fleeing abuse from their drunkard fathers. But no

Lady Lammermoor. So it was that the victories that were achieved by the Bow Street Runners were followed from time to time by losses.

The day before the wedding, Daniel Ball's wife, Jenny, arrived with a special fitted coach to take him back to Liverpool. We helped pack his belongings, and Sir John visited his bedside to bid farewell.

Yet, the time was drawing near to our wedding, and I sensed Sir John did not wish to detract from the festivities and so did hide his frustration at Lady Lammermoor's escape. Whilst Lady Fielding and Clarissa paid no mind but to wedding arrangements . . . (assisted by Molly Donnelly as dressmaker and pastry chef). Therefore with Sir John's generosity, we prepared for the celebration to be held at the Crown and Anchor.

★　★　★

'Whooo-ah! Bring on the krummhorns!' Mr. Donnelly exclaimed as he rose to his feet at the side of the Crown and Anchor reserved for our festivities and held his mug high before draining it.

A modest menu, to be sure, but what it lacked in courses it made up for in quantity.

There was God's own plenty there for all to eat and enough good claret that all might leave the table tipsy if they chose.

On the stage of the Crown and Anchor the harpsichordist, Mr. Benjamin de la Borde, was playing for the crowd a selection titled 'The Enchanted Forest.' But that night I had no focus for music, nor much for what was happening round me. I felt somewhat like a hopping frog, greeting and accepting congratulations from the Donnellys, Sir John and Lady Fielding, Dr. Johnson, who had just arrived; from Joseph Deekin and Hannah; from Will Patley and Annie Oakum and Abigail Hardy.

To begin the gift-giving, Hannah did open a cloth bag and took out a small wood rack containing four bottles. Her husband did then address Clarissa: 'Please allow us to make this humble offering from our apothecary for your future happiness. Here is Thymol of Squill for dyspepsia, lavender for headache, another for flagging energy, and alas — one to cure dark humors.'

'We shall have no need of *that* one,' said Clarissa in a muffled tone (and with a squeeze to my knee). However, she was most gracious to the Deekins in accepting their gift with both hands and setting it beside her. Seeing Mr. Deekin, and being in a rather lively state, I was tempted to inform Clarissa that Mr. Deekin had put her into a trance and commanded her to bite through the imaginary ropes that bound her hands and kept her from writing — a fact I had vowed never to reveal. To divert myself from this subject, I called for a hush and reached under the table to bring out and offer Clarissa my own gift.

She took the book and opened it to reveal the gilt-edged card I'd inserted into the text. I had tried in vain to follow the inspiration of Andrew Marvell and write Clarissa a love poem, but discovered — after many attempts — that I was not a poet. A *billet-doux* would better suit my bride.

'Read it us! Read it!' shouted Mr. Deekin, as Clarissa extracted the note.

'A missive from the amorist?' Dr. Johnson put in.

To my surprise and delight, Clarissa read my card in silence. I will share with you, reader, the modest outcome of my writing labors. Here is what I had put down:

My dear wife —
I have but one wish on our wedding day, and it was inspired by thoughts on this poem by Andrew Marvell. I wish for world enough and time — not that we may grow old together, but rather that we may grow

younger. Here we are, two seventeen-year-old lovers. By the time we're through, we'll be babies in our playpen together.

I love you, and I always will.

— Jeremy

'This is most private,' said Clarissa, her eyes looking into mine. And then we kissed in proper loving fashion. And with that I began to smile. How silly I must have looked. And at that moment I did understand why it is said that love is a form of madness. This new fact of matrimony, to be most candid, had me fretting about the night to come. I knew not what to expect from Clarissa nor from myself.

'See here, see here,' said Dr. Johnson, breaking the awkward silence, as he reached to take both my hands in his. 'Well and good, lad.' Then he turned to address Clarissa: 'As we have turned to such moments,' said he, 'I believe I have a gift for the bride as well. At the urgings of the Fieldings I have spoke quite recent with a printer, one Thomas Neale, who is searching for a likely manuscript to publish in installments for his weekly pamphlet under the title the 'New Adventurer.' So I have taken the liberty of showing Mr. Neale a few chapters of *The Orphan's Quest*, which Lady Fielding did also read and take pleasure in. And I can say with some certainty that he has planned to make you a generous offer, and has asked me to deliver this message with his congratulations.'

'Oh, thank you. Thank you — you dear, kind man!' shouted Clarissa, her eyes wide in amazement as she rushed to embrace Dr. Johnson.

And so the talk flowed on in celebration of this news. But the surprises were not yet complete, for who should arrive at our gathering but my recently found benefactor, Joseph Hanway. He presented us with a package that from its shape could be but one thing. Clarissa and I removed the paper to find an umbrella with handle of fine mahogany burl.

'Mr. and Mrs. Proctor,' intoned he in the spirit of a toast, 'let my gift perform as a shield from life's unexpected cloudbursts!'

'I'll drink to that!' shouted Gabriel Donnelly.

'Let's all drink to that!' called another voice.

Just at that moment Dr. Johnson lifted his lemonade and muttered this aside to Joseph Hanway: 'Just *don't* make it tea.'[1]

---

[1] Hanway had made a violent attack on the habit of tea-drinking, which was answered by Samuel Johnson.

Of a sudden, Sir John stood. The room quietened: even the harpsichord fell silent, or perhaps Mr. de la Borde had finished a final cadence.

'This day belongs to the young,' said he, 'and I shall toast them now.'

'Hear, hear. Speak on, sir,' seconded Dr. Johnson . . .

'Please, Jack,' said Lady Fielding, as she did grasp her husband's arm most firm, 'allow me first to give a little speech.'

'But of course, my dear Kate,' said Sir John in a most gentle tone. 'I'll not stand in the way of my own dear Lady.' Then did he ease himself back into his seat next his wife.

'As my good husband has said, this day belongs to the young — but the young owe much to their elders; and in the instance of Jeremy and Clarissa, one man more than any other. And they are not alone in this debt.

'Most of you here today know that I have a son named Tom Durham. And he is a fine lad, indeed. Nay, a lieutenant in the Royal Navy. But what I wish to say happened long ago. You may believe me,' she said to us all with no further explanation, 'when I tell you that when I saw my son, my only child, taken from the courtroom in chains to what seemed his certain death — that, my dear guests, was the darkest moment of my life.' (Reader, so painful were these memories that her eyes did fill with tears and her voice begin to tremble.) 'He was then but a boy, younger than Jeremy Proctor was when he came to live with Sir John, and Tom's young life was to be taken — and for what? For a few shillings, perhaps a pound (obtained in the course of a robbery), that he intended to give me, his mother, so that we might not starve further. In all truth, I cared not whether I lived or died. Nay, I wished to be dead and would, I'm sure, have ended my life — had it not been for Jack.'

(She referred to Sir John. So she called him, and so had the first Lady Fielding, as well, during those few weeks I knew her before her death.)

'Jack had urgently petitioned the Lord Chief Justice for the lives of the three boys, out of respect to their young years — the eldest was fourteen. As you know, Sir John has managed to save others as young for a life on the sea in the Royal Navy . . . '

'Hear, hear. Hear, hear!' A round of quiet applause was given. Then:

'One of these three boys, the eldest, John Dickey, could not be saved. He was hanged at Tyburn two days after his fellows set sail from Portsmouth on the H.M.S. *Adventure*.'

Lady Fielding continued only a bit further

in her tale, explaining that Sir John had not informed her of his efforts on her son's behalf until they were successful.

'He wanted to arouse no false hopes in me, should they fail,' said she. 'It was probably best so, yet had he known the depths of my despair he might have thought otherwise. Yet when he summoned me to Bow Street and informed me of his success — that is, his partial success — it was as if he had given me my life, given me a reason to live. It was the kindest act ever a man could do for a boy and his mother.

'And to think that that same good, kind, generous man should take me for his wife, knowing my history — that is, to me, a fair miracle of fortune. As 'twas for you, Jeremy and Clarissa Proctor, to find a home at Bow Street as wards of Sir John. There is no telling what fate has in store for any of us. And we have waited for this day a long while, for you must surely have known that Jack and I have for quite some time hoped and, at times, prodded you two to be together and to one day marry and fulfill our great hopes. Now you have.' (She smiled then at us the warmest of smiles and thus sat again at her place, breathing a sigh.)

Sir John stood.

'All of you know this already. Jeremy came

to our household eleven years ago. He has been as a son to me. I have never told him this before — perhaps I should have. And as for his character, may I say justly, that he has wisdom beyond his years.

'I have never known this young man to cut a corner merely to his own gain, or jump the road of truth to make his path one pace shorter. And as you know, though I cannot see his face, I am told he is a handsome lad.' There was scattered applause, which he held off with a palm and moved his raised glass in the direction of Clarissa. 'As for Clarissa Roundtree — who is now Mrs. Jeremy Proctor' — Clarissa squeezed my hand tight — 'I have known this young lady in our own household somewhat fewer years than Jeremy, but not the less in intimacy. And, may I say that her father, whom I had occasion to know, would be as proud of her as I am. She is a young woman of great spirit and talent, and strength of character. Indeed, she has voiced her opinions freely, whether in accord with mine or not. She is a woman who will cede naught of the space on which she stands. Let all heed this, Jeremy especial.'

There was first a titter and then, of a sudden, the room filled with laughter. I was well dizzy by now, with emotion as much as a plentitude of wine. It was then that Dr.

Johnson took me aside to tell me, as he explained, what every groom must know. He spoke softly in my ear until my cheeks grew hot. Dr. Johnson leaned his considerable girth closer and spoke again.

'Sir,' asked I when he finished, 'is that word in your dictionary?'

He burst into laughter, nay guffawed, so that Lady Fielding looked round at us. 'England is not quite ready to *read* the word, my lad; but believe this — the wise Englishman has no reluctance to perform.'

So it was that our wedding party dispersed with the final exchanges from all of the well-wishers. It was indeed the happiest occasion of my memory — a gathering of friends and colleagues who had become for Clarissa and myself our true family.

* * *

And so, after a brief honeymoon, Clarissa and I soon found lodgings quite near Bow Street, where we would set up on our own (after Abigail was suitably prepared to handle the Fielding household). Until our removal, we stayed on for a time at Bow Street, where I continued to work as Sir John's clerk and Clarissa as Lady Fielding's secretary.

One evening a visitor burgled through the

window of Number 4 Bow Street — 'twas my old chum Jimmy Bunkins, who had returned from the New World as a stowaway, a grown man now, with ever the boldness of his youth. He informed me that he and Black Jack Bilbo had been sailing as privateers for the colonists and were both now wanted by the Crown for their deeds. It would have been treason, without doubt, a hanging offense, had he been discovered — and surely trouble, too, for myself and all in the household. Should I tell Sir John that Jimmy was there and risk his life for a principle — a principle I was not myself ready to apply? After a restless night, I risked asking Clarissa's advice. And with not the slightest hesitation, she said I should hide Jimmy.

But I simply could not thumb my nose at the law in such a way. I plucked up courage and brought Clarissa with me to speak to Sir John in his study. Once we had explained the predicament, he sighed deeply and thought upon it. We waited with trepidation, but before long Sir John smiled: 'You are soon to be an officer of the court, Jeremy, with great responsibilities to bear. Virtue would demand full application of the King's laws and customs . . . but are we to hold to this principle alone? What do I think? That we must never allow ourselves to accept the law as an engine that cannot be steered.'

'But *you* know about Jimmy now, sir,' insisted Clarissa. 'What Jeremy decides, all of us must decide together.'

Sir John smiled. 'I have decided that Jimmy Bunkins is a fine lad, a friend of a great friend, and must soon visit a cousin somewhere far away.'

Clarissa did laugh and embrace him, and I sighed with relief.

* * *

A letter soon after arrived from Daniel Ball, which I have kept all these years and will now share with you:

My dear esteemed and justly famed colleague and friend, Sir John.

Allow me, first of all, to express my gratitude for all that you have done for me at my time of distress. You will be pleased to know that I am well and have fully recovered the use of my arm.

Permit me now to elucidate the events of the last few months. These are events of some import for all of us. Not long after I recovered the use of my arm, I was called away from home by one of my constables. We mounted in haste for the docks, where a vessel of French origin did set sail for the port of New Orleans in the New World. The ship had caught the tide that afternoon and was four hours to sea when my constables were called to the dock to find the prostrate corpus of a tall man, who had been murdered by gunshots to the belly and head. And nearby Constable Wiatt did find a second corpus, this of a shorter man, killed in the same manner.

Perhaps you have already guessed the identities of these two. With my own eyes I did recognize them to be Thomas Hyde and Henry Howell. And after further questioning of a stevedore who had brought the last of the cargo aboard the ship, there is little doubt that Lady Lammermoor did embark for New Orleans. The witness did tell of a tall lady of imperious manner, in cloak and hat, with much luggage hoist aboard. If I were to hazard a guess, I would say that Lady Lammermoor had found that her wounded and bungling associates were far more impediment than aid, and thus used her cunning to rid herself of them.

I have decided not to pursue further investigation of this matter and will leave it rest here. I still have but two constables at my disposal; yet I stand ready to do whatever you command; and I should be happy to perform whatever is within our power to serve you.

I remain your loyal, admiring, and obedient servant, Daniel Ball, Magistrate, City of Liverpool.

Reader, as I write this for your enlightenment in the last decade of our century, I have but one further reminiscence, and I am near as old, as I write this, as was Sir John when he lived it.

Thus it was a day before my examinations, and we sat in his darkened study when he announced: 'Jeremy, name a letter of the alphabet.'

'S, sir.' There were two S's in Clarissa. I could think of no other letter — having already used C and L.

'Right — tell me of the Star Chamber.'

'*Camera Stellata*,' said I. 'A secret court that was begun in the sixteenth century, though it had roots much earlier, to avoid the corruption of open court, where there was undue influence by the powerful and prosperous. Punishments could not include death. But because the Star Chamber met in secret, it was subject to much abuse, particularly under Henry VIII and Elizabeth I. It was increasingly used in ecclesiastical matters and was abolished by the Long

Parliament of Cromwell in 1641.'

'Excellent.' He placed his hands flat upon the desk and said: 'I believe I can do no more for you now.'

And with that, 'twas as if I were at once cut loose on a rough sea in a small boat alone — my captain no longer near to guide me.

★   ★   ★

And so even now I continue to have recourse to this: *There is so much misery in this world, Jeremy, and so little charity, that I would not have you harden your heart to anyone. As you grow to be a man, you will hear many tales of misfortune and injustice from individuals, and some may prove to be false, told simply to gain a shilling or some favor. But the next tale you hear may be true, and the innocence you perceive in the teller may be as real as real can be. So let us help as we can, and not look too deeply into motives.*

He quoted that last as if it were an ancient saw, a proverb known to all, yet I had never heard such words of wisdom before he uttered them, nor have I heard such since.

We do hope that you have enjoyed reading this large print book.

Did you know that all of our titles are available for purchase?

We publish a wide range of high quality large print books including:
Romances, Mysteries, Classics
General Fiction
Non Fiction and Westerns

Special interest titles available in large print are:
The Little Oxford Dictionary
Music Book
Song Book
Hymn Book
Service Book

Also available from us courtesy of Oxford University Press:
Young Readers' Dictionary
(large print edition)
Young Readers' Thesaurus
(large print edition)

For further information or a free brochure, please contact us at:
Ulverscroft Large Print Books Ltd.,
The Green, Bradgate Road, Anstey,
Leicester, LE7 7FU, England.
Tel: (00 44) **0116 236 4325**
Fax: (00 44) **0116 234 0205**

WATERY GRAVE

Bruce Alexander

Recently married to the widow Kate Durham, Sir John Fielding, blind Magistrate of the Bow Street Court, presides over a peaceful household, with the imminent return of his stepson from duty on board the HMS *Adventure* promising greater happiness. However, Tom Durham's homecoming is marred by rumours of mutiny among the crew's upper ranks, and conflicting reports surrounding the captain's death overboard. Was it an accident, or was it murder? When Sir John is asked to investigate the mystery, he discovers considerably more than he bargained for . . .

X